BROKEN BLOOD

BROKEN BLOOD

The Rise and Fall of the Tennant Family

SIMON BLOW

faber and faber

LONDON · BOSTON

First published in 1987
by Faber and Faber Limited
3 Queen Square London WC1N 3AU

Photoset by Wilmaset, Birkenhead, Wirral
Printed in Great Britain by
Mackays of Chatham Kent

British Library Cataloguing in Publication Data

Blow, Simon
Broken blood: the rise and fall of
The Tennant family
1. Tennant Family
I. Title
929'.2'09411   CS479.T4/

ISBN 0-571-13374-6

To my mother, Diana

Contents

List of Illustrations

Acknowledgements

Many people have helped during the writing of this book but I would like to express special thanks to the following: the Marchioness of Bath, James Beck, Daphne Bennett, Graham Bush, Ian Campbell, Paul Chipchase, Lord Crathorne, the late William Dunlop, Lord Egremont, Baroness Elliot of Harewood, Michael Luke, Laura, Duchess of Marlborough, Michael Moss, Lord Neidpath, the Hon. Lady Palmer, Kenneth Rose, the Dowager Duchess of Rutland, Pauline Lady Rumbold, Professor Norman Stone, David Tennant, Charles Tennant, Julian Tennant, the late Hon. Stephen Tennant, the Hon. Tobias Tennant and Baroness Wakehurst.

I would also like to thank the following for kind permission to use papers which are in their possession: Mrs Noel Blakiston, Lord Bonham-Carter, Viscount Chandos, Mrs Simon Hodgson, Eileen Hose, Lady Mary Lyon, the Earl of Oxford and Asquith, the late Hon. Stephen Tennant, the Earl of Wemyss and March, the Duke of Westminster and Laurence Whistler.

Finally, I would like to express my gratitude to Kenneth and Bryce Alexander of Tennants Consolidated Limited, for their generous financial assistance, and also to the Society of Authors for a travelling grant.

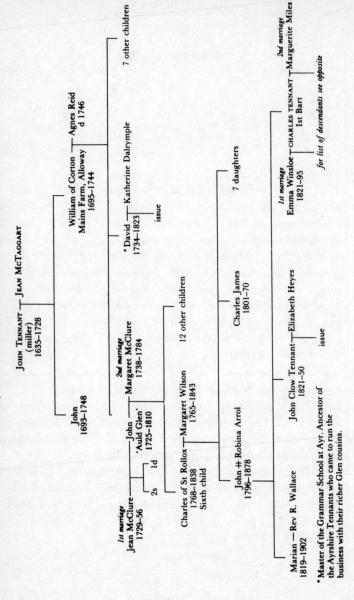

TENNANT FAMILY TREE

The Early Tennants to the children of the wealthy Sir Charles Tennant 1st Bart

JOHN TENNANT (miller) 1635–1728 ⊤ JEAN McTAGGART

John 1693–1748

William of Corton Mains Farm, Alloway 1695–1744 ⊤ Agnes Reid d 1746

7 other children

*David 1734–1823 ⊤ Katherine Dalrymple

issue

1st marriage
Jean McClure 1729–56

John 'Auld Glen' 1725–1810

2nd marriage
Margaret McClure 1738–1784

2s   1d

Charles of St Rollox 1768–1838 Sixth child ⊤ Margaret Wilson 1765–1843

12 other children

John ++ Robina Arrol 1796–1878

Charles James 1801–70

7 daughters

Marian — Rev R. Wallace 1819–1902

John Clow Tennant 1821–50 ⊤ Elizabeth Heyes

issue

1st marriage
Emma Winsloe 1821–95

CHARLES TENNANT 1st Bart

2nd marriage
Marguerite Miles

for list of descendants see opposite

*Master of the Grammar School at Ayr. Ancestor of the Ayrshire Tennants who came to run the business with their richer Glen cousins.

xii

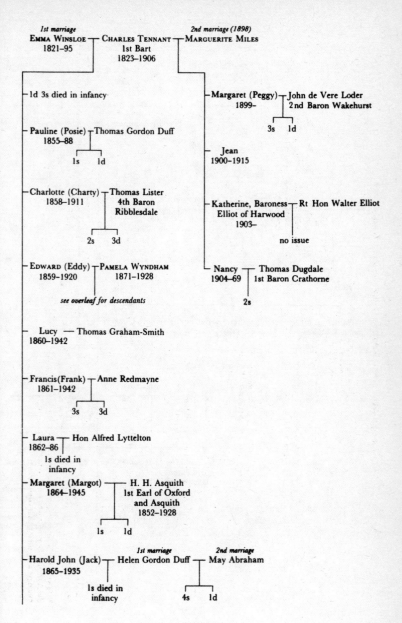

1st marriage
EMMA WINSLOE
1821–95

CHARLES TENNANT
1st Bart
1823–1906

2nd marriage (1898)
MARGUERITE MILES

1d 3s died in infancy

Margaret (Peggy)
1899–

John de Vere Loder
2nd Baron Wakehurst

3s 1d

Pauline (Posie)
1855–88

Thomas Gordon Duff

1s 1d

Jean
1900–1915

Charlotte (Charty)
1858–1911

Thomas Lister
4th Baron
Ribblesdale

2s 3d

Katherine, Baroness
Elliot of Harwood
1903–

Rt Hon Walter Elliot

no issue

EDWARD (Eddy)
1859–1920

PAMELA WYNDHAM
1871–1928

Nancy
1904–69

Thomas Dugdale
1st Baron Crathorne

see overleaf for descendants

2s

Lucy
1860–1942

Thomas Graham-Smith

Francis (Frank)
1861–1942

Anne Redmayne

3s 3d

Laura
1862–86

Hon Alfred Lyttelton

1s died in
infancy

Margaret (Margot)
1864–1945

H. H. Asquith
1st Earl of Oxford
and Asquith
1852–1928

1s 1d

Harold John (Jack)
1865–1935

1st marriage
Helen Gordon Duff

2nd marriage
May Abraham

1s died in
infancy

4s 1d

xiii

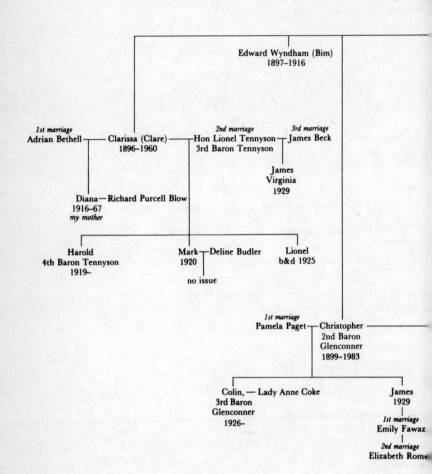

Edward Wyndham (Bim)
1897–1916

1st marriage
Adrian Bethell——Clarissa (Clare)
1896–1960

2nd marriage
Hon Lionel Tennyson
3rd Baron Tennyson

3rd marriage
James Beck

James
Virginia
1929

Diana—Richard Purcell Blow
1916–67
my mother

Harold
4th Baron Tennyson
1919–

Mark—Deline Budler
1920

no issue

Lionel
b&d 1925

1st marriage
Pamela Paget—Christopher
2nd Baron
Glenconner
1899–1983

Colin, — Lady Anne Coke
3rd Baron
Glenconner
1926–

James
1929

1st marriage
Emily Fawaz

2nd marriage
Elizabeth Rome

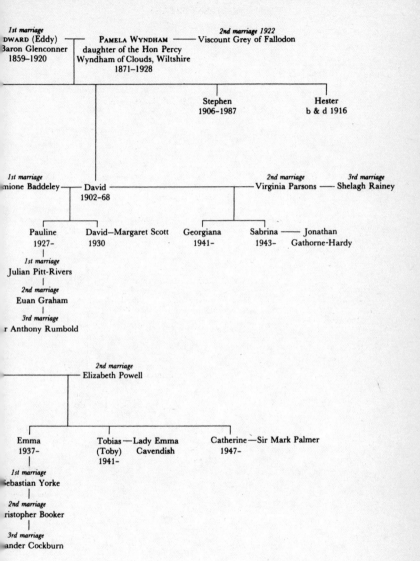

1st marriage
DWARD (Eddy)
Baron Glenconner
1859–1920

PAMELA WYNDHAM
daughter of the Hon Percy
Wyndham of Clouds, Wiltshire
1871–1928

2nd marriage 1922
Viscount Grey of Fallodon

Stephen
1906–1987

Hester
b & d 1916

1st marriage
mione Baddeley

David
1902–68

2nd marriage
Virginia Parsons

3rd marriage
Shelagh Rainey

Pauline
1927–

David—Margaret Scott
1930

Georgiana
1941–

Sabrina
1943–

Jonathan
Gathorne-Hardy

1st marriage
Julian Pitt-Rivers

2nd marriage
Euan Graham

3rd marriage
r Anthony Rumbold

2nd marriage
Elizabeth Powell

Emma
1937–

Tobias—Lady Emma
(Toby)   Cavendish
1941–

Catherine—Sir Mark Palmer
1947–

1st marriage
ebastian Yorke

2nd marriage
ristopher Booker

3rd marriage
ander Cockburn

I

Not Quite the Clean Potato

Throughout my childhood I lived with an absence. When friends of mine spoke of visits to a grandmother I had nothing to say. One grandmother did not like me because she claimed that I had the temperament of the other, and I never saw the other. This absent grandmother – my mother's mother – was the Hon. Clare Tennyson, but her maiden name was Tennant. She was the only daughter of the first Baron Glenconner and, though my family did not see her, I soon realized that she was a well-known figure in country-house society. 'My dear, it's Clare's grandson,' elderly dowagers would pronounce with startled curiosity, as they eyed me up and down searching for similarities. They were startled because my grandmother never mentioned her offspring and she had a reputation for discarding children. For this reason she never took her grandchild to the ballet or the theatre, as most grandmothers did, and I cannot claim to have had even a single word addressed to me by her. This startled the dowagers further when they found that I bore a marked resemblance to 'dear Clare', and of this I was forever being reminded. 'He's a Tennant,' they would say, and though my paternal name was Blow, I soon gave up trying to recover my lost paternal ancestry. But if I was more Tennant than anything else, I began to wonder who the Tennants were. Should I be proud, worried, or ashamed? What influence was this blood likely to have over my destiny?

In spite of my grandmother's absence throughout the 1950s we

1

went to stay frequently with her brother in Scotland, who was then head of the family. The Tennant seat was in the Peeblesshire Border country, and it was always a great excitement catching the night sleeper from Euston – where steam clouded the station – to arrive next morning to the silent stillness of rolling hills. The approach to Glen was by a road flanked with moors until the house suddenly appeared like an Arthur Rackham fantasy. Steep greystone walls swept upwards into turrets, and from the sides of the house battlements and gargoyles menaced. An archway like that on a toy fort led to a compact courtyard and the front door. Turn one way and heathered hills dropped down to the garden's edge, turn about and turrets, pinnacles, and soaring chimney heads jostled for notice. Glen did not have the quiet consistency of other houses that I knew, at peace in their landscape. It was a house of contradiction. Glen was assuming and gentle, proud and self-questioning – and beyond that, a little unreal. Only later did I understand it through the story of my grandmother's people.

The house, I learnt when quite young, was the earthly dream of a Victorian merchant prince. It had been built in the 1850s by my great-great-grandfather, Sir Charles Tennant. Inside, it was more regular than on its exterior and the dream within was not fairy pinnacles, but pictures. Constables, Turners, Gains-boroughs, Romneys and Reynoldses covered the walls, and although by the time I came to visit the collection had diminished, the walls were not bare. The dream was also of comfort, and the style of furniture either French or rich Victorian. There was none of the Tudor or Jacobean that gives the look of land long held. Glen was a house of sudden money, and made from the best that money could buy. A visitor in the days of its making had noted how money seemed 'to flow in (and out) of Glen as easily as the brown burns flowed down the hillside'. I sensed this too, but I did not know from where the money had come or why.

The pictures dominated. Everywhere were gilt frames and tableaux; as a child I was unaware that these were paintings of importance. It did not occur to any of us as children, bent on our own amusements, to question. One Christmas my cousin Toby had been given a repeater gun which shot out a harmless fluffy ball. It provided hours of fun. The idea was to see who could line up all the balls on top of a large picture which hung in the hall. Toby, my brother David and I fired away like trained marksmen. The gilt frame was our target and we hardly looked at the painting. I remember there was a bridge with people on it, but if we had been told it was Constable's *Opening of Waterloo Bridge* it would not have made any impression.

These Tennant cousins were the fourth generation to live at Glen. They were my mother's first cousins, but because of various marriages and divorces some were far closer in age to David and myself. My grandmother's brother – whom we simply called Uncle Christopher – had been previously married and so his children fell into separate groupings. There were Colin and James, the children of Uncle Christopher's first marriage, now in their middle twenties and therefore adults. They lived in London and went to grown-up parties. Emma, the eldest child of my uncle's second marriage, was also ahead of us and too near to adolescence to be a companion. She had schoolgirl friends of her own, played sophisticated music on the gramophone, and waited anxiously to be a débutante and meet Society. Our playmates were her younger brother and sister, Toby and Catherine.

In our games and pastimes we were typical country-house children. We fished for trout in the loch and Toby showed us how you could catch them with your hands in the burns. He was an adept sportsman and lived for scrambling over the moors. He and David would set out early rough shooting and return late in the afternoon. In the winter we skated on the lake below the house or tobogganed on the hills. When night came we played Racing Demon or He. The Glen variety of He – known to us as kick-a-peg – required the maximum number of players and the village children joined in our excitement. And sometimes Emma, Colin and James would share in this fun with us. Everybody scuttled from this room to that, along passages, down stairs and up stairs

3

to avoid the He. We cried warnings to one another, and Scots accents mingled with public school: 'Down the back stairs'; 'In the Oak Room'; 'Up the twiggly-wigglies'. Glen, with its fifty rooms, turrets, and winding stairs, was the ideal place for this game of country-house dodge.

I liked riding more than shooting and I was miserable on one visit because there was no riding at Glen. It was arranged that I should ride a hill-pony from the farm. But the drive was frozen that morning and as we slipped under the arch the pony grew more and more excitable. Half-way down the drive he whipped round and flew zigzagging back. I noticed nothing except my hands gripping not the reins but the cheekstraps, until we swerved to a halt at the front door. Glen was not for budding horsemen. Margot and my grandmother had gone to Leicestershire for that.

We saw the adults for meals, walks and when they participated in our games, or we in theirs. Uncle Christopher moved around the house with a benign, patriarchal smile and wanted us all to be happy.

I do not know when it was that I began to realize that the Tennants had been heard of outside Glen. They had a reputation for being 'fast', intelligent and breaking the rules. By many of the diehard gentry and aristocracy they were considered rather too recent, and the blood not settled enough to be dependable for marriage. My mother's paternal family were a case in point. The Bethells were ancient Yorkshire squires who had stood by their estates and had little time for the unusual; my grandfather's marriage to a Tennant was viewed with apprehension. But in the more alert London drawing rooms the Tennants may have surprised but the doors were not closed. Laura, Margot and Charty – my great-grandfather Glenconner's sisters – were the three names spoken of in connection with the Tennants establishing themselves across the Border. They were three high-spirited Scots girls who had broken down the conventions which were dulling London Society of the 1880s.

4

Long before Colin brought the Tennants a contemporary notoriety for his activities on his West Indies island, Mustique, the Tennants had attracted the attention of newspaper columnists. It had started with those three sisters in the 1880s and the impact they made on fashionable society. Before then, the Tennants had been square-cut Glaswegian merchants, and the family unknown beyond a merchant circle. Now, with the emergence of the sisters, they became sought-after guests on the lists of leading country houses. When Charty married that pre-eminently aristocratic peer, Lord Ribblesdale, their photographs were hung in West End shop windows like royalty. I came to gather that in the space of years the Tennants had bridged what was then an imponderable social gulf. I was impressed by the speed of their arrival, but at the same time I was warned that it was blood of which to be wary. The solid, agricultural metaphor of my great-grandfather Bethell was passed on to me: 'Not quite the clean potato.'

In my Glen childhood, although I did not know many details of Tennant history, I knew that the Tennants had their place in smart society. My cousin Colin was evidence of this. As a child my horizons were London – which was home – and the relations we visited. The journeyings did not lack for variety, but Colin brought news of a distant, exotic world from which age and money excluded me. Suddenly he would arrive – a Cadillac Ford Thunderbird parked outside – and with him came stories of glittering balls, clever fun and a very easeful way of living. With Colin, Glen became a Xanadu of charades and dancing. The gramophone spun and immediate entertainments were improvised. I cannot have been more than ten when I was dancing a Charleston to Colin's guidance.

Princess Margaret's name was heard, and I understood that she was a close friend of his. It was rumoured for a time that they might marry. Then one year Colin brought his future wife, Anne Coke, to Glen. I remember her as a pretty blonde girl. During an evening entertainment I danced with her and felt for a moment part of that gilded group. Later there was a wedding at the stately home of Anne's parents, Holkham Hall in Norfolk. It was attended by the chic of society and relayed on the Pathé News. My mother and I travelled up on a special train laid on for friends and relations. At the reception I stood behind Princess Margaret and the Queen Mother and was surprised by how short royalty were.

But what impressed me most was discovering that I had a great-aunt who was on the stage. It was in the church that my mother pointed her out in the next pew and whispered to me: 'That's Hermione Baddeley, huffing whisky!'

It was at Colin's wedding that I saw my Tennant grandmother for the first time. People found it strange that I was already at my preparatory school and had not met my own grandmother. But I had heard many stories about her and sometimes my mother would imitate her voice for us. It was a rather clipped voice with a sarcastic undertone. At home we had a dreamy Cecil Beaton picture of her and in my imagination I liked to attach this harsh, cold voice to the sweet face in the photograph. Clare was a legend to me, not a loving grandmother, but her fame, I was told, was her beauty. Her life had been spent staying in very large country houses – like Blenheim, Wilton and Compton Wynyates – where equally large house parties could admire her. And, indeed, it was true that with her beauty and sharp wit she had become a publicized personality. I had been told, too, that my grandmother had never aged, and that now at sixty she looked no more than forty. There had been three husbands, but she now lived alone.

On that wedding day, guests still filled the state rooms and I was standing at the main door of the house with my mother. I was gazing around in disbelief at Holkham's great hall with sweeping staircase and marbled columns: it was empty, and the echo of stone floor and marble column was barely stifled by the strip of red carpet which ran down the stairs to the door. As I stood there at my mother's side, an elegant and smartly dressed woman suddenly broke from the top of the staircase. My mother nudged me. 'Look . . . my mother. I want you to walk past her. I want her to know who you are.' I did as requested, and in my grey school suit I walked hesitantly, but none the less observantly, towards her. But as we passed my grandmother did not turn her head to see me. I noticed only a second's contraction before her powdered features returned to ice. And then she walked on, as unknowing to her own daughter as she had been to me, and out into the June sunlight.

Given this puzzling relationship between mother and daughter – and my own genetic proximity to the family – I plied my mother with questions about the Tennants. She also had childhood memories. She remembered being danced round the nursery at Glen by her nanny on Armistice Day in 1918, but she had few memories of her Tennant grandfather, Eddy Glenconner, who had died when she was four. After Eddy's death in 1920, his widow, Pamela, had married the former Foreign Secretary, Sir Edward Grey, who was then Lord Grey of Fallodon. My mother recalled her grandmother and step-grandfather particularly vividly. She had gone frequently to stay in the two houses they occupied: Wilsford, the second Tennant seat in Wiltshire, and Fallodon, the Grey home in Northumberland.

Wilsford was a stone-built manor house set in Wiltshire's lush Avon valley. It had been designed especially for Pamela by my architect grandfather, Detmar Blow. At Wilsford Pamela would talk to my mother of her adored eldest son, 'Bim', who had been killed at the battle of the Somme in his twentieth year. She indulged freely in spiritualism in an attempt to bring Bim back from the dead. Often in the mornings she would sit on her granddaughter Diana's bed and talk of her conversations with him. Pamela also liked the ethereal, and often read fairy stories to my mother. But at the sad passages she always cried. Stephen, Pamela's youngest son who was still at home, would cry too, and the tears quickly spread to my mother. Pamela encouraged such sensitivities but they seemed far removed from the sensitivities of the earlier Tennants who had toiled in industry; it was these Tennants who had provided the money for this haven where Pamela could weep so copiously.

As I learnt about the Tennants' industrial background, I found it hard to relate the heathered, country life at Glen to the smoking chimneys in Glasgow – and the fast lives of my grandmother and her brothers were surely another world to the solid, pronounced gait of the merchant forebears. My great-uncle David married a theatrical star and opened a London night club. His dark good looks flashed across the countryside from a glamorous car or dropped out of the sky in a plane. His sister Clare bathed in milk and lay for hours on a sofa to preserve her beauty – her name the daily diet of the gossip columns. And their brother Stephen, who lived at Wilsford and made it a bejewelled sanctuary, and was himself an astounding extravaganza. These Tennants cancelled the industrial background for ever and the wishes of more staid relations who might have preferred that the family's consolidation be kept to the recognized paths.

Perhaps, then, the fishing and shooting of my Glen visits was not a fully accurate account of the Tennant character. And, indeed, perhaps these pastimes could not have worked themselves very deep, since they had only been practised for a handful of generations. But when I stayed with the Bethells in Yorkshire these traditional country-house sports had been handed down through generations over several centuries. At Glen the landed record was not so complete; the gentrification of the Tennants had been but recently achieved. Since these two families make up a large portion of the person I am, their direct contrast has always held my interest. If, for instance, one sets the Tennant progress against the settled outlook of the Bethells one can see how the circumstance of history had also contributed to their opposite temperaments.

The Bethells had been securely landed since the late sixteenth century at a time when the Tennants were still Ayrshire peasants fighting poverty. It was not until the end of the eighteenth century when a young boy, Charles Tennant, left home to apprentice himself as a weaver, that the Tennants were offered their breakthrough with the discovery of his chemical bleach. But the industrial age was on, competition tough, and the Tennants had to move fast. This they did, and by the 1830s they had established the largest chemical concern in the world. In the meantime, the Bethells had not moved at all. Protected by land, and happy in their hunting and racing, they had no reason to. Permanence of place had bred a calmness in the Bethell character. But it was otherwise with the Tennants. Out of the forging of that chemical empire had come a restless energy constantly in need of outlets.

I have often wandered across the park at Rise reflecting on this diverse background. Rise Park was a sensible seat of solid aspect and again in contrast to the restless architecture of Glen. From the lake, with its mass of water lilies, I would look back at the old Bethell mansion and try to piece together my mother's childhood, split between Rise, Glen and Wilsford. My Bethell uncle no longer lived in 'big Rise' as we called it. After the Second World War the family had moved to a smaller house at the far end of the park. Leased now as a convent, the old house, emptied of Bethells, spoke to me only of ghosts and the past. Sometimes I would lie in the long grass of summer and conjure up the scene of what had been. Out of that door had come my grandfather to hunt his hounds – then kept in the adjacent kennels – across his beloved Holderness drain country. My Tennant grandmother would have been there too, but at an earlier date, and she would have missed much of the hunting. I liked to follow the half-mile of drive that wound through the park and dream back the flow of carriage and car from vanished house parties. I wondered why my grandmother had not stayed in this sporting household. I knew she loved hunting, but I did not know then of her nature.

It was from the Bethells that I had inherited most of my passion for riding, but otherwise I came to accept that I must be very Tennant. 'Simon is *so* Tennant,' I can still hear my Blow grandmother muttering with dismay. I was highly strung, head-strong and hot-tempered – all these I was assured were Tennant characteristics. But surely this was only the surface of the Tennant character? Underlying these strains there must be that grit which had founded a chemical empire. So was there, I asked myself, any link now that could be traced back to that pioneer Charles Tennant who had stood at the forefront of Scotland's industrial revolution? Or was there even a strain left from those Ayrshire Tennants who had withstood poverty when many a similar family had been trodden to oblivion? It is true that by the 1900s the Tennant blood had been altered out of recognition. Money, followed by a title and an aristocratic marriage, had turned the Tennants' direction. The children of Eddy and Pamela Glenconner were no longer practical-thinking people grounded by the realities of commerce, but brought up as over-blown aristocrats, adrift in the luxury of Edwardian England. Thus with each succeeding Tennant generation had come fresh circumstances. I realized that if there was a Tennant temperament the pressure of rapid change must be taken into account.

I grew older, and the childhood visits to Glen became a memory. There had been a lavish débutante ball for Emma, where no cash was spared. Emma, like Colin, now belonged in a sophisticated young set far distant from the scuttle of He and the cries of village children. The cousins went their different ways and we saw them less frequently. Bonds that had seemed eternal were under threat, as happens with the end of childhood. Uncle Christopher had turned sixty and decided to retire from both the business and Glen. He handed Glen and the estate over to Colin and left for Corfu. But Colin's interests lay in his island in the tropics and Glen was used less often. After so short a time the Tennants appeared already to be severing their roots – or was this no more than the natural outcome for such a family? Had the speed of their arrival really been too fast? I began to think back. There must be individuals to study who would provide possible answers.

The mystery of my grandmother reasserted itself. Clare had died at Glen some years before Uncle Christopher left. At sixty-four she was not old, and had died in Christopher's arms. I still had not met her. Apart from my encounter at Holkham there had never been more than the occasional sighting. Once, from the top of a bus going down Sloane Street, my mother had pointed her out. 'That's my mother!' she had exclaimed, and the two grandchildren had peered down to the pavement. I spotted a short but elegantly dressed woman who walked with a Mayfair casualness. Young as I was, she seemed already to disclose to me a life of narcissism lived between the pages of Society magazines. But who was this woman who denied her own daughter? Who did not speak to her only grandchildren? I carried her blood and the characteristics of her family. It was reason enough for my curiosity to increase.

I thought back to Glen. Could the making of Glen, I asked myself again, have been one of the stepping stones in the altered course of this family? This fantasy seat had been built by a Scotsman born of a background unused to the pleasures of life. With the building of Glen, Sir Charles Tennant had given the Tennants their first taste of carefree spending. He had made the Tennants feel secure enough to pause. Although Sir Charles, as a man committed to money, would have seen his house of pinnacles and turrets as no more than the necessary storehouse for his vast wealth, its provocation was clear. Among the rich his dream might not be unfamiliar, but as a Scotsman had he overlooked the dogma of Calvin in his country? First of all, let us return to those early Tennants who had nothing and expected nothing; whose only dream was in their evening prayer.

2

Poverty in Ayrshire

In the beginning the Tennants were poor and had to live with the realities of that condition. The first recorded Tennant to have sufficient savings for his own headstone was one John Tennant, miller, born 1635 and died 1728. He is the family's founding ancestor, and my seven times great-grandfather. Tennant's modest home was near Alloway in Ayrshire, a village now celebrated as the birthplace of Robert Burns. Today there are no visible remains of Tennant's mill house, but if you probe deep enough through the plantation of conifers and tall nettles overgrowing the spot a pattern of stonework emerges. The landscape too has altered; enclosed fields and tarmac roads have replaced moorland and rough tracks. Two features, however, have resisted change. The sweep of the Carrick Hills westward to the sea and the flow of the Doon below the miller's house.

John Tennant's tombstone is in the Auld Kirk at Alloway. The ruined kirk, with a great sycamore jutting out at one side to shadow it, is about as romantic a place to be buried as anyone could wish. Abandoned for preaching centuries ago, the Auld Kirk has been immortalized by Burns in his folk epic *Tam O'Shanter*. It was in the graveyard that the witches danced jigs and hornpipes to the music of an attendant devil. Burns drew on local legend for his poem and in John Tennant's day superstition and belief in the occult were widespread: Calvinism had arrived in Scotland at the time of the Reformation through John Knox and preachers still spoke of hellfire and damnation so that many of the rural poor, believing themselves damned, turned to witchcraft. Others, like Tennant, accepted their lot and put their trust in a happier hereafter. A crudely carved inscription on the reverse side of Tennant's stone gives us a glimpse of his bleak earthly condition and spiritual aspirations. Beneath the doggerel can be seen his adherence to Calvin's doctrine:

Passenger we here who lie
Own it is just that man should die
And bless God who so freely gave
The Faith which triumphs ore ye grave
When glorious Jesus Christ shall come
To give the world its endless Doom
We rest in hope that this our dust
Shall then arise among the just . . .

The stone is considered the most interesting in the Auld Kirk for on its front is a carved tableau of Tennant's work at Blairston Mill. There is the miller's horse with its panniers and set above, a skull, an hour-glass and a crown, implying the kingdom of heaven. There are the tools of the blacksmith's trade too, for his son John, a smith, was buried there later. There are also John the younger's two boys, Charles and William, who died young from drowning. Poverty and accidental death make a sad monument, but given the depressed state of Scotland at that time the Tennants raised at Blairston had every reason to look to the hereafter.

Plague, famine and ignorance were all that the first John Tennant would have known in his lifetime. Famine struck not only through a cycle of inclement seasons but through primitive methods of farming. The human diet was chiefly drawn from crops of oats and barley, and if the harvest failed there was starvation. Seven years of repeated famine occurred from 1696 to 1702 and the pattern persisted until well into the eighteenth century. A Reformed Scotland took it as God's anger at man's sinfulness. Not long before those seven fateful years, a minister had prophesied from the green braes of Upper Bankside in Clydesdale, 'You shall see cleanness of teeth and many a pale blue face which shall put thousands to their graves in Scotland with unheard of fluxes and fevers and otherwise, and there shall be great distress in the land and wrath upon this people.'[1]

But there were reasons for this nation's inert state and the people's simplistic interpretation of the new Faith. Previous to the Reformation the Roman Catholic Church had collapsed – a decline resulting in widespread spiritual and material corruption. The monasteries stood half empty, what monks remained were openly unchaste, and the monastic incomes had long been diverted into the hands of profligate laymen. When priests attended the altar they were either illiterate or too drunk to read the services in either Latin or English. In many counties churches had fallen derelict (Berwickshire alone numbered twenty-two) and for the mass of people there was neither religion nor education.

The Reformation provided a religion and gradually a rudimentary education for the people, but otherwise progress remained static throughout the seventeenth century. Holding back any agricultural progress were the warring of clans and self-interest of the lairds and chieftains. A laird's tenant farmers could find themselves in a compulsory alliance with him, obliged to supply victuals to his private army, and by these elaborate webs of allegiances and loyalties risking good relationships with neighbours. Preoccupied with feuding, the lairds gave no thought to the need to revitalize the land, and Scotland could not prosper until the warring ceased. 'Rest not untill ye roote out these barbarous feides,' wrote James VI to his son in 1597, 'their barbarous name is unknowne to any other nation.'[2] But the lairds saw the situation differently: to kill a neighbouring clansman had become a test of masculinity. 'He was a verie active man, he burnt and harried Sleat for his pleasure,'[3] stated a contemporary about the chief of the Mackenzies of Kintail. And clan warfare was not restricted to the Highlands. Close to the Tennants three established Ayrshire families – Cunningham, Montgomery and Kennedy – carried on a feud of plunder, burning and bloodshed for more than a century.

None the less, surrounded by poverty and a pitiful neglected landscape, Tennant the miller survived. He witnessed the seven years' famine and saw the peasant farmers driven off the land to beg. He would have known the custom of letting blood from starving cattle to mix with the evening meal to stretch it further. He would have observed sights that the contemporary historian, Patrick Walker, described, 'I have seen some walking about till the sun-setting, and tomorrow about 6 o'clock in the summer's morning found dead, their head lying on their hands, and mice and rats having eaten a great part of their hands and arms.'[4] Tennant must often have wondered when it would be his turn to take to the roads.

But it is possible that as a miller John Tennant did not experience the sufferings of starvation as acutely as his fellows. The miller was a necessary figure in the rural community for the tenant farmers were obliged by law to have their grain ground at the mill and to pay a fee for the grinding. This meant that the miller always had the guarantee of some income, although in bad times it would have been slight indeed. It was his son, William, who took to the land and knew all the difficulties that faced a small tenant farmer in the first half of the eighteenth century.

William's land lay not far from Blairston – a mile or two up the river towards Alloway and on the same bank of the Doon. At the Mains Farm the unsatisfactory 'run-rig' system of farming was practised. It was the accepted method, and not questioned then, but under it no farmer could hope to make advances. In 'run-rig' each field was divided into strips and each strip cultivated by a different tenant. There was no rotation of crops nor attempts to fertilize the grasses. In England progress was being made, but not in Scotland. The good land was exhausted by constant sowing while the poor soil was left untended and wretched. With the land either weed or under cultivation there was no proper grazing for cattle and other stock; even in summer they looked weak and sickly. In winter the beasts stood in their sheds close to death, and when spring came the horses and oxen had barely enough strength to pull the ploughs. The teams stumbled into bogs and furrows through weakness, while the cattle had to be lifted from their winter confinement – so undernourished were they – and set to totter on the sparse, new grass.

There were few who recognized the appalling inadequacies of such farming. The landlords were mainly indifferent and the peasant farmer bound by a mixture of exhausted tradition and fierce superstitions. No farmer ploughed his strip until late spring and, fearful that their crop might be destroyed by wild mustard and thistle, he often left the sowing until June. 'It was not too late to sow when the leaves of ash cover the pyot's [magpie's] nest,' the saying went. Of course, the weeds could have been cleared, but the country people saw them as a sign of Adam's fall and dared not tamper with the divine curse. When the crops were finally ready to harvest the autumn gales blew, and half the produce was wasted. Meanwhile the landlords were content to see their fields badly cultivated, remarking that since they were paid in kind they had no steady money to encourage improvements. Prejudice, stubbornness and superstition had made a society that lived on the brink of dissolution.

It was, therefore, no pastoral idyll that greeted William Tennant but rather a terrain unenclosed, hedgeless and undrained. His whitestone cottage house was primitive and built in the style of the peasant farmer of that date: stones roughly lodged together and whitewashed, an earthen floor and a roof thatched with turf made up the Tennant living quarters. It had two rooms and in the main room a peat fire burnt, the smoke carried out through a hole in the roof. William and his wife Agnes slept in that room in their box-bed, a traditional sleeping arrangement whereby the bed was partitioned off from the room by sliding panels. Light came into the dwelling through two deep-set windows, and in winter added warmth came from the cattleshed which adjoined the house.

Country people had little contact with an outside world and at home an absence of proper roads restricted social life to a radius of a few miles. But the farmer's day was a long one – often from four in the morning till eight in the evening – and at night relaxation was round the peat fire. For company there was the family and, in keeping with this simple vision, it was frequent for many offspring to be born. William Tennant sired nine children and in their humble cottage, the Tennants made their entertainment. Like all poor Scottish families, their staple reading was the Bible and beyond that they devoured whatever learning was available. And if a later description of William is to be believed, the children must also have profited from their father's gentle, dry outlook. 'An admirable specimen of the douce, staid, pawky type of Ayrshire farmer,'[5] is how local posterity assessed him.

In spite of John Knox's intention that there should be 'a school in every parish' it was a slow process. Following the Union of Crowns in 1603, Scotland found herself involved in a series of political and religious quarrels with England which lasted until William of Orange came to the throne in 1689. As a result, many of Scotland's internal policies suffered, but so far as education went there was the further problem of training sufficient teachers, raising the money to pay them, and securing a school-house in each parish. It was not until the 1730s that a schoolmaster came to Alloway, using the Auld Kirk as his schoolroom. However, there was already a growing number of Scots who wanted to learn and improve. At the Mains Farm, with help only from the visiting minister, the young Tennants taught themselves to read, write and enquire.

William died in 1744 aged forty-eight and the responsibilities of the family fell to his eldest son. Although no more than nineteen, John Tennant had begun farming at Laigh Corton – another village near Alloway and again a short distance from Mains Farm. John's younger brothers and sisters moved there but most were to leave the land, and several to disappear from record. James went to the West Indies, Robert and Thomas became merchants, Alexander an innkeeper and David a schoolmaster. It is in the lives of David and his eldest brother, John, that we see the Tennants first accepting the challenge of opportunities offered by a country that was finally starting to move.

At the age of twenty-one David Tennant was appointed English master at the Burgh grammar school in Ayr. Apart from one year in the Auld Kirk schoolroom, he had received no formal education, for even with education becoming available the children of tenant farmers were used as labour on the land. David had done most of his learning himself, seated by the peat fire in winter evenings. When he joined Ayr grammar school in 1755, he went to a school that was considered among the more modern and progressive. In the early phase of Scotland's Reformation education had concentrated on literacy chiefly for the purpose of piety. Writing and arithmetic were not thought necessities. But Ayr was a seaport, inhabited by practical men who owned ships and dealt in commerce. To them, geography, mathematics and bookkeeping were all essential. By the 1740s the grammar school had a curriculum in motion that was revolutionary in breadth, and the duties of the three principal masters, were stated as, 'One of them is to be wholly taken up in teaching to read English, and that according to the newest and most approved method. The business of another is to teach Latin and Greek and the province of a third is to teach Arithmetic, Book-keeping, Geography, Navigation, Surveying, Euclid's Elements, Albegra, with other Mathematical Sciences and some parts of Natural Philosophy.'[6]

David's job was teaching the 'new method' of English, which for the first time meant a systematic study of grammar. The hours were hard: seven days a week for twelve months of the year. On Sunday after the sermon he was to teach the principles of the Christian religion and, 'Before and after each day's teaching and before and after each Sunday afternoon's religious instruction, he was publicly to pray to God.' Concluding his duties, the school council said, 'he was to teach gratis two children who would be nominated by the Council'.[7] His task was indeed onerous, but the post was both an honour and a large step forward, and David did not flinch.

Partly by marriage to the daughter of a solicitor in Ayr, and partly through his respectable status David began to move among the professional classes. Two of his wife's sisters had married retired shipowners, and a third had married a distinguished cleric; a brother-in-law was Minister in Ayr and the Reverend William Dalrymple of Burns's poem 'The Kirk's Alarm'. Another was Sheriff Clerk of Ayrshire and married to an heiress. But David held his own. In 1772 he was made Master of the grammar school, a post he held until 1796, when the school became Ayr Academy. His appointment was announced through the streets of the town by 'Beat of the Drum'.

David Tennant had shown that there was a way ahead for a family that might feel itself trapped in rural obscurity, and although his brother John did not hold an official position, he was equally to show the rewards to be found in a changing agricultural scene. At last improvements and the breaking of prejudice had begun – a beneficial outcome of the Act of Union of 1707. The Scots had been understandably sensitive about the Act of Union and the loss of a national identity but the irony was that union with England provided the stimulus for Scotland to emerge from its moribund plight to compete in a modern world. After the Union, energetic noblemen and lairds travelled to England to import ploughmen and tenant farmers to their estates so that advances might be made and adopted by their countrymen. Gradually the 'run-rig' system was done away with, fields were enclosed, land drained and manured, wasteland fertilized and payment for tenanted land made in money rather than kind. The English approach to farming and organizing an estate became the new ideal. Relationships between landlord and tenant grew less distant. 'The relationship of master and tenant, like prince and people, implies a reciprocal duty and mutual affection,'[8] stated Lord Gardenstone in 1779.

As education embraced a wider cross-section of the population, superstitions began to lose ground. A clear-headed generation was coming to the fore, determined to survive and not to be defeated by threats of damnation. It was not that they were less religious but that they read the other side of the coin on the ethics of predestination. Religious anxiety must be dispelled by self-confidence, and self-confidence can best be achieved through worldly endeavour. Since God had created the earth and its society, it was sensible to assume that if one led an industrious life within the community, one was more likely to win his ultimate approval. By the mid-eighteenth century such defeatist comments as one merchant wrote to another in 1724 were less in evidence: 'You seem to be most uneasy about the misfortunes of a bad market and do not submit yourself to the province of a Divine hand which orders all things as He seeth meet. You seem to spurn against your disappointments. You are to make the best of a bad market. You can, which we see is the fate of an honest dealer. Mercats is sometimes up and sometimes down.'[9]

John Tennant was among the clear-headed when he accepted the Countess of Glencairn's invitation to become factor over the Glencairn estate in 1769. It meant leaving the farm at Laigh Corton and making the slow journey in a springless cart over seven miles of undulating countryside to the new farmhouse named Glenconner, near the village of Ochiltree. With him journeyed eight children, his pregnant wife, household belongings and farm beasts. But the change was worth it. Elizabeth Glencairn had been a childhood friend of John Tennant and she knew about hardship. She was the daughter of a carpenter and had been adopted by a friend of her father who had made his fortune with the East India Company. On her marriage to Lord Glencairn he had given her a large dowry which included the estate at Ochiltree. Aware of the dreadful destitution of the Scottish poor and the tenant farmers, she soon became the benefactress of Ochiltree. In Tennant she saw a farmer keen for progress and an old friend whom she wanted to help.

Besides being factor to the Glencairns, John Tennant now farmed 130 acres at Glenconner. In accordance with landlords who wished to better their properties and encourage their tenants, John Tennant's lease covered nineteen years (six had hitherto been the longest) with mention of rotation crops and fertilizing. But 'Glen', as he came to be called, became a part of Ochiltree folklore. He was to be remembered for his goodness, common sense and open heart. Robert Burns, a neighbour and friend of the Tennant family, wrote of Glen in 'An Epistle to James Tennant of Glenconner':

> My heart's warm love to guid auld Glen,
> The ace an' wale of honest men:
> When bending down wi' auld grey hairs
> Beneath the load of years and cares,
> May He who made him still support him,
> An' views beyond the grave comfort him!
> His worthy fam'ly far and near,
> God bless them a' wi' grace and gear!

You can still look out across the land that John Tennant farmed from the farmhouse of Glenconner. The house is whitewashed but was refaced in the nineteenth century when a second storey was added. However, the rough stone-built byre where Tennant kept his cattle is there unaltered, and the name has not gone. You still ask for Glenconner. And the names of Ochiltree, the surrounding villages and rivers take you back to Glen's day. They have been made legend in the verse of Burns. The towns and villages of Cumnock, Auchinleck, Mauchline and Auchenbay; and the rivers Lugar, Kyle and Burnock Water.

Robert Burns was often at Glenconner, but his friendship with the Tennants dated back to Alloway and Laigh Corton. Robert's father William Burnes (the 'e' was later dropped) had built his cottage at the top of Alloway while working as a gardener there.

On Robert's birth in 1759, Glen had signed as witness on the baptismal register. Later, William Burnes leased a farm at Mount Oliphant, a mile or so distant from Laigh Corton. From these two villages the children of William Burnes and John Tennant attended school at Alloway, under the supervision of John Murdoch, a tutor recommended by Glen's brother, David. Murdoch, a bright young man, was not just the new schoolmaster in the Auld Kirk, but specially hired by Tennant, Burnes, and a few other farming families to instil a love of learning in their children. Murdoch introduced them to Milton and Dryden, Gray and Addison, and as to his method of encouraging a fluency with English he has written: 'As soon as they were capable of it, I taught them to turn verse into its natural prose order; sometimes to substitute synonymous expressions for poetical words, and to supply all the ellipses. These you know, are the means of knowing that the pupil understands his author. These are excellent helps to the arrangement of words in sentences, as well as to variety of expressions.'[10]

The desire for literacy was peculiar to the Lowlands, for in the Highlands no development was possible until the early nineteenth century. The obstacles there were the impossible geography and the Gaelic tongue, which no one beyond the Highlands understood. In the Lowlands there were not a few peasant farmers who were keen to educate themselves and their children. William Burnes, for instance, procured books on geography and astronomy for his boys, and a bookish neighbour found them a copy of Richardson's *Pamela*. As the boys helped their father on the farm, he liked to discuss learning with them. Robert's younger brother, Gilbert, has left the following portrait of his father: 'He conversed familiarly on all subjects as if we had been men; and was at great pains, as we accompanied him in the labours of the farm, to lead the conversation to such subjects as might tend to increase our knowledge, or confirm us in virtuous habits.'[11]

The same was true of Glen. It was to Glenconner farm that Burns came to read in manuscript his first collection, *Poems Chiefly in the Scottish Dialect*. Glen was one, among others, who brought the poems to the notice of the Earl of Glencairn, through the young Earl's mother Elizabeth. James Glencairn became a beneficial patron to Burns and much beloved by the poet. Glen, his children and Burns also discussed philosophy and religion, and their influence on man's conduct. Burns passed to Glen a copy of *Letters Concerning the Religion Essential to Man* by the Swiss theologian and philosopher Marie Huber, which dealt with such topics as Justice, the Nature of Faith, and Sincerity of Conduct. On the flyleaf the poet wrote: 'A paltry Present from Robt Burns the Scotch Bard to his own friend & his Father's friend, John Tennant in Glenconner. – 20th Dec: 1786.'

Religion had not lost its special place in the households of these enquiring Lowland families. The Bible was as respected a volume as ever, although it was not purely for the Christianity it had to impart that it was read. It was now enjoyed for its history and literature. Robert Burns maintained that much of his earliest knowledge of ancient history was from the Bible, the reading of which was a ritual in the farmers' houses. Burns had in mind his father when he wrote of it in 'The Cotter's Saturday Night'. The ritual was first to sing a psalm, then for the head of the family to read a portion of scripture, and lastly to kneel in prayer:

> The priest-like father reads the sacred page,
>   How Abram was the friend of God on high;
> Or, Moses bade eternal warfare wage
>   With Amalek's ungracious progeny;
>   Or, how the royal Bard did groaning lie
> Beneath the stroke of Heaven's avenging ire;
>   Or Job's pathetic plaint, and wailing cry;
>   Or rapt Isaiah's wild, seraphic fire;
> Or other holy Seers that tune the sacred lyre.

In his farming Glen liked to keep himself in the vanguard of progress. He enclosed his land, drained his fields, rotated crops and started to grow turnips, potatoes and other root vegetables. Previously, any food other than the traditional and drear oats 'meal' was viewed with suspicion, but now Dr Johnson's definition of oats as 'a grain which in England is generally given to horses, but in Scotland supports the people', no longer held good. The diet was more plentiful and varied, famine receding, and by the end of the century Lowland farmers were in advance of their English equivalents. They read whatever modern books and pamphlets on farming they could find, and when the *Farmer's Magazine* began circulation, Lord Brougham wrote to a friend, 'In England the gentlemen alone take it. In Scotland it is circulated amongst the farmers fully as much as the landlords.'[12]

Glen did not travel far afield from Ochiltree, but when he did it was usually to observe agriculture. Making a visit to the Lothian district – one of the most advanced farming areas in the Lowlands – Robert Burns wrote this letter of introduction on Glen's behalf to his friend, Robert Cleghorn:

> My Dr Sir,
>   Give me leave to introduce the Bearer, Mr Tennant, to your acquaintance. – He is not only one of the most respectable farmers, but also one of the most respectable men, both as to his character and connections, in Ayr-shire. – He is on a tour of pleasure thro' the East part of Scotland, or rather on a tour of information; for he is a keen Farmer, & as such, I have taken the liberty to put him under your instruction for an afternoon when he comes to your Country. –[13]

Burns's letter was written from his farm at Ellisland in 1790. He had taken a lease on this farm in Dumfriesshire two years earlier acting on Glen's advice. Asking for Glen's opinion, he had written then from Edinburgh: 'I go, on my return home to take a decisive look of a farm near Dumfries; where, if you will do me the favour to accompany me, your judgment shall determine me.'[14] Soon after Burns wrote to his amour of the moment, Agnes M'Lehose, 'A worthy, intelligent farmer, my father's friend and my own, has been with me on the spot: he thinks the bargain

practicable.'[15] As it happened, Burns's venture into farming
proved a disaster, and the blame was sometimes attributed to
Glen for his advice. It is true that the land was in poor condition
but the lease was favourable. Glen would have seen the intensive
cultivation needed as a challenge, and it is probable that he did
not take into account that Burns's temperament was unsuited to
the wholehearted commitment required. The result was that
Burns intended to be conscientious, but with the demands that
his rising reputation as a poet laid on him and a nagging
ambition to play a part on a larger stage, he lacked that necessary
single-mindedness.

It is certain that Glen would have been upset by Burns's failure
at Ellisland, but Burns never lessened in his esteem for his friend.
It is likely that he blamed himself and his own confused sense of
direction when he wrote, 'So much for Farming! Would to God I
had never engaged in it!'[16] Indeed, the Burns family were not
fortunate on the land: Robert's father had died an early death
through his struggle to make a living first at the farm at Mount
Oliphant and later at Lochlea, a village some ten miles north-east
of Ayr. At Mount Oliphant William Burnes was plagued by bad
land and a hostile factor, and at Lochlea by a lawsuit. He may
well not have had the farming aptitude of John Tennant, but
recurring troubles wore him down. His last years were spent in
litigation with his landlord, emptying his purse and his hope.
When he died in 1784, John Tennant had a pony sent over from
Glenconner to help carry the body back to the Auld Kirk at
Alloway where Burnes had wanted to be buried. It was yet
another link with Glen, as Robert led the Tennant pony with
another that supported his father's body.

Like his father, Glen sired a large family. He had sixteen
children: three borne by his first wife, who died at twenty-seven,
and the remainder by his second. That Ayrshire Tennant blood
proved strong and thick and of the sixteen born only one died in
infancy. The tradition was still that the boys should work on the
farm and the daughters in the house until they were old enough to

shape their own lives or to marry. Once grown up, most of the boys went their separate ways: one to the navy, one to Cape Town, one to Ireland and one to become a preacher and evangelist minister in India. 'Preacher Willie', as Burns had dubbed him in his letter–poem on the family,[17] was to write a lengthy book advocating the introduction of education and Christianity in that country. Only two of Glen's sons stayed behind in Ayrshire, close to the soil: John became a successful and independent farmer, while James was content as the miller of Ochiltree.

By the 1780s the Tennants were ready to move beyond the confines of a purely rustic existence – an instinct, anyway, in one that he had a contribution to make in a Scotland suddenly alert with potential. Some of that potential had already been realized by the 1780s: David Hume had written his *Treatise of Human Nature* (1739–40) and Adam Smith his *Wealth of Nations* (1776). In chemistry, Joseph Black had discovered carbon dioxide and was now working at Glasgow with James Watt on a theory that was to lead to the harnessing of steam power. Thomas Telford was designing bridges and roads, while Robert and William Adam, Colen Campbell, Sir William Chambers and Charles Cameron were practising architects, the last-named designing palaces for Catherine the Great. Although after Burns the country's literature suffered an eclipse until Sir Walter Scott, in almost every other area Scotland was taking an international place. There were some who said that this enlightened Scotland could only bear comparison with the new Athens and the Age of Pericles.

That burst of enthusiasm to learn which had filled the houses of a farming peasantry had not been in vain. Glen never left Ochiltree and died there a patriarchal figure of the community at the age of eighty-three. Yet as he quietly tilled his fields, Scotland stood on the eve of dramatic change. Not far from Ochiltree were towns and cities waiting for the new industries. Many of the inventors and industrialists who were to bring about this urban revolution were the sons of simple country folk. And Robert

Burns in his letter–poem to the Tennants had remarked on the ninth child of Glen, 'And no forgetting wabster [weaver] Charlie, I'm tauld he offers very fairly.' It was in this son, Charles, that the purpose bred by Calvin and curiosity nurtured in a farmhouse was to take the Tennants out of obscurity. The fortunes of the family lay with a fifteen-year-old boy who had left the farm of Glenconner to apprentice himself as a weaver in the village of Kilbarchan, a few miles to the south-west of Glasgow.

3

Making Bleach

With Scotland breaking free from a depressed past, this newly enlivened nation turned its attention to what became its most significant home industry – linen. From early in the eighteenth century the Scots had been at pains to improve an industry that could give the country fresh commercial impetus. The decision to support the linen trade proved to be a wise one, for by the end of the century both Scotland's leading exports had badly fallen away. The manufacturing of tobacco and sugar had been severely disrupted by the American War of Independence when bands of French privateers roamed the Atlantic sinking the trading vessels. The tobacco and sugar lords never recovered and by the 1780s the linen and cotton kings were replacing them. But the first obstacle that had faced the linen improvers was to lift it from a homespun craft to a national industry that could compete in a world market.

At the outset, opposition to Scotland's revitalization of its linen trade came from the English wool merchants. Wool had long been England's established cloth industry and the merchants did not want competition from their impecunious neighbour. English cloth manufacturers demanded therefore that Parliament impose a duty on all Scottish linen articles, but one result of this tax was to make Scotland ever more determined to establish the industry. In 1727 the Scottish Government created the Board of Trustees for Improving Fisheries and Manufactures whose aim was to fund and promote home business. Subsidies were at once made available to the linen industry and the benefits were soon numerous: the importation of better Dutch machinery for preparing and spinning the flax; the encouragement to skilled foreign workers to come and teach their methods; and the establishment of spinning schools. Not least was the capital provided for the laying down of bleachfields to accommodate the necessary whitening process that consumed both space and time.

It was some years before Westminster realized that Scotland was not to be stopped in its purpose, and after 1750 its obstructive policies were reversed. An act was passed prohibiting the importation and wearing of French cambrics, while another provided support for weavers of flax and hemp to settle in Scotland. In 1747 the British Linen Company had been founded in Edinburgh with the intention of buying raw flax, supplying it on credit to the spinners, repurchasing the yarn and supplying it again on credit to the weavers. All this was done to stimulate production and so successful was it that the company was able to extend credit to manufacturers as they waited through the long bleaching process. The Scots worked diligently to turn what had so recently been a village and small-town activity into a national industry. By the 1770s Scotland had 252 factories in operation with Glasgow as the linen capital, producing 2 million yards of cloth per year.

When Charles Tennant apprenticed himself at Kilbarchan he went to a traditional weaving village, but one that had changed with the times. In the seventeenth century it was a village of thirty to forty weavers; at the date of Tennant's apprenticeship in the latter 1780s there were 380 looms and a population of 2,500. Charles Tennant was learning his trade in an advanced weaving centre, for Kilbarchan was near to Paisley, the capital of Scottish weaving, and it was in Paisley and its neighbourhood that weavers earned a reputation for literacy and radical thinking. A weaver's income was good around Paisley and afforded the weaver opportunities for leisure. And this he did not waste in idleness. The weavers formed political and literary societies – in reading they had a keenness for Milton, Bunyan and Addison, and in politics for the writings of Thomas Paine. They discussed religion too, and the many sides of Calvinism. Among the artisan classes, they came to be considered the most progressive, and nowhere was this more in evidence than in the Glasgow districts.

The weavers still worked from their stone-built cottages and then passed the yarn on to the manufacturers. At Kilbarchan, Tennant would have learnt to weave on the most modern of looms and he soon knew every phase of the linen-making process. And yet, fast as the weavers might turn out the cloth, there remained one insoluble problem: there existed no method whereby the bleaching of the yarn might be done in hours rather than weeks and months. With an industry that had assumed national importance, the bleaching of cloth had changed little since the days of the pharaohs. The linen was still boiled or 'bucked' in water or a weak alkali. After that it was laid out in the open to whiten or 'croft' in the sun's rays, but if the sun was dim or intermittent – as it usually was in Scotland – this process could last for months. Then it was washed using wooden scoops and lastly it was 'soured'. Only in the final stage had an advance been made: in 1750, Dr Home, an Edinburgh scientist, discovered the use of vitriol in place of buttermilk for souring the linen. Steeping the fabric in sulphuric acid proved that the same effect could be achieved in twenty-four hours as soaking in buttermilk for two or often as much as six weeks. Home's discovery reduced to four months a process which for centuries had lasted seven or more.

But year by year, as the industry became dominated by large manufacturers investing sums of capital in this promising trade, the pressing need to find a chemical bleach increased. The urgency redoubled in the 1780s, when cotton began to replace linen. Cotton fibre was drawn from the flowering top of the flax plant, could be spun and woven easily on new machinery and, not requiring the lengthy treating of linen, it was cheaper to manufacture. It could also be woven to imitate the expensive and fashionable silk muslin. Seeing the vast commercial possibilities for cotton some linen producers changed over, while others manufactured both.

David Dale, the son of an Ayrshire shopkeeper, was a leader among the cotton men. He had built up a small business as a seller of yarn when he switched to cotton manufacture. Acting partly on the advice of Richard Arkwright, inventor of the spinning frame, Dale sited his cotton mill near the Falls of Clyde at Lanark. The water power that could be drawn from the falls was ideal and in 1786 production began. Within a few years several more mills had been added and soon there were over a thousand employees. Many were former destitutes and David Dale built houses and provided food and clothing for his employees. His housing and welfare schemes laid the foundations for New Lanark – a pioneer venture of an idealistic industrial town which was further enhanced by Dale's social reformer son-in-law, Robert Owen.

Advances towards production of a chemical bleach were gradual. In 1774 Carl Scheele, a Swedish chemist, discovered that chlorine had the properties of a whitening agent and could eliminate the unreliable laying out of the cloth under the sun's rays. But chlorine had dangerous side-effects. Pajot des Charmes, a French chemist and inspector of manufactures, has left the following description: 'Its action is sometimes so strong that the operator will fall down senseless. Running at the nose, asthmatic affection of the chest, headache, tears and smarting of the eyes, bleeding at the nose, and even the spitting of blood are the ordinary inconveniences to be expected.'[1] He tried to shut out the fumes by wearing protective headgear but he found that 'these means were only palliatives'. It was not until a well-known French scientist, Claude Louis Berthollet, experimented by adding alkali to the chlorine that it became possible to use the liquid with any success.

The bleaching problem was discussed throughout the industry and prompted by the possibilities of a solution, Charles Tennant left Kilbarchan to study the issue. Having served a further bleaching apprenticeship, in 1788 he acquired some bleachfields of his own. Tennant was ambitious to forge forward for he realized that if an answer was found the floodgates would open. To assist him with the capital outlay, he bought his bleachfields in partnership with a friend – a Mr Cochrane of Paisley. Early each morning the twenty-year-old Tennant was to be seen spraying the strips of cloth and his dedication and appearance were noted by a neighbour. He had a domed head, a broad brow and hooded, deep-set eyes shaded by thick dark eyebrows. He wore side whiskers and, despite his firm build, it was noticed that his manner could be hesitant and nervous. That neighbour was William Wilson, a merchant and factor to Lord Glasgow, and as befitted his professional status he knew many in the trading classes. Impressed by Tennant's endeavour, Wilson eventually overcame his initially unfavourable reaction to a bleachfield so near his home, and after a while invited him to his house. It was here that Tennant would have made his first contacts with those who were to play a significant part in the making of his career.

William Wilson's son, John, was a manufacturer of alum, an important substance in dyeing cotton. John Wilson's alum factory, which was close to Tennant's bleachfield, had a number of partners, of whom a senior was Charles Macintosh. Unlike Tennant, Macintosh had received a formal education in chemistry at Glasgow University, he had studied under the scientist William Irvine and later under Joseph Black. His father, George Macintosh, had originated an important dyeworks and Charles had grown up listening to talk of chemicals and science. John Wilson was often at his father's house and he brought with him colleagues like Macintosh and Dr William Couper, an eminent Glasgow physician.

For the first few years, though, Tennant worked alone in the bleachfield. It is not known whether he attended the Glasgow lecture halls where scientists explained their discoveries to an interested public but had he done so he might have heard such scientists as Daniel Rutherford talk of his discovery of nitrogen, or Thomas Hope of strontium. And for a young man anxious for knowledge, the journey to Edinburgh would have been no obstacle. Here Tennant would have found the legendary Joseph Black, installed in the chemist's Chair since his departure from Glasgow in 1766. Black, who is regarded as the father of modern chemistry, was famous for his engaging lecture-room manner. He liked to hold his audience in suspense with a smile quietly playing at the corners of his mouth as he divulged his information. He was admired for his cool and clear presentation of a scientific problem, and of his intelligence and clarity his friend Adam Smith remarked, 'No man has less nonsense in his head than Dr Black.'[2] He was revered in France too – a nation that was leading the world in scientific advance – and there the scientist Antoine de Fourcroy referred to him as 'le chef et le Nestor de cette grande révolution chimique'.[3]

While Tennant was educating himself in science and chemistry, the impact of ideas from France was being felt throughout Scotland. A natural offshoot of the desire for civil liberty and equality in France had been a thirst for knowledge and the breaking of new ground. A group of French chemists (Crayton de Morveau, Lavoisier, Berthollet and Fourcroy) composed chemistry's first official nomenclature, and a fairly constant exchange continued between chemists in France and those in Scotland. Nor did the Revolution go unfelt, for the Scots, with a rising professional and merchant class, wanted a land free from the tyranny of the corrupt regimes that had oppressed the French. They saw that the threat could come from the oligarchy of the British establishment. France and Scotland shared an empathy that extended into science. Glasgow had its French bookshop, and it was here that Charles Tennant bought a number of books on chemistry, teaching himself to read, as others did, in French.

In 1795 Charles Tennant married William Wilson's daughter, Margaret, and around that year he went into partnership with Macintosh, Couper, James Knox and Alexander Dunlop. The last two were sales manager and accountant to the new bleach company that was eventually known as Tennant, Knox & Co. There is no record as to whether the company used the Berthollet process but since Tennant knew of it, this must seem likely. In the meantime Tennant persevered in his quest for an absolute bleach solution. He discovered that if slaked lime was mixed with water to form a suspension and chlorine gas passed through it, the result was a chlorine liquor. The process was similar to Berthollet's combining alkali with the chlorine, except that the lime and water were continually stirred to ensure the maximum absorption of the dangerous fumes. Several bleachers used Tennant's wet bleach and found it the most successful so far. In the first instance, Tennant would demonstrate his invention to bleachers for a £200 fee, if necessary travelling beyond Glasgow to give demonstrations. The following description has survived of him in Ireland: 'The apparatus itself may be seen at work at the bleach-green of Charles Duffin, at Dungannon. A Mr Tennant who works with him, and who it seems, is very expert at the process, may be employed at the different bleachers, until they get into the method of managing it themselves.'[4]

An example of the close contact with Europe was the passing on to Tennant of Claude-Louis Berthollet's advance. James Watt had learnt of Berthollet's discovery while visiting him in Paris, and later told Tennant, for as Tennant moved more among Glasgow's professional men – many of whom he met in his father-in-law's house – his circle of contacts widened. Much of his research was done by word of mouth besides the reading of journals or possible attendance at lectures. There was a great keenness to impart information, for one discovery could suddenly lead to a variety of others. Science and the machine age were in their infancy and amateur, scholar and merchant dealt freely together in an excitement of what the future might hold.

In 1798 Charles Tennant was granted a patent for his 'bleaching liquor', but close to the answer as it was, there remained drawbacks. In liquid form it was bulky to transport and also, like most liquids, its strength could only be guaranteed for a period. What was needed was the durability of a bleaching powder, and Tennant and Macintosh now set their minds to this. Within a year they had arrived at the right and conclusive substance: by simply passing the chlorine over moist slaked lime sufficient of the gases could penetrate the lime, which could then be dried to become a bleaching powder. In 1799 a second patent was therefore granted, giving the substance the registration of 'bleaching salt'. The patent was taken out in Tennant's name, as previously, which later caused controversy as to who was the actual inventor. Was it Tennant, or was it Macintosh? According to Macintosh it was he 'who invented the substance' and it is true that he gave Tennant the final idea, but equally it was Tennant who exercised it. Writing of the incident, the Glasgow historian, George Blair, put it like this:

> Although the application of the lime in a dry state was a great improvement, suggested, it is understood, by a hint from Mr Macintosh 'to try the experiment', yet the original application of even the dry lime appears to have been made by Mr Tennant; and it is not the person who offers a casual suggestion, but he who puts it into practice in the steady prosecution of a settled object, that is really entitled to the credit of any important invention.[5]

None the less, Tennant owed a large debt to Macintosh. It was Macintosh who had the academic training and who had been among the first of industrial chemists to travel to Europe and observe bleaching and dyeing there. He had an interest in a wide range of chemical concerns and knew most of the significant people in this developing industry. When he finally left the Tennant, Knox partnership he went on to invent waterproofing, from which the name 'mackintosh' – but with a mistaken 'k' – is derived. At the commencement of the partnership with Tennant, Macintosh was closely involved, having a high stake in the partnership shares, but the largest shareholder was, with reason, Charles Tennant.

With the bleach powder formulated, the next step was to find somewhere suitable for a chemical factory. The selected site was of 2$\frac{1}{3}$ acres on the northern side of Glasgow city. The advantages of the choice were that the land lay on the north bank of Junction Canal, giving quick access to the Clyde and Forth waterways; on part of the area there was lime – the vital ingredient of the substance; and lastly, land on that side of Glasgow was still cheap. The locality was called St Rollox, a corruption from the name of an itinerant holy man from France, Roque, who had passed that way in the twelfth century. But from now on St Rollox was to be identified not with holy travellers but with high Tennant chimneys, erected to carry the soot of chemical waste out into the atmosphere.

The Glasgow of 1800 had not yet shed the rural appearance which had earlier led a visitor to call it, 'one of the most beautiful small towns in Europe'.[6] Around St Mungo's cathedral clustered rustic cottages with thatched roofs, and grassy moorland still swept round the city on nearly every side, while much of the architecture in the city's centre was grand and classical, dominated by a piazza where merchants conversed. Until recently the merchants had been the tobacco princes, but gone were those confident men in powdered wigs and scarlet coats, who were described by a contemporary as strutting 'like so many actors on a stage'. In their place were the cotton merchants, and with them Glasgow was to alter. In 1780 its population stood at 40,000 and by the end of the century that figure had doubled. The promise of higher wages from the new industries brought in handloom weavers from the outlying villages, agriculture labourers and the country poor. They filled the inadequate housing of this undeveloped and part-medieval city, and there began the crowding that resulted in the appalling condition of forty years on. Gradually the outskirts grew dotted with factories, and by 1800 the city itself held a dozen cotton mills. Chemical plants, making chiefly sulphuric acid, were in operation too; but Glasgow's chemical skyline, grouped on the city's northern edge, was soon dominated by one factory alone: the St Rollox bleaching complex.

It was the cotton and its dependent chemical boom that brought riches to Charles Tennant, and steadily extended the boundaries of his newly erected works. He realized that the products required for making the bleach had their additional outlets elsewhere: the principal commodity that he manufactured on a large scale only three years after the founding of St Rollox was, inevitably, sulphuric acid. With Scotland's industrial revolution firmly under way, the comment of the German chemist, Justus Liebig, that 'we may fairly judge of the commercial prosperity of a country from the amount of sulphuric acid it consumes',[7] was not missed by Tennant. He could sell it to most textile manufacturers and metal processors. But the initial concentration had to be in the marketing of the bleaching powder.

Tennant, Knox's approach to selling the powder was far in advance of its time. A system of agencies was devised to publicize the company and facilitate customers' orders, and soon there were branches throughout Great Britain. Sir Walter Scott immortalized the Dundee branch in *The Antiquary*,[8] when he described the scene at the fictional Fairport post office. '"Eh, preserve us, Sirs!" said the butcher's wife, "there's ten, eleven, twal letters to Tennant & Co. – Thae folk do mair business than a' the rest of the burgh."' And an instance of Tennants' agency policy is well illustrated by the following letter to an interested customer:

26th June 1801   St Rollox Bleaching Salt Works
Mr Walter Crawford   Glasgow

Sirs

   We have your esteemed favour of 20th inst.
We shall be extremely happy to have you as a customer for our Bleaching Salt, & to afford you every information as to

its use that you may desire. But having appointed Mr James Ferguson of Aberdeen as our agent we are unwilling to let our own sales interfere in his district & which our friends would derive no benefit by, since the prices of our Agents are always the same at which we ourselves sell.[9]

Mr Ferguson can supply you also in Blue Test Liquor.

We are, respectfully,
Yr most obliging servants
Tennant, Knox & Co.

Scott's reference to the demand for the new chemical bleach is an example of how St Rollox was so successfully to expand, guided by the energetic business acumen of Charles Tennant and his partners, for year by year sales increased, and as they increased Charles Tennant drew further away from his Ayrshire ancestry. He continued to correspond with the two brothers who had stayed on the land, and in the evenings he liked to reminisce on his Ayrshire childhood and those visits from Robert Burns. But his energy, ideas and instincts were reserved for the future. As the nineteenth century dawned, Charles Tennant stood ready to make St Rollox a landmark in an age where commercial opportunity promised to be infinite.

4

The Largest Chemical Empire

Throughout the eighteenth century Britain had been laying the foundations for an industrial revolution. The extensive colonial wars that had dominated so much of that century had been carried out with one end in view: commerce. By establishing a network of colonies across the world Britain was to ensure for herself vital export and import markets. The gradual control of India through the East India Company was to bring a limitless supply of cotton flax; from Guadeloupe came sugar; the conquest of Canada opened up fish and fur trading; Senegal brought gum; and from Manila came the China tea trade. In turn Britain exported her manufactured products to the colonies, and although trading conditions altered according to the different climates of peace or war, the pattern was set. At the end of the eighteenth century, Britain had outpaced both France and Holland to lead the world with her commercial empire.

By the early nineteenth century industrial change and a need for progress were altering the predominantly landed structure of English society. Modernization in agriculture was taking labourers off the land and emptying the villages. The enclosure acts, which were to make farming more efficient and more profitable, often had the less fortunate result of depriving villagers of their common land and creating a new village poor. These disturbances brought unrest to the countryside, for while the rural unemployed hung around the villages waiting for occasional

39

labour, rioting broke out. In desperation and to show their protest, groups of unemployed burnt the hayricks and destroyed the new threshing machines that were depriving them of work. Many drifted away from their rural roots to the rapidly expanding towns. But as yet there was neither sufficient employment in the towns nor adequate dwelling space.

It was against this background of upheaval that Charles Tennant and his partners were developing the first great chemical factory. The advance at St Rollox had been steady and impressive. In 1799, the year of commencement, 52 tons of bleaching powder were produced at £140 per ton; in 1820 it was 333 tons at £60; and by 1825 it was 910 tons at £27. Added to this was the output in sulphuric acid, which by the 1830s had reached 200,000 lb a week. In 1816 Tennant started to manufacture soda on a large scale. Soda was a vital substance for the making of soap, which in turn was a natural by-product of the bleach ingredients, and therefore a further chief product of St Rollox. But it had not been possible previously to exploit the full advantages of soda production until the salt tax had been dropped. The best salt came from France and the government had no wish to help the French while the Napoleonic wars lasted, hence the tax. Salt, again, was a necessary ingredient of soda, and as soon as it was once more available Tennant lost no time in erecting his soda plant.

The expansion of St Rollox was mainly due to Charles Tennant's business acumen and entrepreneurial spirit. Macintosh, who had many other interests, acted as scientific adviser but played little part in the firm's commercial activities. In spite of the invention dispute, it was clearly Tennant who was principal creator at St Rollox. Writing a memoir of his father, Macintosh's son later stated that without 'the talent and industry brought to bear upon the business by the late Mr Charles Tennant the results, both as regards the partners of the St Rollox works and the public interests, might have been very different from the actual results'.[1] In 1815 Macintosh left the partnership and Tennant acquired control of the company. The other partners remained but the business, formerly Tennant, Knox, was renamed Charles Tennant & Co.

With the growth of St Rollox, Tennant became rich. In Glasgow his citizen status had risen but as yet the class into which he had moved had no social recognition. Britain was still dominated by a governing landed oligarchy who defiantly ignored the new town rich like Tennant and his kind. Many of the landed might draw incomes from the coal or iron found on their estates, but they did not hold with the notion that the expanding industrial towns might deserve some say in the Government of the country. Neither Manchester, Glasgow nor Birmingham had any representation in Parliament. Power, in the eighteenth century, lay with a handful of Whig families, and those who benefited were either their paid sycophants or their relations. Bribery was quite accepted as a vote-catcher, while the relations filled 'rotten boroughs' – seats without electors. Some land-owners had as many as fifteen relations taking their seats in Parliament, and this Whig system of supremacy stood good into the nineteenth century. But it could not last. In France there had been a revolution, the prolonged Napoleonic wars had near-bankrupted the country, and Britain's unemployed were rioting. And beyond these disruptions there had arrived a new and influential town class who wanted a voice.

The French Revolution had given Britain's rising classes an incentive. It had shown that it was possible for oppressive government to be overthrown, and a restless radicalism spread through England and Scotland. Soon almost every town had its Radical club; the best known were the Friends of the People and the Union. They were influenced by the writings of Thomas Paine, and in particular the *Rights of Man*, which spoke against monarchy and aristocracy as archaic and obstructive elements in his looked-for free society. Paine had written the *Rights of Man* in response to Edmund Burke's *Reflections on the French Revolution*, a treatise that defended the ancient constitution and attacked the revolutionaries for the drastic measures taken. Burke was the true spokesman of Whig belief: England must be governed by men of breeding and property, by which he meant the large landowners. Those great Whig landowners who had Burke's confidence were Russells, Cavendishes, Pelhams and Fitzwilliams. Like his father, Burke's son Richard did not trust the motives of the rising classes. Writing to his employer Lord Fitzwilliam, whose seat was Milton, near Peterborough, he warned, 'Think when you walk the streets of Peterborough that they lie under the stones and that they will come out of the rotten tenements you have purchased of Mr Parker to lord it over the lord of those tenements.'[2]

But at St Rollox, as the chimneys, warehouses, sulphur and soda plants were extended, Tennant gave himself fully to the Radical cause. He held firmly to all the sentiments of equality expressed in *The Rights of Man* and he was an active member of the Friends of the People. He wanted universal suffrage, religious freedom and, as a stimulus to business, free trade. He supported vigorously those causes backed by the Radicals which expressed their own lack of freedom. An instance was the request from George IV to divorce his wife, Queen Caroline. The King's cruel treatment of her since their marriage was notorious, and although she now roamed abroad finding pleasure where she could, she was seen by the British people as a badly wronged woman. At the outset the King had married her while already in secret marriage to Mrs Fitzherbert; he had then formed numerous other alliances, and finally had thrown her out. But it was this fresh act of humiliation which brought the Radicals rallying to her side. In Glasgow, Tennant was among those who met to petition against the King's proposed action.

A gathering of Glasgow's foremost Radicals took place in the Black Bull ballroom to discuss the issue on 13 December 1820. Select in number, the group was described as consisting of fifteen or so of 'the leading magnates' in the city. The plan was to oppose immediately the conservative body of Glasgow magistrates who had forwarded an Address to the King, commending his petition to divorce. Tennant and his friends argued that the Address did not represent the true opinion of the people of Glasgow, the people had not been consulted. The group left the Black Bull to speak with the chief magistrate and request that a public meeting be held in the town hall to hear the people's feelings on the matter. To hold a public meeting without permission from the magistrates was illegal, and permission was denied. At this point Tennant took the initiative. 'We will get our own *Trades'* Hall,' he told the magistrate. 'Try if you *dare*,'[3] was the reply. But the Radicals did dare; a public meeting was held, the attendance was large, and a petition protesting at the divorce went to London.

The petition was circulated for signing to a number of Radical centres, among them the St Rollox Chemical Works. It was not the only occasion on which Charles Tennant made a stand for the Radical cause and the unheard classes. Popular feeling rose in Glasgow in the years preceding the passing of the great Reform Bill in 1832. There had been a gradual weakening in both Tories and Whigs in some of their reactionary prejudices. The Tories were in power during most of the 1820s, and in 1825, as an antidote to violent rioting, they conceded the right to strike to the people. In 1829 the Catholic Emancipation Act was passed, allowing Roman Catholics certain liberties following the strong restraints that had existed since the departure of James II in 1688. Thus, there were signs that the landed oligarchy was prepared to make moves towards bettering the conditions of the dispossessed, but at the mention of parliamentary reform they were implacable. The right to vote could not be entrusted to the people, nor could representation in the House of Commons. By 1830 the spreading cities were filled with protestors, and in Glasgow 100,000 marched through the streets calling for reform. Tennant was of their number.

It has been said that Wellington could have kept the Tories in power had he been less adamantly against reform of the franchise. But Wellington was not a politician, he was a soldier, and beyond military affairs his vision was often limited. In 1830 his Government lost the election and the Whigs returned under Lord Grey. Although most of Grey's cabinet now saw the necessity for electoral reform, there were still many diehard Whigs who had to be coaxed. 'Sacrifice one atom of our glorious constitution, and all the rest is gone,'[4] mumbled the elderly Lord Eldon from the Upper Chamber. And there was a moment's hesitation in the passing of the final Bill, at which point revolution threatened throughout the country. But bringing their lordships back to reason came Lord Brougham. This clever, astute lawyer, who had been raised to the peerage and now sat as Lord Chancellor, explained once more how the Bill had been designed to give franchise to the new class, but not to the whole populace. He urged them to support it, since it was this new industrial class which was most likely to guarantee their lordships' future. He put it quite succinctly:

> . . . If there is a mob, there is the people also. I speak now of the middle classes – of those hundreds of thousands of respectable persons – the most numerous and by far the most wealthy order in the community; for if all your Lordships' castles, manors, rights of warren and rights of chase, with all your broad acres, were brought to the hammer and sold at fifty years' purchase, the price would fly up and hit the beam when counter-poised by the vast and solid riches of these middle classes, who are also the genuine depositories of sober, rational, intelligent and honest English feeling. Unable though they be to round a phrase or point an epigram, they are solid, right-judging men, and, above all, not given to change. . . . Their support must be sought, if Government would endure – *the support of the people as distinguished from the populace*, who look up to them as their kind and natural protectors. The middle class, indeed, forms the link which connects the upper and lower orders, and links even Your Lordships with the populace, whom some of you are wont to despise . . .[5]

The second and final Bill was at last passed on 4 June 1832. The completion of the 1832 Reform Act brought rejoicing across Britain. For many it was not the final answer, for the working man still had no right to vote, but at least the iniquitous system of rotten boroughs had gone and the extended vote embraced a far wider section of the population. Industrial Britain had been recognized and Scotland – so important in the Industrial Revolution – need no longer complain that she was England's poor relation. Applying the Reform Act's yardstick of voting to anyone who lived in a house of a £10 annual value, Glasgow's electoral roll rose from a select thirty-three to 7,024. There was representation in Parliament too for the growing cities: Birmingham, Manchester, Leeds and Sheffield all returned members for the first time. One hundred and sixty-eight 'rotten' seats had been swept away and replaced by over a hundred new constituencies. Two of these new seats belonged to Glasgow.

On the night of the passing of the Reform Act the city of Glasgow broke into celebrations. Bonfires were lit and gas torches flared from every house. Bells were pealed and civic buildings such as the Royal Exchange were dressed with the figure of Britannia while the word 'Reform' blazed out in gaslight. But whether the illuminations were by gas or candle, a contemporary observer noted how 'in a trice the whole city might be said to be flashing with fire'.[6] From the mansion of the Lord Provost three thousand gas torches encircled the motto of the city, 'Let Glasgow Flourish', while from Charles Tennant's brand new house at 195 West George Street were hung paintings of the King, the cabinet, and the people. Beneath these paintings was written, 'Hail, glorious reform!' The only enemy that Glasgow had that night was the Duke of Wellington, who had refused to vote for reform. In the streets his effigy was burnt.

Charles Tennant was considered one of the leading spirits of Glasgow's Radical and reforming movement. He had made available a warehouse at St Rollox as the meeting place for Glasgow's most radical group, the Crow Club. At the point at which the concluding of the Reform Bill had seemed to hesitate, Charles Tennant had again gone – this time with his two sons, John and Charles – to join the demonstration of 120,000 who had marched through the streets carrying banners that read 'Liberty or Death'. But by the success of the Reform Act Charles Tennant now had his place. He was then in his sixties, but since he had given no other sign of active socialism, the question arises as to what extent he was fully committed to improving the general state of society. There was still much to be done for the urban multitude, but in this area Tennant had taken no direct part. Was there, by chance, a degree of self-interest in his Radicalism? The answer is not straightforward. Obviously his continuing fight for Free Trade was self-interested, but he would have been a foolish businessman not to wish it. Naturally he had no desire to return to that struggle in Ayrshire. Yet from his childhood poverty he retained a strong sympathy for others who had not left that condition. On his death it was written, 'Mr Tennant was all his life a Reformer, and of him it may be truly said, that he steadily maintained to the last those political opinions with which he set out.'

Tennant was not a pioneer social reformer in the sense that Robert Owen was. At St Rollox there was no emphasis on the 'ideal community' as at New Lanark, with its housing scheme and education centre for the employed, although an influence from there must have rubbed off – as it did in a number of Scottish factories. St Rollox had its own school for the education of the children of its employees. When the gases and fumes from the chimneys and other chemical departments seemed likely to be dangerous, precautions were taken. Tests to eliminate any danger were carried out, and a medical officer was engaged full time. Certainly, Tennant was a kind and humane man, and he had a public conscience, but his real drive lay with his chemicals and the expansion of the business. That Tennant was a Radical fits the historic context but was not the driving force of his character. With his Radical sentiments on one side, and his accumulating wealth on the other, Charles Tennant was the perfect example of the paradox that had led his newly established class to fight for acceptance and recognition.

By 1830 St Rollox had spread from its original $2\frac{1}{3}$ acres to nearly 50 acres, and the workforce had risen from twelve men to over 300. Tennant agents acted throughout the country, and there were now two bases in Ireland. In London there was an office in Upper Thames Street. St Rollox was spoken of as the largest chemical works in Europe, if not the world. It was now supplying an ever-larger range of manufacturers with its products. Of the importance of the new bleach, Justus Liebig wrote in 1843:

> But for this new bleaching process, it would scarcely have been possible for the cotton manufacture of Great Britain to have attained its present enormous extent – it could not have competed in price with France and Germany. In the old process of bleaching, every piece must be exposed to the air and light during several weeks in the summer, and kept continually moist by manual labour. For this purpose, meadow land, eligibly situated, was essential. Now a single establishment near Glasgow bleaches 1400 pieces daily, throughout the year. What an enormous capital would be required to purchase land for this purpose![7]

Thus Charles Tennant was among the first to link science with manufacture. To do so with success needed timing and awareness. Tennant had shown how it could be done. In the pre-industrial era it had been difficult to market any new produce through lack of efficient transport and communications, but by the early decades of the nineteenth century this was changing. There were the improved roads of Telford and McAdam; the strengthening of the canal network; and, in the 1820s, the arrival of the railways. And to make his products available Charles Tennant did not lose a moment to pursue the advantages of this progress. But he also wanted to learn about and investigate all industrial advances, since most of them became of service to him. In 1825 he went on a trip to the north of England to study coal and rail developments. Thomas Grainger, a Scottish railway engineer who accompanied him, has left the following account of Tennant's energy and curiosity:

> In the course of this excursion, his desire to see everything in the district that was interesting and the fatigue to which he subjected himself are incredible. Early or late his activity never failed, and rather outdid that of his younger companions. On arranging one evening in Newcastle to start next morning to see the various works at Sunderland, while we were hesitating about the hour, he at once resolved to take the earliest coach, at 4 a.m. which we did. But the energy and vigour of his mental powers – his keen and rapid perception of the nature of the various engineering, mechanical and mining operations which rose successively under our observation, and his just and accurate estimate of their value, and comprehensive views of their extensive appreciation in commerce and the arts, which he descried afar off – were what more especially called forth our admiration and respect. Nor did he confine himself to what was to be seen above ground; he descended one of the deepest coal-pits in Northumberland. I shall never forget the morning on which we, along with Mr Nicholas Wood, the eminent coalviewer, rigged out in coal-pit dresses (and odd figures we certainly were) descended the principal pit of the Killingworth Colliery.[8]

At St Rollox Tennant had initiated a fleet of schooners to carry goods along the canals as far as London. By the mid-1820s the works were consuming over 30,000 tons of coal a year and it had become both expensive and slow to transport such a quantity up the Monkland Canal or along the roads by cart. Tennant, therefore, stood as one of the chief sponsors for the Garnkirk and Glasgow Railway – Glasgow's second industrial railway, aimed at bringing coal from the Lanarkshire collieries to Glasgow's industries. The original two steam engines were made at the Stephenson works in Birmingham; one was named the *St Rollox* and the other the *George Stephenson*. The line was made of the most modern iron rails and built as straight as possible; its final stopping place was conveniently opposite Charles Tennant & Co. The railway was given an impressive opening ceremony on 27 September 1831 to mark this proud step forward in Glasgow's industrial history; the day before, the *Glasgow Herald* stressed the excitement of this forthcoming event:

> The extreme novelty of this exhibition – the first of its kind in Scotland, and we may say the second in Britain, cannot fail to excite anxiety to witness it – which will show in our own land the great *march of movement* so much and so justly desiderated by our southern brethren; and as economical and expeditious transit is of the first consideration, we must view this as one of the highest benefits to every class of the community.[9]

A large crowd gathered for the opening, as had been anticipated, and the day was recorded in four lithographs by a local artist, David Octavius Hill. One of the lithographs shows St Rollox, its chimneys and warehouses dominating the background, while in the foreground is the engine *St Rollox* pulling open carriages and its 200 invited guests; in the opposite direction travels the *George Stephenson*, also with banners waving and guest-laden carriages. That evening a dinner was held, once again at the Black Bull in Argyle Street. It was an evening of fine wines, toasts and speech-making. The dinner of the railroad's proprietors and their guests was reported in another Glasgow newspaper, the *Courier*. We can imagine the confident presence of those industrial merchants as 'Mr Cunningham's excellent band contributed not a little to the hilarity of the evening, by playing a variety of appropriate and favourite airs.'

The multiple activities of Charles Tennant had made him a

well-established figure in Glasgow's merchant circles. His neo-classical residence in West George Street had replaced the more modest dwelling where he and his family had previously lived at the St Rollox works. Since 1817 he had been a member of the respected Merchants House, the meeting place and guild for the prominent tradesmen of the city. The Merchants House – which still exists – dates back to the late sixteenth century. It was founded on strong religious principles, with the intention of instilling integrity and fair-dealing into its members. On a wall of the meeting room was a wooden board on which were inscribed in gilt certain quotations from the Scriptures: 'Do not discommend those commodities that are very good, which you are about to buy so that you may bring down the price of the commoditie and get it for less than it is worth. . . . Proverbs 20.14: '"It is naught, it is naught, saith the buyer: but when he is gone on his way, then he boasteth." So should not the seller over praise or commend a commoditie when it is naught.'[10]

Charles Tennant would have looked frequently at that board. But at the same time there had come another voice to Scotland in the writings of Adam Smith. This Professor of Moral Philosophy at Glasgow University, who had talked with Voltaire at Geneva, had brought a new understanding to the purpose of making money. With the publication of *The Wealth of Nations*, Smith rid the Scots of any guilt that may have lingered over the pursuit of commerce. To 'truck, barter, and exchange', Smith explained, had been common to all men since the founding of the human race. Man was born a dependent creature and to survive he had lived by dealing. 'Give me that which I want, and you shall have this which you want'[11], were the terms of human barter. Thus in ancient days he who made bows and arrows had done so in exchange for cattle or venison, and so it had progressed as man's ability to better his standard of living had increased. To advance from an agricultural society to an industrial one was part of the progression. Profits, Smith said, were beneficial to society because they enabled industry to expand and thereby guaranteed greater employment; the riches earned by merchants were not to be gainsaid. Merchants generated an enthusiasm and the competitive spirit, and it was through their labours that an ever-prospering economy might be built. *The Wealth of Nations* gave to men like Tennant a moral back-up for the creation of their industrial empires.

Tennant continued to grow richer on his labours, but he was not personally extravagant. As one who had worked hard to make his fortune, he knew that money once spent was not always so easily replaced. Nor did he seek any higher social position. His two sons were educated at Glasgow high school, and he kept in frequent touch with his less well-off brothers, and concerned himself with the lives of his nephews, nieces and cousins. If necessary he would help his poorer relations with gifts of money, and his only irritation was the careless use of that money. He advanced loans and gifts to his brother Robert's family, but clearly without the looked-for result. This annoyed him. On 26 March 1827, Charles wrote to his brother John in Ayrshire:

> By way of Loan and otherwise I am in advance for Robert's family here, upwards considerably of £2000, and were it to be attended with the desired effect of rendering them more independent I should have less reason to regret, but instead of doing so, I fear it may have generated a tendency to expense not altogether consistent with their situations.[12]

Towards the end of Tennant's life a flicker of that fervent early Radicalism returned to him. In July 1838 he was offered a knighthood by the Prime Minister, Lord John Russell, for his contribution to the manufactures and commerce of Great Britain. Charles Tennant replied gratefully to the offer and thanked for 'the very flattering notice it contains of the slight service I have rendered to the Manufactures and Commerce of our Country'. However, the knighthood was declined for, as he put it, 'reasons too numerous and peculiar to be mentioned in this note'. There exists no further correspondence on the matter, but his decision must be obvious. As a lifelong member of the Friends of the People, and an adherent of Thomas Paine who had advocated the abolition of all titles, to accept the honour would have been inconsistent with long-held principles and Tennant was at all times a man of integrity. He never ceased to believe in the new era he had seen born, and that the possibilities for an ever-fairer society must lie with liberal thinking. To this extent he remained a committed Radical.

A few months later, on 1 October 1838, Charles Tennant died at his home. He was seventy-one. At the date of his death the St Rollox Chemical Works covered nearly 100 acres and employed 500 men. The recent expansion was partly due to a relaxation of import duties – for which Free Traders had so fiercely fought – and in particular the total abolition of the salt tax, which had so hampered the soda trade. The demand for bleaching powder had continued to increase annually, and as sales rose the price per ton continued to be lowered. Apart from Tennants' novel system of agents and representatives, the company now had branches in Liverpool and Manchester. His quick eye for improvement had not failed him, and it was an attribute that he passed on to his eldest son, John. Starting from nothing, Charles Tennant left behind him a personal fortune of £90,000, which by modern standards would be worth £5 million. He had secured his descendants against poverty for a long while.

On his death the Glasgow newspapers and public comment were full of praise for Tennant's enterprise and energy. The *Glasgow Argus* of 13 October 1838 spoke of 'his own inborn energy of character and clear intellect', and went on to remark how Tennant, 'by wedding science to manufactures, has at once extended their field of action, and elevated them to the rank of a liberal profession, with all the deep sustained power of a comprehensive mind'. And of his radicalism, John Strang, writing a little later in *Glasgow and its Clubs*, said, 'His purse, his leisure, and his great influence in society were all freely and indefatigably employed in the furtherance of liberal principles and opinions, in the progress and practical application of which he believed the best interests of society to be chiefly concerned.'

Tennant was buried on Glasgow's necropolis – the city's resting place for the distinguished. The necropolis rises to a hill behind the cathedral, and from the summit its mausoleums and monuments descend on either side of winding lanes. The Tennant mausoleum stands on the very height of the hill – for it was one of the cemetery's first tombs – and raised on a large stone plinth is a statue of Charles Tennant seated. From his chair Tennant looks out beyond the cathedral and the river Clyde towards St Rollox. The face is contemplative but filled with determination, even certainty. Today the chemical works have gone, replaced by high-rise apartment blocks, but the face still gazes out to the acres of land that saw the making of a fortune, a new social class and a dynasty.

5

A Fortune and a Concubine

High Tennant chimneys now crested the skyline on the northern limits of the city. Tennant warehouses flanked long stretches on either bank of Junction Canal, and the St Rollox shipping fleet had grown to be the most extensive in Glasgow. Dependent on Tennant products were the many textile mills that had sprung up in and around Glasgow. The Scottish cotton industry had now truly taken off. By 1850 the mills numbered 149. But it was not only St Rollox and the cotton industry that had advanced: Glasgow was changing, too. A multitude of other new industries had also arrived, and the infamous era of overcrowding and tenement building had begun. Streets of houses were erected quickly in an attempt to cope with the rapidly increasing population, but the unceasing flow of migrants filled the city at all points of the compass, and the number of new houses fell far short of demand.

The speed with which St Rollox had grown and developed was but one instance of how Glasgow now began to transform itself from an eighteenth-century town of broad pavements and leisured walks to a dense, industrial city. Soon Glasgow would represent not just this burst of inventive energy that had taken Scotland from its dark ages; it would come to symbolize the distress that followed everywhere in the wake of industrialism. Although those who owned the new iron foundries, potteries, mills, chemical factories, shipbuilding yards and engineering works lived in clean and upright dwellings, for most it was different. For the majority of the labouring class there was no space. In the hope of a better living they had come in from the countryside, and following the Irish famine of the 1840s, they had come from there too. Their search for betterment, however, too often ended as this contemporary witness saw it:

> I have seen human degradation in some of its worst phases, both in England and abroad, but I can advisedly say, that I did not believe until I visited the wynds of Glasgow, that so large an amount of filth, misery and disease existed on one spot in any civilized country. . . . These places are, generally as regards dirt, damp and decay, such as no person of common humanity to animals would stable his horse in. . . . It is my firm belief that penury, dirt, misery, drunkenness, disease and crime culminate in Glasgow to a pitch unparalleled in Great Britain.[1]

Alongside the poverty went the epidemics. Typhus and cholera – two water-borne diseases – struck fiercely during the first half of the century. In 1832 a severe cholera outbreak claimed thousands of victims; in the cholera hospital 79 per cent of the patients died and 3,000 were found dead in the city. The epidemics were caused largely by stagnating sewage and contaminated water supplies. Sewage outlets in Glasgow were frequently no more than an open drain which ran down the centre of narrow lanes – the wynds – while on either side rose rat-infested lodging houses. If the poor could find no other accommodation it meant living in these warrens of decay and disease. And beyond this there were the appallingly contaminated public wells into which both sewage and industrial waste flowed. These irritants of epidemic should have been enough, but the river Clyde, a once-clean river, had become the refuse pit for every new industry.

St Rollox was a chief offender in the pollution troubles. From early days the factory had thrown out noxious fumes and court actions had been brought against the company. An instance of this occurred in 1822 when a number of nearby residents had grouped together to complain. The book of their complaints survives. The residents said that the smuts dropped by the discharged smoke blackened the vicinity and that the fumes brought on coughing and sickness. One plaintiff, John Turnbull, a druggist, gave the following statement on the damage done to his plantings:

> Last year his potatoes and other crops were greatly hurt and during the present season several thousand of seedling beeches along with six thousand seedling thorns have been entirely destroyed. The witness has not the slightest doubt that this was occasioned by the works. When the wind blows in a direction from them he not only feels a most offensive smell in the gardens but can distinctly observe the stream of gas passing over it. . . .[2]

The foul fumes and smuts discharged from the chimneys came from the making of sulphuric acid, which necessitated the burning of massive quantities of coal. Charles Tennant – and his son, John – were aware that there was no easy solution to the problem. In those pioneer days there was no method whereby the smoke could be 'cleaned' before it passed into the atmosphere. Tennant's choice was either to close down the works or to play for time and prevaricate. Tennant took the latter course as another plaintiff's statement shows:

> The smell of the works is at all times very offensive when the wind is north and makes her sick and inclined to vomit. Her son says it affects him too, but not so much. She thinks the injury increased since the high stalk was built. Whenever the wind is in the north it pours down upon her. She considers this wholly to arise from the manufacture of vitriol – and if Mr Tennant would give that up, she would let him carry on the other things as he pleased. Mr Stewart told her Mr Tennant had promised to give it up some years ago – but doubts this now as she sees new buildings going up.[3]

It would have been too much to expect Tennant to sacrifice such an important part of his business, but the outcome for him was good. In none of the cases brought against Charles Tennant & Co. did the plaintiffs ever make an impression. The Tennants firmly held their ground until their pursuers were prepared to settle for a small sum. St Rollox was too closely linked with Scotland's revitalized identity for any more serious action to be taken. This comment from two bleachers during the 1822 inquiry makes this clear: 'They also state that such is the present extensive dependence of the bleaching Trade in Scotland, upon the produce of the Defenders Establishment, that it would occasion a national calamity where it suspended only for a few weeks.'[4]

But by the time John Tennant succeeded his father the problem of chemical waste had increased to an alarming degree. With the growth of the factory the spread of fumes and smuts had redoubled. John Tennant had long been aware that a solution must be found. 'I've got it . . . I've got it!'[5] he was overheard to mumble during a Sunday sermon. At St Rollox he would build the tallest chimney in Britain, if not in Europe; a chimney that would carry the fumes and smuts so far into the atmosphere that they would be lost for ever in the higher skies.

With the building of the chimney in 1842, St Rollox became a distinctive landmark of industrial Glasgow. Its foundations were sunk 20 feet below the surface, resting on a base of sandstone rock, while the whole chimney tapered upwards to a full height of 435 feet. It stood three times the height of Nelson's Column in Trafalgar Square, and no view of Victorian Glasgow was complete without it. It was the wonder of the new city and a sign of fulfilled promise for the age. The chimney was known simply as Tennant's Stalk – stalk being the term employed for the tall industrial chimneys. It entered into local folklore as a symbol of the impossible: 'Until Tennant's Stalk down Buchanan Street walk,' went a song.

It was sad, though, that the great chimney did not have the

57

effect that Tennant had so desired. The chemical filth may have been sent further into the atmosphere but still it came down again, only a little further afield. A pall of yellow smoke hung continuously over the area of the works and now it spread beyond them. A contemporary cartoon was made of St Rollox where behind a density of smoke could be seen blackened brick stalks. The ironic caption read, 'A clear day at St Rollox'. A civil engineer, George Dodd, contributing in 1847 to a book *The Land We Live In*, portrayed the realities of the works and working scene at St Rollox in words that might have come from Charles Dickens:

> They are, necessarily, black and dirty; and some of them are as infernal in appearance as we can well imagine any earthly place to be. The heaps of sulphur, lime, coal, and refuse; the intense heat of the scores of furnaces in which the processes are going on; the smoke and thick vapours which dim the air of most of the buildings; the swarthy and heated appearance of the men; the acrid fumes of sulphur, and the various acids which worry the eyes, and tickle the nose, and choke the throat; the danger which every bit of broad-cloth incurs of being bleached by something else – all form a series of *notabilia* not soon to be forgotten. The buildings occupy an immense square, from which shoot up numerous chimneys. Many of these chimneys are equal to the largest in other towns, but they are here mere satellites to the monster of the place – THE Chimney.[6]

And yet St Rollox was also a monument to the kind of progress to which every industrialist would aspire. Another writer, J. D. Burn, who in his book *Commercial Enterprise and Social Progress* had noted the changes that were occurring in Britain's new industrial cities, viewed St Rollox with impressed amazement rather than Dodd's horrified alarm. He begins his assessment of the place with nothing short of the highest praise:

> If there was no other manufacturing or commercial

establishment in Glasgow than the stupendous works of Charles Tennant & Co., it would be a place of commercial importance. This chemical laboratory stands alone in its greatness, not only in Great Britain, but there is nothing equal to it in the whole world.[7]

Then Burn continues to give us a description of the various departments – the soda, soda-ash and chloride of lime departments, the soap manufactory (60 tons a week) and, most intriguing of all to him, the sulphuric acid section. 'We pass', he remarks, 'between two mountains of sulphur, each of which contains 5,000 tons.' He is taken up a flight of steps which places him 100 feet above the surrounding buildings. Below him he sees 'fifty-eight lead chambers for receiving the sulphurous gas, and converting it into vitriol'. Each of these reservoirs holds 21,000 cubic feet of gas. Burn descends again where, 'We are once more on the solid earth, and much of it is melting in our presence. Men are moving about like spirits in the fitful glare of the fiery furnaces; some are breaking up the mountains of crystallised soda, others again are bearing immense loads of salt into furnaces.' Burn may see St Rollox as an inferno but one that is more blessed than damned.

Concerned as John Tennant was about the pollution, he was first and foremost a hard-headed, practical man running the most successful chemical business in the Western world. He would not have seen St Rollox with the imaginative sensations of the above writers. Of course he wanted the well-being of his employees otherwise he could hardly have carried on; medical supervision was provided and should any serious illness occur the employee was sent to Glasgow's Royal Infirmary. Working with chemicals could be vary hazardous: a chief chemist at St Rollox bore the nickname 'Sniffer' Crystal as his nose had been partially burnt away through the sniffing of chemical mixtures. Tennant would have minded about this, but he minded as much about the price of his chemicals. 'Well, what's to be the price this year?'[8] was the question he waited to ask his head man every January. As productivity increased the price could be lowered, sales would once again strengthen, and profits would gross.

John Tennant was precisely the sort of man that the Industrial Revolution might have planned to produce. He believed in the age to which he had been born as totally as the great Whig landowners had previously held faith in their estates. When Tennant travelled it was for business and pleasure was always secondary. The arts and the visual side of life meant little to him. Journeying to Italy and Sicily to inspect some sulphur mines he had acquired, he wrote home with the cry, 'Let me see no more Italian gardens!'9 On moving to his father's house in West George Street he was not sparing in his hospitality but the company was mostly made up of fellow businessmen and politicians. It is said John Tennant once entertained the visiting Chopin – but that would have been because of his distinguished position in the city. It was the dream of the Radical Richard Cobden that Britain should be governed by its new merchant class rather than by its hereditary aristocracy. The merchant class were in touch with economic reality. They wasted no time in foolish indulgence. Had this been so John Tennant would have been a leader among his own kind.

And yet there was another side to him that has defied explanation. At twenty-two he had taken up with a woman of no known background who had already lived with two other men. One of these men was a well-known Glasgow physician, Dr Bulmanno, and the other a businessman named McCulloch. The woman's name was Robina Arrol and she already had two children by one of her former lovers. How Tennant met her remains a mystery, although it seems likely that she would either have been passed on to him or that they met at a place of public entertainment. From the outset they lived together, and were never legally married. According to a boy who worked in their first house, John placed an engraved plate on the door announcing, 'Mr and Mrs John Tennant', but this was for decency's sake and short-lived. There was clearly more than one aspect of the situation that embarrassed John Tennant but no record of his attitude survives. He appears not to have mentioned Robina to anyone; when the 1861 census was taken in Glasgow, he wrote boldly alongside his name 'unmarried'.

Understandably, perhaps, the rest of the Tennant family did not take kindly to the arrangement. For a family that was in the process of establishing itself it was hardly a forward step. John's mother strongly disapproved and so did his younger brother, Charles James. But it was only the convention of marriage that John had flaunted; when his three children were born he brought them up with affection and responsibility as would any normal father. Robina seems to have played little part in their upbringing; it may have been a more patriarchal society then, but one would expect to find some evidence of her influence. There are no letters to her from her children and none from her to them. She is not even mentioned in John Tennant's will. And when she predeceased him from consumption she was not buried in the new Tennant vault on the necropolis. Robina came into and went out of the family, leaving her genes, but little else.

It was not until after his mother's death in 1843 that John Tennant moved to the family mansion in West George Street. Before that he had lived in a house close to the factory – and it would seem that he continued to use that house as a secondary residence throughout his life. When the 1861 census was taken he was in fact staying at Garngad Road and not West George Street. In keeping with his practical outlook, there would have been moments when he considered it necessary for him to be on the spot, but West George Street was the family home where Tennant kept a good table and where his children – when they were in Glasgow – went.

What, one asks, was the Tennant house in West George Street like? Outside it was indeed substantial with a broad portico supported by double Ionic columns. It stood at a cross-section of the street, looking solid and rectangular. But how much did the interior reflect the way of life of a busy and successful Glasgow merchant? The house had as many as four to five sitting rooms all furnished with sensible dark pieces so as not to over-excite the imagination. This description of the dining room has been left by one of John's grandsons:

> The dining-room was large and bore all the embellishments one associates with the early period of Queen Victoria's reign. Solidity, what might even be termed handsome solidity, had been the aim of the decorator, and he had made a bull's eye. The mahogany tables, the pillars, the chairs, the curtains, the pictures, the sideboard and mantelpiece betrayed no weakness, no infirmity of delicacy anywhere. When to this you add the blazing gas jets and a glorious coal fire, I trust the picture is complete.[10]

Yet of the many downstairs rooms, only two were properly used: the dining room and a marble-floored smoking room. In one, Tennant dispensed a generous hospitality of food and wine, while in the other, heavy with cigar smoke, he discussed commerce, politics or movements on the stock market with his fellow merchants. West George Street, therefore, perfectly fulfilled both a residential and mercantile purpose.

John's and Robina's three children were Marion, John and Charles. They were born in 1819, 1821 and 1823 respectively, and spent little of their childhood in Glasgow. Tennant decided that they would be better off in Ayr, and it was here that they grew up, looked after by a Tennant cousin, Elizabeth Turner. It might be tempting to conclude that Tennant did not want Robina to bring up his children: a woman of unknown background, with a shady history, might not be thought the ideal mother – yet I doubt that this was Tennant's reason. More likely he wanted his children to grow up in a healthy place, and what could be better than a seaside town? Ayr was pretty and unspoilt – a town that did not know the meaning of pollution. Also, for the Tennants Ayrshire was full of cousins: it was the land of their roots.

Tennant sent his two sons to the Ayr Academy, where his great-uncle David had been headmaster. The school now had a reputation as one of the best in Scotland, but when they were about ten Tennant moved his sons to an independent private school run by a seceder minister, the Reverend Archibald Browning. Browning's school was at Tillicoultry in the central Lowlands and took in around forty day boys and boarders. Why should Tennant have wanted to change their education? The answer reveals something about Tennant. Browning was famous for instilling independence in his pupils; he taught them to act and think for themselves rather than by the slaves of received ideas. He taught them, in brief, to question.

It was planned that both John and Charles should enter the business, and their father wanted sons who could act in a tough, commercial climate. He did not want yes-men for sons, or sons who might be in any way effete. He needed sons who would be down to earth, yet individual; and the school at Tillicoultry seemed to promise this where the accent was on the shaping of character rather than enforced godliness. That the boys clearly knew their father's attitude is indicated in this extract from a letter written (at a slightly later date) by the younger son, Charles, to his sister Marion: 'Write to me as often and as long letters as you feel inclined but to my father be brief – you know this is his desire – he is a man of few words, and long pious reflections, and expression of excited sentiment do not harmonise with a mind so active and practical and so much employed.'[11]

The nonconformist aspect of Browning would also have appealed to Tennant. Whatever the fears of fire and brimstone that had persuaded his early ancestors to hold life at naught and to place all hope in the hereafter did not touch John Tennant. Busy with commerce, he was fulfilling that side of the Calvinist text that preached the worthiness of a useful life; the hereafter could wait until another day. It was not that Tennant was either an agnostic or an atheist, but that St Rollox was his religion. The preachings of Adam Smith were more real to him than the sermonizings of Presbyterian ministers. Hence he could dream up his stalk in church and on another occasion confuse the Lord's Prayer with the twenty-third psalm.

In spite of his unconventional domestic arrangement, the Tennant family were fortunate in having John at the head of St Rollox. Had control fallen to his younger brother, Charles James, their wealth might well have been short-lived. Although in early days he had been a partner in the firm with John, by 1850 the partnership had been severed. The two brothers quarrelled, probably because Charles James was more interested in the fineries of a gentleman than in the business. His money was spent on his dress, maintaining a country estate and a pretty wife. For his dandified ways he was known as 'the Vipe'. He took care not to meet any of the poorer Tennant relations left behind in Ayrshire, claiming that he really did not know 'these people'. And the last thing he wanted was for the well-bred image he presented of himself to be tainted by associations with trade. A Glasgow cousin of the Tennants, David Murray, well known as an antiquarian besides being a solicitor, kept a book of notes on the Tennants, and of his memories of Charles James he had this comment: 'He walked smartly, with his head in the air, as if all the world belonged to him, and prepared to knock any one over who might venture to dispute his claim.'[12]

But St Rollox rested firmly with John, and the bid of Charles James to make the Tennants gentlemen came to nothing, for his marriage was without issue. Instead John, content to be known as 'merchant' or 'manufacturer', saw St Rollox through its period of greatest prosperity. Sir Robert Peel's budgets of the 1840s all favoured the new merchant class: although a Tory, Peel was a rich cotton spinner's son and the interests of the new class were close to him. He knew that it was the energy of the industrialists that could give Britain a thriving economy, so he cut import duties thereby winning the long-fought battle for Free Trade and, more as a symbolic than economic victory, repealed the Corn

Laws. The effect of Peel's trading measures was soon felt at St Rollox. By the 1850s Tennant chemicals were being sold in Europe, the West Indies and the USA.

It was the repeal of the Corn Laws that made the landed class realize that they were no longer the dominant power. Much as they disliked every aspect of Free Trade, they particularly resented a cut in duty that seemed to hit directly at their own interest. Now foreign corn would be bought and not theirs. But the argument was not so simple, and since England was almost self-sufficient and the foreign supply limited, the actual economic slight was not so great. None the less, the industrial merchants were now being given preference over them. Lord George Bentinck, speaking for his class, exclaimed, 'What I cannot bear is being sold.'[3] The landed chose to forget that many of their families had benefited – and continued to benefit – through marriage into trade, and they developed a renewed horror of the business classes. Throughout the nineteenth century and beyond, few opportunities were missed to mock those of trading origins.

Secure in Glasgow – the very citadel of industrial progress – the Tennants remained unmoved by this landed spite. When John Tennant replied to the census he calmly put down, 'Manufacturing chemist, soap & etc,' while he listed in his employ '887 men and 807 boys'. The boys' ages ranged from twelve to sixteen and they did the manual work. They were educated at the St Rollox school and many would have been the children of the adult employees. Given the heat from furnaces and the quantities of sooty grime, St Rollox must have looked like a scene from the worst industrial excesses as described by Charles Dickens: the boys half-clad and toiling under loads, the men hot and begrimed from furnaces. But it would be wrong to assume that the conscience of every 'ironmaster' was as blunt as that of Josiah Bounderby of Dickens's harsh satire *Hard Times* (1854). Dickens needed to speak strongly because there were terrible ills, but Tennant was not blinded by his own greed. St Rollox may have had a reputation for its foul smells, but it was not known for

brutalizing its employees. Admittedly, though, John Tennant did
not stray far beyond the conscience of his day; like many others,
he believed that in the great industrial adventure lay the ultimate
cure for every ill.

The faith that most mid-Victorians held in the Industrial
Revolution is perhaps hard to understand today, but we cannot
judge them accurately without that understanding. It even
influenced Tennyson to write in 'Locksley Hall', 'Saw the
heavens fill with commerce, argosies of magic sails . . .'. And J.
D. Burn wrote enthusiastically about St Rollox and its surrounding area:

> When the works of Mr Tennant were first established at St
> Rollox, they were completely isolated and stood alone in
> their fragrant glory. What a change has come over the
> dream of that once dreary locality. The whole district for
> miles is now teeming with manufacturing life; potteries,
> glassworks, saw-mills, iron-foundries and machine-shops,
> coal depots, earthenware manufactories, railway stations,
> and a busy hard working and commercial population
> occupy almost every inch of the ground.[14]

John Tennant died in 1878 aged eighty-two. He could feel
proud that he had not only increased the fame of Charles
Tennant & Co. but given St Rollox an added distinction through
the highly trained and often well-known chemists he employed –
unusual, at this date, in a bleaching works. It was just 100 years
since his father, Charles, had journeyed to Glasgow in pursuit of
his discovery. The Tennants had established a leading place in
merchant society, come to exemplify the rapid pace of Scotland's
progress and Glasgow felt honoured by them. They were an
integral part of the new city that was winning international
renown. In a book entitled *One Hundred Glasgow Men*, the
anonymous author could write of John Tennant,

> He was almost the last of our great merchants who were first
> and foremost Glasgow men. He refused to follow the custom,

now become too common, of looking on Glasgow simply as a disagreeable place where money is to be made, being in it as little as possible, and giving all that is in one to other places far away. His interests and pleasures were alike centred in Glasgow; his most intimate friends were here; he lived among us all his life, and at last died here in the house that his father had built.[15]

But it is not quite true to say that John Tennant never thought of leaving Glasgow. Around 1850 he did, in fact, make a bid for a 4,000-acre estate in Peeblesshire, but the estate went elsewhere and Tennant was the under-bidder. Though why should Tennant, who was so committed to his business, wish to buy a property some sixty miles away? I do not believe that he wanted to set himself up as a landed gentleman, but the reason could have been the new levy, income tax. An income tax had been introduced during the Napoleonic wars, but Peel's levy was to be permanent. At first it was only sevenpence in the pound, but inevitably it grew. A merchant like Tennant would have had more income than he needed to spend and one answer was to put that money into land. With the money in land it would not be taxed, and the likelihood was that its value would grow.

John Tennant did not think again of buying land, but he kept a shrewd eye on his fortune. At his death he was worth a little more than £5 million; most of his fortune was in St Rollox and he left partnerships available to his near family. These were for the children of his elder son John, who had died of consumption – a legacy of his mother Robina – at the age of twenty-nine. Robina's other pronounced trait – a less harmful one – was her tight curly hair, which she passed to her younger son, Charles, who was now to control the destiny of the family. It is said that this woman – of whom we have so little knowledge beyond one surviving miniature – had a good intelligence, but the truth of her qualities we shall never know. John had made an excellent job of destroying all the evidence.

There were signs that the Tennants were to alter course. John was the last St Rollox Tennant to make Glasgow fully his home. Other Tennant cousins migrated there from Ayrshire, but the line that had established the name was now restless to move on. During his long minority, Charles had been expanding his interests, and those of his family, across the world. The Tennants were ready to cross the Border: Mincing Lane and Grosvenor Square were to become their new homes as much as St Rollox and West George Street.

6

A Great Entrepreneur

The man who put in the successful bid for that Peeblesshire estate was none other than John Tennant's son, Charles. 'How much money have you got, Charlie?' was the query of the surprised father. The reply was, '£90,000' – or over £14 million by today's figures. John Tennant must have been amazed by such a sum and he responded in the true, dry humour of a merchant: 'The devil you have!'[1] But this was exactly the amount that the thirty-year-old Charles had already made independent of his rich background. Clearly, this young Tennant lacked neither drive nor initiative. John Tennant might well feel proud that the vigorous Tennant genes were still much in evidence.

One reason for Charles's impressive youthful performance was that there had been no question at any time that he should be indulged on account of the family wealth. At sixteen, John Tennant had removed his son from the Reverend Browning's school and apprenticed him to a Liverpool merchant. William Nevett was a dealer in fabrics and Charles's godfather. With him, Charles learnt about dyeing and the quality of materials. After four years there, John Tennant made Charles, along with his brother John, working partners in one of the subsidiary Tennant companies. In 1844, the next year, when he was twenty-one, Charles went to work with the London branch, which was now named Charles Tennant & Sons, still in Upper Thames Street. However, John Tennant did give his son some financial backing. He provided him with an annual allowance of £400, plus £2,000 to make his life with, by current reckoning around £12,000 and £60,000 respectively. It was an attractive sum to spend, but the young Tennant did not dissipate it. Knowing that he would have a long wait before he rose further in the firm, and being the younger son, he decided that he would make a fortune on his own account. These were the early signs of a restless energy that needed to be constantly employed.

Soon after his arrival in town, Charles went to see Mr Overand Gurney, a well-known City banker. He proposed to Gurney that his bank might advance him a loan for the purchase of some shares in the Midland Railway. Surprisingly perhaps – since the railway boom was as hazardous as it could be exciting – Gurney agreed. He must have felt a confidence in Tennant, not only to have agreed but to take only the share certificates as security. But Gurney's confidence was rewarded, for the investment paid off and money fell into Tennant's pockets. So began a career for Tennant where everything he touched seemed to become gold.

For several years Charles stayed in his brother John's house in the Boltons. It was while recovering from a slight illness that Charles wrote the following letter to his sister, Marion, in Edinburgh. Obliged to look at the church that stands in the centre of the square, Charles Tennant suddenly began to question whether there might not be a higher life outside business:

> The Church before me ought to remind me of all that is beautiful and holy, but share lists will obtrude themselves and stir the avarice of all bad passions. . . . I spend my time, of course, principally in reading, poetry is my favourite, and Byron, as you know, is 'my soul's delight', his work and life are the only books I ever asked my father to give me. . . . Business, however, is such an enemy to the Beautiful and Sublime in thought . . .[2]

But these lightly touched doubts were not to last. 'The avarice of all bad passions' triumphed and Charles was soon set on another adventure. This time it was shares bought in 1847 in an Autralian land company. He may have had to wait a year for news, owing to the slowness of communication, but when it came the news was good. His realizable profit was immense and made up the larger part of his fortune. Charles acted fast when he saw a likely opportunity. In 1847 an Act had been passed making it possible to buy large tracts of unused land in Australia. Speculators at once bought property in vital areas, such as those controlling water supplies, and thereby holding a monopoly over developers. The assets of this land could then be resold at vast increases. But first of all the speculators needed backing, and it was just such a company in which Charles Tennant had bought a large stake of shares.

It suited Charles Tennant's temperament to make money so quickly. He was twenty-five and already a millionaire many times over. His success came in part from an absolute self-assurance and confidence, boosted without doubt by the financial solidity his family had already achieved. Byron now became a glimmer on a far horizon as he threw himself into the speculative arena. But like many who both make and preserve their fortunes, a fraction of a per cent lost or gained mattered deeply to him. He had the boldness to take risks underpinned by a scrupulous attention to detail. His character was well expressed by his short but always immaculately dressed figure. With his quick movements and need for rapid answers, he had not time to waste on the shortcomings of this world. The pace of commerce and the thrust of dealings on the market were his precise measure, and he required no other. Later, his daughter, Margot, was to see him thus: 'He had the courage for life and the enterprise to spend his fortune on it. He was kind and impulsively generous, but too hasty for disease to accost or death to delay. For him they were interruptions, not abiding sorrows.'[3]

Charles lost no time either in finding himself a wife. During his illness, which was the result of a swelling on his leg, he had gone to take the waters at Malvern. In 1849, he made a second visit and met there, also for the second time, a young girl named Emma

Winsloe. Emma was there in the care of her mother, who some time past had been deserted by a spendthrift husband. Richard Winsloe was the son of a Devon vicar and his mother, Catherine Walter, was the daughter of the founder of *The Times*. Emma's mother had been brought up by her paternal grandfather, an Admiral Monkton, who had served under Admiral Howe on that Glorious First of June in 1794. But Richard Winsloe had spent what money his wife had, leaving Charlotte Winsloe nothing but an allowance of £200 a year from the Devon vicar. On this she struggled to bring up and educate her two children.

Because of her father's negligent ways, Emma had grown up to know hardship. With their mother, the two children had led a wandering existence. France was then cheaper than England and for a time Emma and her brother had lived in Le Havre. After that, their mother had taken them to Paris where Emma had learnt to speak French fluently, and, at her convent school, lacework. It was the kind of background – respectable but poor – that might have equipped her to deal admirably with a life of petty economies, but it was not to be. In August 1849, some months only after they had met again, Charles married her; the anxious, rather withdrawn girl became the wife of one of England's richer young men. It was also the first marriage that the Tennants had made outside Scotland.

Charles now began to think about giving the Tennants more permanent roots. Until then they had been quite content with their newly established place in the metropolis, but Charles was not one to hoard his riches. He saw in his imagination a setting more idyllic than the smog-filled Glasgow landscape. In 1853 he put in his successful bid for the Peeblesshire estate, known as the Glen. What he bought at first was a property of just under 4,000 acres, centred by a modest house, which sat in the bottom of a valley flanked by heathered hills and wild moors. The setting was perfect, but the house was not what Charles envisaged. To achieve the touch he desired, he employed the fashionable Scottish architect David Bryce, to build him a house in fantasy baronial style. Glen was modelled on the style of Glamis, and up it went, with turrets and gargoyles menacing. With its fairy-tale quality, Glen excellently expressed the rich man's need to escape.

Charles was still only thirty when the Tennant seat was built. But it was before Glen had been started that Charles had already begun a family, and he was to show himself as fecund a producer of children as he was energetic for business. His first child, Janet, was born in 1850, but lived only sixteen years before dying of tuberculosis. Three more, Charles, John and Charles, were born, but all died in childhood of the same disease. The legacy of Robina was working itself out. The first child to live into adult life was Pauline, known as Posie. And after her came Charlotte – Charty – and Edward, or Eddy. There followed another five children – three more girls and two boys – the last being born in 1865. This new generation of Tennants, raised on fresh air and rustic tranquillity, knew little of Glasgow. To them, it was a strange, dark city where people toiled in sad conditions. Glen, where there was time to ramble and dream, was their reality.

Meanwhile, in Upper Thames Street the Tennant interests were spreading. For a long while now the company had considerably extended their activities from simply agenting the bleaching powder. They were now widely employed as commission agents, exporting a large variety of goods to Europe, notably tallow, for the making of candles. They also exported their own alum, acid and vitriol. By 1850, Britain's industrialists were approaching the boom years: years when the benefits of Free Trade could be gloriously reaped. Between 1850 and 1870 exports rose from £71 million to £200 million while imports trebled from £100 million to £300 million. During those years, Britain stood alone in the world as a trading power, which was extremely beneficial to the Tennants. Nothing, it seemed, could dim their ever ascending star.

In 1866 Charles Tennant involved himself in a venture that was to gain him a reputation far beyond the confines of St Rollox and the stock market. Brimstone, the chief source of sulphur, was largely found in Sicily, but over the years the mines had been passing into the hands of the British. For instance, in 1838 John Tennant and a Liverpool colleague, James Muspratt, had jointly bought one there. In that same year Ferdinand of Naples, annoyed that Europe and Britain in particular should be exploiting his kingdom in this way, placed a heavy duty on all exported sulphur. Next, he gave the monopoly on all exported sulphur to a Marseille firm. Lord Palmerston, Britain's Foreign Secretary, was furious. Acting, as always, on his own initiative, Palmerston first sent a threatening note to Naples. The King chose not to listen, so Palmerston commanded the Royal Navy to seize Italian coasting vessels. In retaliation, Ferdinand sent 12,000 troops to Sicily, but the British proved the stronger force; in 1840 the monopoly was cancelled.

The price of sulphur may have fallen, but the British chemical manufacturers were scared. Sicily could no longer be depended upon; they must look elsewhere for their mineral. After several false starts, British manufacturers turned to using Spanish pyrites – now the best-known source of sulphur. But the Spanish pyrites had an additional advantage – it also contained copper. At present the pyrites was imported from Spain in its raw form; what the manufacturers badly needed was a mine where the minerals could be refined on the spot. At last, in the 1860s, they saw their chance.

In the south-west corner of Spain lay the greatest sulphide deposits in the world. These mines had first been worked for their metals by the Tartessians, natives of the area, who produced, around 1000 BC, a civilization famed throughout the ancient world. Next, came the Phoenicians from faraway Tyre and Sidon, who needed Spanish silver to finance their trading to the Orient. They held the monopoly of the metal market of Tartessus for two centuries, but when Nebuchadnezzar laid siege to Tyre in the sixth century BC, the Phoenician empire was broken and their control of the mines ended. The mines were now famous with the traders of the ancient world, and from Greece there followed the

Phocaeans – a powerful maritime people – who brought wine and olive oil in exchange for the precious metals. But in 535 BC the Carthaginians conquered the Phocaeans, destroyed the city of Tartessus, and took over the mines. Three hundred and fifty years later, the Carthaginians were overcome by the Romans. The history of the mines was as dramatic as the wealth they contained.

The Romans mined the area for over 400 years, drawing from them silver, gold, copper and iron. When they left, after the fall of their empire, the mines lay idle for a thousand years. Many thought the Romans had exhausted them, but in fact they had only taken an outer surface. Modern mining methods could strike deeper into the rocks, where thousands of tons of pyrites waited to yield up its copper and sulphur. This was how it appeared to Ernest Deligny, a French engineer, sent in 1850 to investigate the prospects. It was Deligny who named them the 'Mines of Tharsis', partly because the local hill bore that name, but also because of the Biblical Tarshish, a once-thriving ancient colony that was supposed to have inhabited that place. Thus Deligny no longer saw before him a sleepy fishing village, but a new town filled with a Tharsis workforce.

But the French company that had employed Deligny eventually fell into difficulties. The problems ranged from poor administration to the sheer cost of reworking the mines. The company did not have the money: for example, they needed funds to build a railway that would take the goods to the sea. This lack of finance was not helped by internal quarrelling and finally it was decided to sell out to Britain, where the chemical and engineering industry led the world. Headed by Charles Tennant, a number of the larger British manufacturers had grouped together. They negotiated terms and in 1866 formed the Tharsis Sulphur and Copper Company. But it was Tennant who was their mentor, force, and guiding light.

Under Charles Tennant, the dream to revive the mines was realized. To carry out the scheme required the kind of entrepreneurial dash that Tennant so firmly possessed; risking large sums of capital in a venture on foreign soil was unheard of at this time and Charles had to persuade his father into the scheme. He may have already made a fortune in his own right, but John Tennant still sat as head of the family. After some hesitation, he saw the point of the plan, and soon Charles was writing back from Spain: 'All day I have been on a stretch in this extraordinary mine. I can quite understand the gentleman who said there were two things worth seeing in Spain – the Cathedral at Seville and the *"ciel ouvert"* at Tharsis.'[4]

The mines at Tharsis turned out to be a great success. There was copper and sulphur to be had in plentiful supply, and it came at a time when both could be used in a multitude of developing industries. Two mining villages grew up round Tharsis, populated by 1,200 Spanish workmen. Again, it was Tennant who saw to much of the organization, and he recruited the management from Scotland. The Scots had a reputation for getting a job done, and they could keep a disciplinary eye on any idlers. A school, a Roman Catholic and a Protestant Church were built. Tharsis became virtually a self-sufficient community, a little piece of empire in the middle of Europe. And sitting at the head of this empire with supreme self-confidence, was Charles Tennant.

The achievement of Tharsis paved the way for other operations, with Charles Tennant backed by the same syndicate. He now had the greatest names in the chemical industry firmly behind him: men like David Gamble, Henry Deacon and John Williamson, all the possessors of important chemical plants. Six years after the opening of Tharsis, they founded the Steel Company of Scotland, with Tennant once again as chairman. Tennant enjoyed the honours they paid him: business, like politics, is to do with power, and Tennant clearly enjoyed the position he had arrived at so early. There is something almost theatrical in S. G. Checkland's descriptions of Tennant conducting a Tharsis meeting:

He was bowed out of the Tharsis boardroom by his fellow directors as though they were facing royalty. He dominated

76

any negotiations in which he was involved, looking over a high-bridged patrician nose with eyes that could transfix, and pursing a sharply defined mouth. . . .[5]

Later in his book, Checkland mentions one of Tennant's many winning touches: 'Tennant was especially effective at shareholders' meetings – disclosing just enough to create a sense of participation, but withholding any data upon which embarrassing questions might be based.'

'Rich, modern, and busy' were the words Margot used, when many years later she portrayed her father in a novel.[6] And, indeed, as Tennant's commercial fame grew, so did the list of companies on whose board he sat. By the end of his life he was chairman of fourteen different companies and a director of nine others. From some of their names it could be said that Tennant sat at the head of the speculative wealth of the nineteenth century. There were: Mysore Gold Mining Company, Champion Reef Gold Mining Company, Coromandel Gold Mines of India, Nine Reefs Company, Balaghat Gold Mining Company, Sudan Gold Fields – and so the progress reads on, through chemical companies and steel, to the railways of America. Such enterprises kept him ceaselessly on the move; his letters home indicate this activity. 'Just in from City after 6 Boards & one Shareholders' meeting',[7] goes a typical letter.

As Charles pursued his business pace, his children were growing up at Glen among all the comforts he had established there. He filled the house with books and, by the time they were young adults, with pictures too. Margot said that she and her sisters got their education from the books in the Glen library, although they also had a governess and the boys, instead of being educated in Scotland, were sent to Eton. Charles had created a background whereby his children might have the benefits of the country-house upbringing, but for the Tennants there was a slight difference. They were Liberals living in a Tory stronghold; they were not popular, therefore, with many of the neighbours.

The duller, stiffer, more conventional kind did not visit Glen. The children's friends therefore tended to be the various adult personalities who passed through the house. This encouraged them, and in particular the girls, to the talkative and questioning.

The three boys – Eddy, Frank and Jack – were put through the system intended to produce gentlemen. Prep school and then Eton made their characters quieter and more conforming than those of their sisters. It also gave them a different attitude towards the fortune that sent them there. They accepted it much as their landed schoolfellows accepted the inheritance of land, and sporting interests meant more to them than the making of chemicals. Charles's third son, Jack, went to serve an apprenticeship in the Glasgow works before going up to Cambridge. His account of his year there is revealing in its implications of the change that had taken place:

> I cannot say that I think my Glasgow experience was a success. After breakfast I trudged up to the works of St Rollox along that interminable Parliamentary Road, some two miles long, and arrived there, I gossiped with a clerk or book-keeper or possibly the works manager for half an hour. I would then go with a foreman over the vitriol plant and test acid of various strengths. I climbed up steep ladders and got my clothes spotted with vitriol, which first made a red mark and then left a hole. Or another time I would go over the saltcake plant or the bleaching powder plant, and I trudged back again in the evening. I got to know something about the manufacture of heavy chemicals, but I had no duties and no responsibilities, and I was not very happy. I knew not a soul in Glasgow, there were no Old Etonians, and I had no companions or recreations.[8]

It is probable that Charles Tennant did not realize the extent to which a public-school education would distance his sons from coping with the challenge of a business empire, but equally, his own vanity would have been to blame for it. It pleased him to know that he was a force to be reckoned with; that he stood a giant among the chemical manufacturers; that the London Stock Market often waited until Charles Tennant had begun dealing. He might not have liked the limelight being stolen from him in old age by a young, energetic son. And, anyway, surely the fortune was solid enough? Beyond a directorship here or there, there would be no need for his sons to tamper with his empire's basic construction. Why not, then, let his sons become country gentlemen? Glen, with its shooting and its fishing was there to be enjoyed, and who better to enjoy it than his own offspring. But like many men committed to the world, Charles had not counted on his own mortality. A day inevitably had to come when the empire he had made, and that to which he had succeeded, must pass into other hands.

In 1881 Charles Tennant bought himself a large town house in London's Grosvenor Square.* Although for some years before the death of his father he had been in control at St Rollox, there were now clear reasons for him needing a significant London base. He had too much business in the City to be kept distant any more from the heart of operations; since 1879 he had been a Liberal Member of Parliament; and in 1880 he had embarked on the greatest speculative adventure of his life – the Mysore goldfields. But he had picked a London square which contained a large portion of England's ancient Tory aristocracy, and the arrival of this trading Liberal family from Glasgow was viewed with disdain by society's old order. Charles, however, was not one to heed the raised eyebrow. He stood, after all, on the heights of the financial universe, and he felt no need to be bowed by the powers of any other. And least of all, perhaps, by the class that had tried to hold 'trade' down, and keep men like Tennant from having their wealth.

At this time, Charles Tennant became friendly with some former Indian civil servants, who told him about disused gold

* Originally 35, it was later renumbered as 40.

mines in Mysore. Tennant's interest was immediate. He saw that, like Tharsis, these mines could be reworked and new gold discovered. He formed the Mysore Gold Mining Company, becoming its chairman. Because his name was on the prospectus, shares soon moved from £1 to £8; but reworking the mines took time and after three years both shareholders and directors had begun to panic. By 1884, with nothing to show and a great deal of capital sunk, the shares had fallen back to 9d. But Charles Tennant remained confident. He bought in huge quantities of extra shares at the new low price, and bought out any dissatisfied shareholder at par. Only £13,000 capital remained to continue sinking shafts in the hope of a major find and his directors recommended that the project be abandoned, but Tennant counselled the opposite. In 1886 gold was struck, and by 1889 the profit return on each Mysore dividend was 75 per cent.

An incident erupted in 1883 with Tennant's Tharsis Company which showed that a man in his position could not afford to involve himself in sharp practices. It was reported that Charles Tennant, chairman of Tharsis, had with a number of directors sold shares in advance of poor end-of-year results and then bought back once the price had fallen. Today, 'insider dealing' – as it is known – is illegal, but in those days it was no offence but considered extremely bad form. A letter written by a shareholder, Alexander Crum, to Charles Gairdner, manager of Scotland's Union Bank where Tennant was deputy chairman, puts the case:

> I am very happy to hear that Tennant was able to make his position clear. – As reported here on Tuesday night he was one of several Directors who had not only sold shares but also, having issued a circular indicating poor prospects for the year, with one consent repurchased their holdings at lowered prices and now enjoyed the big dividends they knew were coming.[9]

The whiff of scandal hit the northern press, and one newspaper reported, 'Several shareholders alleged that the chairman and other directors of the board had trafficked in the shares,'[10] but Tennant was deft enough to extricate himself without any loss of reputation. Charles Gairdner was one of those who stood by him; Frederick Pitman, a Writer to the Signet – a Scottish solicitor allowed to prepare Crown writs – was able to write to Gairdner: 'I have not seen any Glasgow Papers so do not know what has been said about our friend the M.P. from Peebles [Tennant] but his shoulders are pretty broad and I am glad you think he has done nothing that should be found fault with.'[11]

It is possible that Tennant was not at all guilty, but he knew himself to be an easy victim of what he had described in youth as 'the avarice of all bad passions'. Like a gambler, he was addicted to the chance of gain and a quick profit would always excite his alert temperament. The Union Bank, for instance, did not find him as loyal as they might have expected a deputy chairman to be. He only gave his business to them if their rates were better than anywhere else, and that went for a fraction of a per cent. On the other hand, the Bank would not have wanted to lose Tennant's shrewd expertise and knowledge of the commercial world. He not only remained deputy chairman, but went on to become their chairman for more than twenty years. Men like Tennant were not readily come by.

From the early 1870s Britain's economy had been in recession, and complaints about pollution at St Rollox were besetting Tennant afresh – 'A sparrow didn't dare fly over the works', was the comment of one sanitary inspector. Instability in the copper market led the Tharsis dividend to fall as low as $7\frac{1}{2}$ per cent. Tennant's Steel Company of Scotland was finding trade difficult owing to the recession. In the Mysore venture there was, as yet, no end in sight, and the arrival of Ludwig Mond from Germany with his new, improved formula for the making of soda threatened the end of the British chemical industry. In 1884, when all these pressures were at a height, Tennant's health nearly broke. He complained of constant sleeplessness. This Titan among industrialists, so used to having his way, was suddenly confronted with setbacks he was not accustomed to encounter.

After dominating the chemical world for seventy years, St Rollox had begun its decline. The reason was Ludwig Mond. Almost since its conception, St Rollox had used the Leblanc system for making soda – or sodium carbonate. But the Leblanc process was wasteful. It required quantities of sulphur, among other minerals, much of which went to waste. At St Rollox, for instance, there were nearly 100 acres of grey, spongy desert, containing 15 to 20 per cent sulphur, and in some places this desert was 80 feet deep. It was one of the main causes of pollution in Glasgow, draining into the river Clyde where it mixed with acid from the distilleries to corrode the copper sheathing on the hulls of ships. The waste also gave out a particularly malodorous smell.

None the less, in its day the Leblanc system was considered highly efficient and St Rollox had been among the first in Britain to install its plants. Sodium carbonate was an essential product in a chemical factory, and a major raw material in three linked manufactures – soap, paper and glass. St Rollox, therefore, produced several thousand tons of soda each year. But the advantages of the process Mond intended to market were that it required no sulphur, was cheaper to manufacture and there was no waste. This invention of what was called 'ammonia-soda' had come from two Belgians, Ernest and Alfred Solvay, and was known as the Solvay process. In 1872 Mond was granted a licence to set up plants and market it. In that same year, the first in Britain to be offered the new process was Charles Tennant.

But he declined the Solvay system; and with that decision St Rollox lost a considerable fortune. It must be remembered, though, that when Mond approached him, his father was still alive, and it is unlikely that John Tennant would have wished to change from Leblanc. After all, the Leblanc process was continuing to serve the Tennants very well, and as yet the better performance of the Solvay system was largely unproven. Also, a chief outlet for Tharsis sulphur was to the Leblanc manufacturers. Nor is there any record that the many distinguished chemists who were employed at St Rollox spoke in Solvay's favour. Yet its advantages must have been clear. Perhaps the truth is that St Rollox and the rest of the British chemical industry had grown complacent. They had dominated for too long. Within ten years the Solvay system had outpaced Leblanc, and many Leblanc plants were obliged to fold. On Tyneside, for example, of twenty-five Leblanc works formerly there, only thirteen remained. By the early 1880s Charles Tennant had every reason to be worried.

In the winter of 1881, he met John Brunner, Mond's partner, in Bournemouth with the purpose of trying to persuade him to join the Leblanc makers in a price alliance. This did not work, but Brunner wrote back to Mond giving a report of Tennant's distress and agitation:

> He was very very doleful about the prospects of the trade in view of our competition . . . Was it true, he wanted to know, that we could make Alkali at a penny. I replied that it was true. In that case, he rejoined, I might depend upon it as a certainty that they would all go into the Ammonia process, and fight us on our own ground. They would *not* be ruined. I asked how the entire loss of their existing plant was to be distinguished from ruin, and told him we could not and would not increase faster than the annual increase of consumption, and had no wish to sell at such prices as would ruin the trade as soon as a few insolvent people were squeezed out.[12]

Brunner and Mond knew that the day was theirs, and later in the letter Brunner appears to have enjoyed watching Tennant caught in a trap. 'He tried the threatening tack, and got rather warm when I simply sat back in my chair and smiled. . . . Finding that threatening was the wrong dodge, he changed again very suddenly, and gave me an immense amount of soft soap.'

The only answer for the Leblanc soda makers was to merge. Although they could not defeat Brunner, Mond on the soda score, at least they had the market in other products. In 1890, the United Alkali Company was formed, made up of forty-five chemical factories, including, significantly, St Rollox. United Alkali became the largest chemical concern in the world, and Charles Tennant sat as president. Here, he shone in his ability to keep shareholders optimistic that United Alkali was the more successful company. But too often the annual profits and dividend payments disproved this. 'Brunner, Mond can make money and you cannot,'[13] a shareholder cried at one meeting.

These were distracting decades for Charles Tennant, as he watched that chemical empire built by his grandfather diminish. It still had, of course, a sound value, but the high days of expansion were over. For a man of Tennant's alacrity and reputation for never missing a trick, it was an extreme irritant. Writing to his father's Liberal friend Lord Rosebery to congratulate him on a good speech in the House of Lords, Tennant's youngest son, Jack, vented some of the despair: 'The House of Lords wants nearly as much waking up as St Rollox, which is saying a good deal.'[14] Two years earlier, his new son-in-law Lord Ribblesdale who had married his daughter Charty a little before, had advised Rosebery:

> If you go to Glen on the 6th you must cheer Mr Tennant up – business they tell me is b–––––y bad and the groans he was wont to emit on the daily arrival of the post when last I was staying there were truly portentous – very different from the soft purrs he gives when basking under the genial influence of Mr Gladstone's smile, or when descanting on the venial extravagances of his son and heir over the post-prandial Chateau Lafitte at Dalmeny – do you remember?[15]

But there were compensations in store for Tennant as he entered old age. In 1885, at the age of sixty-two, Gladstone recommended him for a baronetcy as a reward for his services to the Liberal cause and six years in Parliament. He had stood first for the Partick division of Glasgow and latterly for his home constituency at Peebles. Tennant had conducted an energetic campaign there, ousting the safe Tory Member, and becoming the first Liberal Member of this Border constituency. Gladstone had become a firm friend of Charles Tennant and he was a frequent visitor to Glen. In his turn, Tennant was a fervent supporter of Gladstone, and backed him on such controversial issues as Home Rule for Ireland. Indeed, Tennant could speak eloquently on ills that were distant from him, displaying the old family radicalism, but it was not as pronounced as it had been. Wealth had modified it. He was bitterly opposed to the introduction of the death duty tax in 1894 and, as the employer of 3,000 men, he had a horror of the spread of trade unions.

The escape from a troubled world of commerce was Glen. As he grew older, Sir Charles – or 'the Bart', as friends and family came to call him – derived relief and contentment from his fishing, his shooting and his collection of pictures. He liked the life of a laird, and planning his estate, even if he had few occasions in which to live it. In between board meetings he would send directions for the planting of trees and shrubs, but he had less time to practise the country-house sports than his sons had. Golf, possibly his favourite pastime, he would practise in hotel bedrooms, but shooting was another matter. There were some who feared the direction in which his gun could go. However, Ribblesdale has left a touching portrait of the Bart bringing the game down at Glen: 'The Parental one dropping on one knee and fetching a high one out of the skies, a sight not to be forgotten, and the murmer of admiration which his retainers and family give vent to, almost touching.'[16]

And it must have pleased Charles Tennant to know that his children were among the most sought after in London Society. This family, who only three generations ago were subsistence farmers on Ayrshire soil, were now pursued in marriage by England's most established aristocracy. Or perhaps he was indifferent. Power he had achieved through commerce, and beyond that he wished for no more than the achievements of Glen – and 40 Grosvenor Square. It was as if Charles had returned to those enthusiasms that commerce had obliged him to banish those many years ago. Had the pursuit of business quite obscured his thoughts on 'the Beautiful and the Sublime'? Where now was that church in Bolton Gardens? Maybe to live among the beautiful and the sublime on a spiritual level was impossible for him, but at least he could possess them in earthly terms. And so with every fine creature comfort – at Glen and in London – Charles shut out the smells and ills of his commercial universe.

A grandchild of the Bart's – Barbara Lister, a daughter of Lord Ribblesdale – later gave vivid recall to Glen as she remembered it in the 1880s. She would go there with her German governess, Zellie, and:

Pepper-pot turrets, high pitched roofs like a French château, it reminded Zellie of Cabours, but there was no indication here of dead or dying grandeur. All was spick and span, superbly groomed and appointed. The gravel was as meticulously combed as the children's curls, the lawns as smoothly ironed as their nightgowns. Only the hills were rugged and unkempt and *Ur – alt*. Everything else was new. . . .[17]

Grandpa Tennant occasionally complained of the immense expenditure of a garden of this size, the coke, the plants, what is termed the sundries. There was one house where pineapples were grown. 'Each pine we eat costs us five pounds,' Zellie heard Sir Charles Tennant say whilst the dessert was being handed round; but he did not often grumble about money. It seemed to flow in (and out) of Glen as easily as the brown burns flowed down the hillside. Zellie had never dreamt of any place where pounds, shillings and pence, less still where marks and pfennigs did not prove an insuperable obstacle to any projected pleasure scheme.[18]

Charles Tennant had removed the family from Glasgow; whether intentional or not, he had severed their industrial roots but made them aware that they were rich. They still owned 195 West George Street, but it was not often visited. Once the Tennants had glimpsed the South and the splendours of sophistication, they could never return to drab, provincial society. They had touched the best in life, and they intended to enjoy it. And the alacrity with which the Tennants had moved was now to be transposed to the quick repartee of the London drawing room.

7

Entering Society

For the rising generation, the London drawing room of the 1870s
had become a very dreary affair. Strict conventions of behaviour
among the English upper classes was leading to the virtual
extinction of character and individuality. There were unwritten
laws on what you might or might not discuss; who you might or
might not see; and where you could or could not go. For young
women it was especially tiresome, as a young lady could never go
anywhere without a chaperone, and development of the mind was
not encouraged. Male company tended largely to be boorish for
any man of sensibility. Everywhere the Victorian cult of
philistinism threatened. Thus it should be no surprise that there
was a younger generation eager to rebel. But it took the arrival of
Sir Charles Tennant's daughters for this to happen.

Lady Frances Balfour, a daughter of the Whig Duke of Argyll
and brought up at Inverary in the old tradition, was to comment
on this rebellion which afflicted her generation: 'Where it broke
down was among the coming generation who grew impatient of
the many bonds and restrictions which admittedly bound them.
The first movement of change undoubtedly came with a family
highly gifted of totally unconventional manners, with no code of
behaviour, except their own good hearts, the young women of the
Tennant family.'[1]

Growing up at Glen in relative isolation from the sophistica-
tions of society had made the Tennant girls different. It was

partly the wildness of the setting and partly that they had only themselves and the local people to fall back on that gave them that individuality which young London Society so craved. Unlike many newly arrived families, the Tennant girls had no wish to ape fashionable conventions or copy the habits of the aristocracy. They were proud of their humble Scots ancestry, their industrial beginnings and the mock-baronial castle where they lived. 'The hills at Glen are my real biography,' wrote Margot, 'I was a child of the heather.'² And her sister Laura wrote in her diary, 'I am proud of being a little Scotch girl. Proud of my great-great-grandfather, an honest farmer – a friend of Burns & a child of Nature.'

Indeed, the Tennants were quite right not to be intimidated by the taboos of the landed aristocracy. To attack the trading families simply on the grounds that they were new and therefore vulgar was like the last cry from a sinking ship. In realizable assets, a family such as the Tennants was far richer than most of the aristocracy, and their wealth was proof that the nineteenth century firmly favoured trade. But as a game of power between two different classes, this fact could only be a further irritant. Yet it was Tennant money that came to the rescue of the nobility's younger sons and impoverished noble families. The Tennant girls had every reason to be themselves.

It was Charty who first attracted the attention of London Society. Her father brought her 'out' some years before he acquired 40 Grosvenor Square, taking lodgings in Brown's Hotel, Dover Street, for the purpose. Charty was tall, good-looking and fair, with the tight curly hair of her grandmother, Robina. She had a habit of making the disarming remark – a characteristic that marked the Tennant girls. At a dinner party she asked Lord Rothschild whether he still thought the Messiah was coming. It was not the kind of question that other young girls might ask, but Charty became admired for her directness. Soon she met Thomas Lister, heir to the Ribblesdale title, and with a face so marked by breeding that he came to be known as 'the Ancestor'. Lister had a humorously ironic outlook, attributable in part to a childhood spent in exile from the family home. His father had lost heavily on the turf, which meant growing up in Fontainebleau and Tunbridge Wells rather than on the family estate, Gisburne, in Yorkshire.

Charty and Ribblesdale – as he became shortly after their meeting – were soon engaged. At their marriage in April 1877 she was nineteen and Ribblesdale twenty-two and far from rich. But Sir Charles took to his near-penniless son-in-law. He paid off the £20,000 mortgage on the Gisburne estate and gave them a house in Mayfair. Further, he made Ribblesdale a director of one of his companies, Nobel-Dynamite. Ribblesdale, the aloof aristocrat whose voice of detached irony can almost be heard aloud in his memoirs, struck a strong accord with his very different father-in-law. Sir Charles always said that Ribblesdale was one of the few who had shown him gratitude, but Ribblesdale was an intelligent man and he would have admired the energy and purpose of the Bart – a sense of direction that his own immediate ancestry would appear to have lacked. And the activities of the Tennant circle must have been preferable to those long, silent rides with his father in the forests of Fontainebleau where no topic could bring hope. However, Ribblesdale never shed an inherent aristocratic hauteur – for him, a combination of melancholy and distance – which the celebrated portrait by John Singer Sargent so notably caught. Though his directorship might have made him part of the business community, his nature was more suited to his other roles – a lord-in-waiting and Master of the Royal Buckhounds. Later in life it was noted by business colleagues that before company meetings he always preferred to lunch alone – in an ABC café – rather than with his commercial associates.

The Tennant girls did not find easy suitors simply on the grounds of money: it was their disregard for prevailing social codes that intrigued. They broke the rules because it did not occur to them that Society could have such stuffy conventions. It was ridiculous that Liberals could not dine with Tories, that ladies may not speak to men in the quiet of their bedrooms or go anywhere unchaperoned. All these rules the Tennant daughters broke quite naturally; and Society's younger generation, thankful that the restrictions had at last been speared, began to follow suit. Adolphus Liddell, nicknamed Doll, who had grown up in country houses to the conventional rhythm, first became a friend of the Tennant girls in the early 1880s and left a record of his first visit to Glen. He found there 'a joy of eventful living that I had never thought could exist except in a book,' and he went on:

> There was no attempt at anything like chaperonage, all the old-fashioned restrictions as to the manner or place of companionship between young men and maidens being entirely ignored; but with such an entire freedom from self-consciousness that after a time it seemed just as natural as it does to suspend the ordinary rules in regard to the attitude of the sexes during a valse, not, however, without a good deal of interesting and sparkling talk in the intervals of the dance.[3]

House parties at Glen became the symbol of liberation among the young generation. Elegant bachelors, wits and bright young things of the day were now regular visitors; George Curzon, Arthur Balfour, Godfrey Webb, Mary Elcho and Harry Cust were frequently to be found there. High spirits marked the occasion, whether it was word games, conversation or general ragging. And spirits could veer from the sophisticated to the nursery – at lunch, one day, George Curzon threw a cutlet across the table at Margot – but whatever the mood it was a blessed release from the staid drawing rooms of their elders. Godfrey Webb had come from an older generation but his friends were the young. He was Glen's wit and court jester, with an admired talent for composing verses on the spot. Usually more than one of the men were in love with one of the daughters. Webb, in spite of his advancing years, fell for Margot's companion sister, Laura. Doll Liddell too was enslaved by her. Harry Cust, the young generation's charmer and womanizer, pursued Lucy, the next sister down from Charty. Life at Glen went on in all directions; Gladstone's daughter, Mary – another frequent visitor – described it as 'the maddest, merriest whirl from morn to night'.

In the background of this liberation was Sir Charles, with his thoughts on stocks and shares, and heavy chemicals. Preoccupied by business, he had little time to devote himself to the shaping of his children, but he was an indulgent parent not given to the narrow outlook of most Victorian fathers. He believed that the young should have freedom and he liked to see his daughters developing personalities of their own – though he drew the line at Margot riding her horse into the house, and he wanted his daughters to marry husbands who could provide for them. He had no time for philanderers; when he caught Harry Cust proceeding towards Lucy's bedroom he threw him out of the house. The incident was worsened in that Lucy was married at the time, albeit unhappily. But as a businessman, reared on tough, financial realities, Sir Charles had a sharp eye that had learnt to distinguish the doubtful from the worthy character. On occasion he might even try to influence his daughters towards the right kind of husband. When Doll Liddell first arrived at Glen he had found the Bart dejected because of a falling market followed by the loss of an agreeable candidate. Liddell explained it thus: 'Sir Charles was somewhat gloomy, as he had favoured the suitor, and the American money market was in an unsettled state.'

Nor did Emma enter very much into her daughters' high spirits. She kept herself remote from smart Society, preferring to visit her garden and her greenhouses. Attending balls or being the mother of these new young débutantes meant little to her, and if her daughters' spirits grew too much for her, she would put them in their place with a quietly reducing remark. She was without worldly ambition for them. She wanted them to be happy, but in an ordinary way; of a retiring disposition, she did not share their inherited vitality. The girls respected their mother, but nothing would obstruct their independence.

It was the youngest brother, Jack, who told the girls one day that they were more like lions than sisters. Certainly the three brothers did not have the fire of their sisters and it was the outspokenness of the latter which established the Tennants in society. It was with the arrival of the two youngest daughters, Laura and Margot, that the name Tennant really caught the attention of dowagers and young alike, though some, like the Benson brothers – bachelor sons of the Archbishop of Canterbury – thought the girls vulgar in their excesses, though even the Bensons craved their company. Others were less critical – or less envious – and the vigour and curiosity of the girls made 'Tennant' a byword for refreshing unconventionality.

Laura and Margot were to crystallize that group of leisured but sensitive country-house people who came to be dubbed 'the Souls'. Lately the group has had a revival of interest shown it, and the circle has become known once more. They included the guests to Glen already cited, along with such families and individuals as the Windsors, the Desboroughs, Violet Granby, George Wyndham and the Pembrokes. Most of the circle were titled, many well connected, and their houses became the natural gathering places for their animated talk, word games and romantic fancy. Of this last Maurice Baring has left a vivid account. Visiting Wrest Park, the home of Lord and Lady Cowper and a frequent Souls' rendezvous, he found that 'a constellation of beauty moved in muslin and straw hats and yellow roses on the lawns of the gardens designed by Lenôtre, delicious with ripe peaches on old brick walls, with the smell of verbena and sweet geranium . . . and we bicycled in the warm night past ghostly cornfields by the light of the large full moon.'[4]

The impetus for the Souls' romantic and intellectual activities had come from Laura and Margot. The two girls, though, were very different in character. Laura was vivacious, melancholic and dreamy; Margot was extrovert, quick-witted and determined. Both were curious and questioning, yet Laura was haunted by the premonition of early death. 'I shan't live a long life. I shall

wear out quick: I live too fast,'[5] she told A. C. Benson. Margot,
like her father, was too impatient to give way to such intro-
spection. She wanted very much to live and find out what
happened in the larger world. There were early signs in Margot
that 'talk' was an important ingredient in life. A visiting Tennant
cousin recalls the seven-year-old Margot saying to him during a
rather quiet carriage ride to Glen, 'Well, Johnnie, have you no
conversation?'[6]

Separated by only a year and four months, Laura and Margot
grew up as a pair. They read, talked and bragged – and at an
early age both tried their hands at novels. At Glen they turned
their bedroom, named the Doocot, into a sitting room. They
covered the chairs with Morris chintzes and the floor with a
Morris carpet. They ordered writing paper with 'The Doocot'
engraved on it. The Doocot was used for entertaining friends after
their parents had gone to bed. Margot has described how she and
Laura would sit up in bed, propped against coloured cushions,
while brothers and friends sat ranged around the candlit room. It
was this kind of behaviour that gave the Tennant girls a
reputation as 'fast', but, in fact, by the light of candles, they were
not indulging in amorous pursuits but discussing books, politics
and reading stories. Nevertheless, to a largely philistine upper
class such activities were hardly less suspect. This attitude was
well summed up by a suitor of the Tennants' friend Mary Elcho,
who had once said of her, 'a very nice filly, but she's read too
many books for me'.[7]

Led by Laura and Margot – though Charty and Lucy were not
far distant – the upper classes now found themselves with a
budding set unashamedly dedicated to heighten feeling and the
artistic consciousness. By the mid-1880s this group of friends was
meeting regularly in one or other of their country houses. Central
among these houses were the Elchos' Gloucestershire seat,
Stanway, a rambling seventeenth-century manor – once an
abbot's residence – built of mellow, golden stone; Wilton, the
Palladian seat of the Pembroke family; Clouds, a new country

house, set near the Salisbury Plain for the Hon. Percy and Madeline Wyndham; Taplow Court on the banks of the river Thames, and the home of one of the Souls' leading hostesses, Lady Desborough; Wrest Park, in Bedfordshire, with its Versailles gardens; and, of course, Glen – a favourite foregathering spot, particularly in autumn. But the group had no membership code, they were more simply, as Doll Liddell wrote, just 'a set of friends, the nucleus of which had been brought together by the social gifts of the Tennant family'.[8]

This new and widening circle shook up the philistine complacency that had dominated upper-class life for so long. Since the dissolute days of the Regency the British aristocracy had been sinking into an intellectual decline. During the eighteenth century there had been tutors, the Grand Tour, and that enterprise required for establishing and enhancing those great classical estates. In the Victorian age of the nineteenth century there had been a tendency among the landowning class to sit back on the stylish labours of their predecessors. Learning was no longer a necessity, nor a virtue. The well-bred nineteenth-century Englishman was, in fact, encouraged to suppress his intellect – if ever he felt it intruding. On the landed estate foxhunting and shooting took an almost moral precedence over hours spent in the library. Books might grace a room but they were not for reading, while in the park a temple could be used for a shooting lunch but not for poetic reverie. And backing this attitude was the Prince of Wales's own stubborn refusal to be educated; with the endorsement of royalty philistinism seemed unassailable. To discuss books or poetry, and further to investigate one's feelings was quite unthinkable. Thus the group's soubriquet, the Souls, had been coined in mocking jest at its sensitive pretensions. But what threw the confidence of the philistines a little was that some, like George Wyndham and Margot Tennant, hunted, while others, like Mary Elcho and Laura Tennant, had irresistible personalities.

Laura, whose enigmatic elfin face was to haunt many of

Burne-Jones's paintings, became the symbol of this new sensibility. Her diary, which she kept from the age of twelve, shows the constant conflict between earthly reality and spiritual flight. She wanted to live only at the very height of awareness; for Laura this meant acceptance of the world's shortcomings and a repeated yearning for the freedom of death. Today her writing might be thought indulgent and perhaps purple, but we must not forget that she was still very young. In this extract from a letter to a friend, she expresses this awareness and foreknowledge. It was written from Paris after watching a funeral pass:

> I always think the body is but a window from which the soul leans out (some farther than others) so that the blue rushing air may refresh it, and the roses and lilies may grow redder in its Presence, and when it has been too long pent up, and the window is very wide open, it waits for some early dawn and steals away silently through the morning, lingering just a little where it loved the garden most, and then melts out of sight like the stars. . . .[9]

Nearly everyone who met Laura fell for her. Although she was not beautiful in conventional terms, her personality answered the spontaneity the young generation sought. Part of her charm was in having a character made up of opposites which her naturalness did nothing to hide. Her friend Frances Horner, another member of the Tennant coterie, described Laura in her memoirs as 'gay and melancholy, flirtatious and innocent . . . with open arms and an open heart for all the world'. Laura had warmth and immediacy, and, given her temperament, it was more than just the conscience of the rich that made her hold a regular Sunday class in the nearby village school. She wanted to understand the lives of the less fortunate; she instigated a home for foundling babies in East London. But always close to the surface was her dream of a perfect kingdom where there was no sorrow or weary earthly cares. Writing to Mary Elcho on the birth of Mary's first son in 1884 she put forward this vision:

I am sure it is $\frac{2}{3}$ born & that the light from the half open Heaven's gate is in his eyes. Why did he want to leave Heaven so much sooner than he need have. Ah! why indeed. Won't he regret the weeks playtime he gave up to come a little quicker into his school – & how hard his lessons will sound after the Angels A.B.C. . . . I firmly believe more things are of my dream life than of my material life. I saw you Mary and spoke with you – you heard me didn't you darling. And I will tell you that I was one of his Lady's in waiting on his silent skyey descent. I fanned the stars that he might not be hurt by their hot breath. I & the West Wind brought him in our arms – and we waited in the green sky because I wanted the floor of his mind to be like the sea's floor 'with green & purple seaweed strewn' & all adorned with mysteries & pearls & corals & deep gold caves wherein dwell the reflections of Heaven & where the music of Israfel is echoed night & day. Yes we lingered by the way & if it had not been that the wind was so turbulent I would have stayed in the land of the rainbow – but on we spun thro' the starry air – & you were like the wind & were glad when we arrived. Ah! me! Ah! me – he will regret it someday – & wish he was playing in his little garden in Heaven with countless unborn souls.[10]

A year later, at the age of twenty-two, Laura married Alfred Lyttelton. She had met Lyttelton first in the autumn of 1884 and the friendship was confirmed by a visit to Stanway that November. An intensely romantic courtship began with Laura referring to Alfred as 'My king, my king!' For Laura Alfred was the ideal hero – a fine cricketer, athlete and not without an intellectual side. He responded well to all her dream conditions – he loved her as tenderly as she loved him – and she could write to him, 'I will descend into the shadow lands of your soul and even into its cold dark caves I will dwell in the byways of your heart as well as in the sunlit pastures that slope towards the sky[11] . . .'

97

And in another letter Laura added, 'You will never ask me to go down to the cellars of life or to get accustomed to the stars.'[12]

As an eighth son of Lord Cobham, Alfred Lyttelton had no inheritance prospects, but he had an income as a barrister, and beyond that he was one of the most popular figures of his day. Alfred had questioned whether Laura might not have been happier 'to have married a very rich man and lived among eldest sons and squires and had large country houses and shooting'[13] but the ambitions of the Tennant daughters were less regular; and Laura cared nothing for such trappings. If she was to marry it would have to be for a romance that would lift her far above this world and, by chance, with Alfred she found it. Once again the Bart attended to any material worries. On marriage, he provided them with a house in Mayfair's Upper Brook Street – only a walk from his own home in Grosvenor Square – and gave her an income of £5,000 a year for life.

Laura's fairy-tale marriage might have been less idyllic had it not been so perfectly cushioned by her father's ample funds. Such ecstatic love is harder for the poor to realize but, as it was, Laura could indulge her high-flown emotions to the full without ever having to touch down on mundanities. Together she and Alfred did the rounds of country houses – mainly Souls' houses, though – with Laura dashing off a note to friends about the inmates. 'Lady Wemyss is a wonderful woman – as a hill to a hay-stack as compared to most women. Jowett (the Balliol professor) was there like a paroquet in a future cherubic state.'[14] Only at the end of that year, 1885, did Laura's old premonition return to her. She was several months' pregnant, and she wrote to her brother-in-law Edward Lyttelton, 'I don't think I shall die, because GOD must know that nobody ever loved children more . . . Only one never knows how bad one's own deeds have been and perhaps I do deserve it – only it would be very hard. I think a great deal about it now and often find myself arranging everything, so as to leave all things neat and well.'[15]

Few of Laura's friends took her anxieties seriously, except for one visitor, a young American named Chapman, brought to see her by Harry Cust. He met her only two weeks after her marriage and he wrote to Gladstone's daughter, Mary: 'They call Mrs Lyttelton a charming woman and they none of them see that she is dying. I wake up in the night and thank God for having given me one half hour of this woman, who calls out all that lies buried, that is best and noblest in us.' And as he sailed for America some weeks later, he wrote again, 'If Mrs Lyttelton is going to have a baby or anything of that sort, I ask you to write and tell me, for I do not want to see her death in the papers.'[16]

Laura died eight days after the birth of a son. It had been a difficult birth, leaving both mother and child exhausted. For a few days she had seemed to rally but the doctor warned that this could be a deception. Soon she began to lose a great deal of blood – the result of an internal injury during birth – and after three days her strength gave out. It was 24 April 1886, and Easter Eve. There appeared to be something almost prophetic about this moment: that Laura, whose diaries are filled with celebrations of heaven, should have died so fittingly at the Easter festival. Her last words, heard by Alfred and her sisters, were, 'I think God has forgotten me,' and then a while later, Margot recalled, 'She gave a little shiver and died . . . The silence was so great that I heard the flight of Death and the morning salute her soul.'[17]

It was only the American visitor who had sensed that extreme frailty – of which Laura herself knew – that had cut her life short at twenty-three. But in spite of the tuberculosis that had killed the eldest sister Janet and was shortly to kill Posie, no mention was made of the disease in Laura's death certificate, though it must seem that once again she had inherited her sickly constitution from her grandmother Robina. The child to whom she had given birth with such difficulty died two years later. Laura's death shook London and later *The Times* remarked that she was 'as widely and deeply mourned . . . as perhaps any woman of the same age has ever been.'[18]

One by one the letters of condolence confirmed the lasting

mark that Laura's personality had made. What particularly struck many was the immediacy of her response to life. The Prime Minister, Gladstone, writing to his nephew, Alfred Lyttelton, said, 'How eminently fine is it of her that in living a short time she fulfilled a long time. If life is measured by intensity hers was a very long life.'[19] Her bachelor friend, A. C. Benson, recalled his first sighting of her at Cambridge: 'I could not think who she could be. She looked so young and yet there was an indefinable sense both in her words and look of having lived so much and understood so much';[20] while Edward Burne-Jones, who had lost a great source of inspiration, spoke for most of her friends when he said: 'We shall all feel it, all of us, to the end of our days: it will be a never healing wound . . . I am as unhappy as an outsider can well be – and so are we all. It is never out of our minds and the year feels darkened hopelessly.'[21] Henry James, recently arrived in London for his final sojourn, wrote in stylistic manner, 'With all of us your wife's delightful exquisite image will remain – a beautiful, clear possession, a human link, a constant tender reference, among those who knew her. She was kind to me, and her memory is sweet.'[22]

Laura died and became a legend – a catalyst of that young London Society ready to break away – but Margot has rightly pointed out that Laura was not 'a plaster saint'. Margot grieved deeply over the loss of her closest sister and called her 'a generous, claimative, combative little creature of genius, full of humour, imagination, temperament and impulse'.[23] But there was a wilful streak in all the Tennant daughters; they had been lovingly indulged by a rich father and they expected their demands fulfilled. When Frances Horner and Charty Ribblesdale made a journey to Oberammergau, a conversation began among themselves and other friends as to who received the most flattery – Frances or Charty. In her journal Frances wrote, 'Of course there was only one opinion possible. To admit discussion even on the subject is absurd . . . We decided that Frances might comfort herself with the conviction that much of the unwholesome adulation Charty received was snatched by her eager grasp and might never have fallen to the share of a more retiring nature.'[24] And in her own diaries Laura had listed among her bad qualities, 'Fond of being praised'. While E. F. Benson, drawing a satirical portrait of Margot in his novel *Dodo*, made the forceful Dodo announce, 'I like wealth and success, and society and admiration.'[25]

As the Tennant daughters conquered Society, Sir Charles was making a spectacular entry into the world of art. Like many rich men, he wanted to see his wealth in a visible form. He had built Glen and bought his London mansion; now, in keeping with other town mansions, he needed paintings to adorn the large rooms of the latter. He preferred the traditional English school to the avant-garde – such as the Italian primitives – and once set on his course he acquired with rapidity. The paintings of Reynolds, Gainsborough, Hoppner, Raeburn, and Romney began to turn 40 Grosvenor Square into a palace of English art. 'I am proud of my handiwork and brainwork at No. 40,' wrote Sir Charles's dealer, William Agnew, and the Bart was very proud too. Often late at night his children would find him examining one of his many treasures in the blaze of the new electric light. 'Doesn't Lady Crosbie look splendid this evening,' he would announce as he gazed at a Reynolds. Though his daughter Margot was to complain that he could never look at the paintings of others dispassionately; she said that he would compare their possessions with his own. But the Bart was ever the businessman, trained by percentage and profit, and it was hard to shed that commercial rivalry to come out on top. To know that he was assembling one of the finest English collections in the country was balm to this vanity.

With Laura dead Margot now became the Tennants' star. Short in height and without a marked beauty, she made up for these deficiencies by the power of her personality. Nevertheless, she liked to say that her skin was excellent and that but for a hunting accident her nose would have been quite straight. She was committed to the world in a way that Laura had not been and she enjoyed friends in high places. At twenty-five Margot was sitting on Gladstone's lap at Hawarden while he read her poetry – the Grand Old Man fell completely under her spell – and a little later she was organizing the visiting list of the revered Professor Jowett, the Master of Balliol. The white-haired Professor took her under his wing and began to educate her. Jowett sensed a mind waiting to be shaped and Margot responded. It was not usual for a Society girl to be eager for learning and she added a new dimension to the bachelor existence of this Oxford academic. Staying at the Master's Lodge, Margot took part freely in those discussions normally the preserve of male company. Jowett called her 'the best educated uneducated person'[26] he knew.

The Souls' group drew together after Laura's death; they had lost almost their originator – although the soubriquet was not coined by Lord Charles Beresford in her lifetime – and they were determined to preserve an identity. Sometimes they referred to themselves as 'the Gang', and Margot would write to George Curzon of a Glen visit, 'We had a nice "Gang party". Elchos Brodricks Staffords Pembrokes Ribblesdales Alfred (Lyttelton) A. Balfour Eddy & myself. No parents – papa at Paris Xhibition mama up with old Duffs.'[27] In London George Curzon held a number of dinner parties for the Souls, the house parties gathered momentum, and by the early 1890s the Souls' influence was known throughout Society and also caught the attention of the national press. Looking back, Daisy, Countess of Warwick – a member of the Prince of Wales's set – admitted that in sophisticated society at least, 'I think they sent us all back to reading more than we otherwise would have done, and this was an excellent thing for us.'[28] But the press tended to treat the Souls' apparent exclusivity with sarcasm. *The Queen* magazine commented in 1894,

The Souls are a set of attractive men and women of the

world, very intimate, and eminently 'in touch' with one another, who have come to believe in themselves as the fine flower of culture, of a rather more delicate pate and more exquisite and subtle taste than ordinary mortals, whom they stoop to mix with when it suits them, but whom they criticise & pity.

The charge of exclusivity has been exaggerated. The sporting gentry of England would have been distinctly ill at ease after a day in a Souls' country house. For the gentry the arts were – and still are, for that matter – suspect. Equally, like any other group of friends, the Souls would have admitted anyone they found sympathetic into their circle. They took up artists and architects, but the plain talk of businessmen or stockbrokers would have been uncongenial to them. Yet given the comforts and connections of their backgrounds, it was hardly surprising that an element of posing should have crept in. Secure in their ancestral houses, they could live far removed from reducing realities. And since it was not done for women to be formally educated beyond some polite social training, many of their intellectual aspirations were bound to ring a trifle false. While those promising young men – like Balfour, Curzon and Wyndham – who stood at the core of the group, invested the Souls with fantasies of chivalry and learning they contributed to the group's effete reputation. 'Care to help me translate a sonnet by Ronsard before breakfast?'[29] shouted Wyndham to his niece, Cynthia Charteris, as he spotted her at her bedroom window while out on his morning run at Clouds. But Margot Tennant, considered the liveliest mind in the group, was not affected. The Tennant daughters had, after all, sprung from the very real world of commerce; there had been not time to breed affectation in them.

Margot's vehicle was wit. It was an attention winner that Charty, Laura and Lucy possessed too, but Margot staked the major claim to it. Her lightning repartees travelled the drawing rooms almost with the speed that she made them. 'She tells enough white lies to ice a wedding cake.' 'Ettie's (Desborough) as strong as an ox, when she dies they'll positively make Bovril of her.' But each remark was totally spontaneous, coming out almost before she knew she had made it. Her quick tongue at times earned her a name for callousness and want of tact, but any intentional injury was quite alien to an instinctively generous heart. The remarks were part of her impulsiveness, a way of striking at the centre and avoiding wasting time in hedging at subjects. She cared, too, for the truth, though this could often be coloured by her own emotion or prejudice. But whatever Margot's points or failings, she brought back to life a near-moribund Society. She dashed convention and received ideas with vigour and bravado; some thought her a decadent influence, but most just stared at her progress in bewilderment. Made up of passionate action – and often in contradiction – Margot defied easy assessment. Searching for words, Frances Horner said of her, 'I only know that we shall never see her like again.'[30]

When not with Professor Jowett, Margot was hunting in Leicestershire. She loved the hard-riding hunting world and wrote, 'I am longing to be galloping, galloping . . . my blood dances as I feel the straining living creatures moving in a sort of rhythm under me.'[31] But the supply of horses had not come as easily as expected. With St Rollox under pressure, this sport of the English gentry perhaps struck her father as a wanton extravagance. 'Don't talk of any more horses,' he had said to her. Frustrated by this indifference Margot had written to his friend Lord Rosebery, begging him to intervene, 'I want you to tell Papa you've heard that I've been riding well (!!) and that I deserve two hunters . . . You don't know how fond I am of hunting & how hard it is and tempting. £150 can't be very much to Papa, can it, he's rich, isn't he?'[32] Margot got her extra hunter and soon many more to follow. She stabled them at Melton, where she fell in love with a foxhunting bounder named Peter Flower.

Flower was a younger brother of Lord Battersea; he had a reputation for seducing women and running into debt. She had met him in 1883 when she was only nineteen and he took an instant hold on her imagination. He awakened physical love in her for the first time, which was perhaps heightened by his dare-devil attitude to all he did. Well dressed and with the sloping shoulders that sportsmen often have, he also possessed what Margot described as an 'infectious vitality'. With the optimism of youth Margot believed that she might alter his worst habits, such as insolvency, and influence some ambition in him. For seven years she stood faithful to him and waited, but to no avail. Finally she admitted that she could not change him and in 1891 she travelled to Egypt with her parents to break the spell. Out there was Alfred Milner, a rising diplomat and politician, who suddenly declared his love to Margot and proposed marriage. But his embraces were too passionate, the affair with Flower still too close, and she declined. Her family were disappointed; Margot was twenty-seven, Milner had seemed ideal, and now time was running short.

Throughout these years Margot spent long periods at Glen with her parents, or alone with her eldest brother, Eddy. Frank and Jack, the two younger brothers, were married, Charty at Gisburne with Ribblesdale, and Lucy mostly in Wiltshire with her irascible foxhunting husband, Thomas Graham Smith. Frequently the sisters met at Easton Grey, Lucy's home, where she kept an open hunting box for her sporting kin. Margot and Charty loved the stone walls of the Beaufort country, but Glen came first for Margot, and for Eddy too. She said that she knew every clump of heather, birch and burn that there was, and Eddy, while big-game shooting in India, when asked what his thoughts were, replied that it had to be Glen. Sir Charles had built strong roots there for his children and now, as the Mysore gold mines began to pay off, those roots appeared ever more solid.

In the same year as she returned from Egypt Margot met Henry Asquith. He was at the time a Member of Parliament and a barrister, but was shortly to be appointed Home Secretary in

Gladstone's fourth Liberal Government. He was also married with five children, but two months after his meeting with Margot his wife, Helen, died. Asquith at once began his courtship of Margot, and after nearly three years of hesitating she accepted him. But the courtship had told on Margot's nerves, as had the years with Peter Flower and the rebuff of Milner's hand. During the period of uncertainty Asquith had written to Frances Horner, 'Her passion long since went elsewhere; and, whomever she marries, her husband will have to win his way. I am under no illusions.'³³ And he wrote to Margot, 'The way of your life shall be as you determine it and your choice shall be my law.'³⁴

Margot married Henry Asquith at St George's, Hanover Square on 10 May 1894. It was the Tennants' parish church from Grosvenor Square – and where all her sisters had been married – but Margot's wedding demonstrated how firmly established the Tennants had become. On the following day *The Times* spoke of the large crowds outside the church, gathered not only for the marriage of one of Her Majesty's principal Secretaries of State, but also because 'of the position held by the bride in London society'. The Tennant daughters had held the centre of the social stage for a full decade and it was reflected by those gathered within. The pews were lined with England's blue-blooded families – Granbys, Pembrokes, Brownlows, Elchos, Cavendishes – many of them Souls' families and many also families who, a dozen years before, would not have spoken to a Tennant. The Tennants now stood not just at the heart of Society, but close to the very centre of government. The register at Margot's wedding was signed by past and present prime ministers, and two future ones: Rosebery and Gladstone, Balfour and Asquith.

It has been said that Asquith changed after his marriage to Margot. His first wife, Helen Melland, knew no one in Society, preferring to lead the unambitious life of a mother and housewife in Hampstead. Asquith had been very fond of her but he must, at times, have asked himself whether she was right for a man of his ambitions. By his marriage to Margot he had immediate access to the foremost country houses in Britain; he also gained a financial independence that was vital to his political career. In the background, now, there would always be the Tennant fortune. Already the Bart had given them a large and handsome house in Cavendish Square, plus the customary settlement to his daughters of £5,000 a year. No wonder Asquith had once written to Margot, 'The way of your life shall be as you determine it' – with all he was to acquire through marriage to her, she had every right to stay in the limelight. Yet it was said by some that it would have been better had Asquith kept to his nonconformist, middle-class origins, rather than adopting, as one put it, 'all the failings of the aristocracy'.[35]

By the 1890s the Tennants had reached a turning point. They could no longer be regarded as straightforward merchant stock – gone for ever were the days when their dining companions were no more than plain-spoken men of commerce. Through their conquest of the London drawing room, their outlook and the way of life they followed had inevitably altered. The security for which they had fought to become rich middle-class citizens was theirs no more. And yet landed though they may be, they had not the sustained growth to call themselves aristocrats. The question was, now that they had deserted the commercial stronghold from which they had drawn their energy, how was that energy and enterprise to find such vigorous sources again?

8

New Aristocrats

Yet in spite of change, Sir Charles still stood at the head of an industrial empire. St Rollox may have lost some ground against Brunner, Mond, but the employment roll still stretched to 3,000 and the great Tennant chimney continued to dominate the Glasgow skyline. Talk of Tennant pollution went on much as before – it was remarked that the fumes of St Rollox killed off bed bugs, and when a new fountain was placed in Cathedral Square, people asked how long it would prevail against the smoke from Tennant stalks. And the West George Street home remained the meeting place for Sir Charles and his group of business confederates. This group – made up mainly of the Tharsis board – were the instigators of several flourishing concerns that came to establish themselves round Glasgow. They were enterprises naturally related to Tennant interests, and chief among them were the establishment of steel and the introduction of dynamite to the area.

With the founding of the Steel Company of Scotland in 1872, Sir Charles and his colleagues became the pioneers of that commodity in their country. The idea was that, for the making of the steel the Tharsis mines would supply the company with their deposits of iron ore. But problems arose. The cost of refining the ore was far greater than anticipated, and by the time the company had arrived at a successful solution, other competitors had entered the field. The rival companies – such as Consett and

Colville – had the advantage since they were run by men totally committed to the development of steel, whereas the expertise of the Tharsis directors had always lain primarily in the marketing of chemicals. Added to this the USA and Germany were now setting themselves up to challenge Britain's industrial lead and by the 1880s, Britain's former industrial supremacy was seriously under threat. Also, the trade union movement had gathered momentum, spreading unrest and hectoring employers to give their workmen more than mere subsistence money. This meant that the Steel Company of Scotland was to find that it had vastly over-extended itself; a large capital sum had been spent on installing the most advanced technological plant on the assumption that the company would be the chief supplier and that wages would remain low. From 1890 to 1894 the company could pay no dividend whatsoever to its shareholders. On the verge of bankruptcy, Sir Charles as chairman begged the shareholders to weather the storm. 'To go into liquidation now would be unworthy of Scotchmen,'' he cried, appealing to their patriotism. But in 1895, the following year, Sir Charles resigned from the board.

The Steel Company survived and went on to flourish, but the Bart had clearly felt himself responsible – in part at least – for the severe crisis. Now into his seventies, was it that his noted acumen had started to waver? Should he, perhaps, have foreseen the competition that was bound to come from within? As railways and shipping increased, steel was certain to become the most sought-after commodity. Or perhaps Sir Charles, moving rapidly from one concern to another, did not always have the time to look fully into each individual situation? In the case of the Steel Company he had let affairs drift in the hands of a brilliant, though extravagant, manager. With his eagerness to make money, was there not a side of the Bart that was always the gambler, trusting to hunches and instinct? Usually his instinct had paid off, bringing him back large returns, but even the man for whom the Glasgow stationmaster held back the midday

London train could make a mistake. Or was it above all that by the 1880s a new commercial world had opened up – a more international one – grounded firmly on a fresh code of economics that had not been applicable during the first industrial wave, when Britain had stood alone?

Certainly, where Sir Charles was concerned, this was largely so. From the 1870s to the middle of the 1890s Britain had been in an industrial decline. Competition from the USA and Germany had led to a fall in prices, while the running cost of plants and machinery increased, and due to trade union action, overheads also started to rise sharply. The high profits of the first industrial era were over, which would have affected St Rollox and other companies in the Bart's control. Sir Charles's economics were based on low overheads and running costs matched by a virtual monopoly of the market. This was no longer possible, and by the middle of the 1890s new business ventures were springing up bringing with them a new technology that could cope with the altered conditions. It would have been expensive for firms like St Rollox to adapt their earlier machinery and gradually the first wave industrialists began to be eclipsed by new organizations. The manufacture of St Rollox soap, for instance, was soon to be headed by the fresh-thinking young businessman, William Lever, and his enlightened factory at Port Sunlight.

The Tennant fortune, however, was already secure, and Sir Charles a millionaire several times over. The Bart may have made a number of mistakes late in life but the record of his youth and maturity must remain impressive. He may not have taken St Rollox into the twentieth century, but history was moving faster than the Bart cared to recognize. Lord Brougham had been right when he had urged their lordships to back the rising middle class at the time of the first Reform Bill: 'Solid, right-judging men, and, above all, not given to change' was how he had described them. And indeed, Sir Charles Tennant now had become a Tory in everything but name. Kind though he was in a private capacity, he had no wish to liberate the people any further. Margot's

stepson, Raymond Asquith, staying at Glen in 1897, recorded Sir
Charles's feelings on the subject, 'My host here – tho' a professed
liberal – is the largest employer of labour in this country and
possessed by an almost maniacal hatred of trades unions and all
their works; debates over the dinner table are, sometimes,
dangerously heated – the house being full of radicals.'[2]

In 1895, Sir Charles's wife, Emma, died. She had never
responded to the great wealth that surrounded her – to the
money that flowed in and out of Glen 'as easily as the brown
burns flowed down the hillside' – remaining always the
straightforward, direct person who had grown up in poverty. And
once again, it is Ribblesdale's daughter, Barbara, who has left the
most vivid portrait of her Tennant grandmother:

> She seemed to be made of old lace, pearls, and delicate
> aigrettes, but under these trimmings she was as simple,
> unassuming, practical, and philosophical as Sophie
> Buhler's own mother. Ostentation irked her, wealth dis-
> comfited her. She felt at home with simple people, chatting
> with the blacksmith's wife, carrying a stick of Vanilla
> wrapped up in her Valenciennes-edged handkerchief, to the
> factor's wife to flavour her rice pudding. Best of all she
> loved her solitary rambles in the garden. When scent-spray
> rain misted the hills and hot-houses, she would pause to
> wonder herself crazy over the beauty of the fringed lip of a
> Cattleya Mossi, or pick one bloom off a spray of orange
> flower to hold it in ecstasy to her pretty aquiline nose.[3]

The death of Emma Tennant meant the closing of a chapter to
her surviving children. 'Mama is dead,' Margot wrote in her
diary, 'She died this morning and Glen isn't my home any more.'
During her last days the children had returned to Glen and
enacted to the full all the rites of a Victorian death. The
daughters took it in turn to read hymns to her: 'Hymns are really
what she likes best,' Lucy wrote, 'They are simple and comforting
and echo what is in her heart.'[4] They read her her favourites: 'At

even ere the sun was set, / The sick, O Lord, around Thee lay'
and 'Weary of earth and laden with my sin, / I look at Heav'n
and long to enter in.' The Bart came to her room, gave a sob, and
departed again. In the evenings Margot arranged a literary game
to distract Ribblesdale; on another occasion Asquith read aloud
from Morley's essay on Robespierre. At the moment of her dying
the Bart read from the prayer book, and Charty recited 'Lord,
now lettest thou thy servant depart in peace . . .' The family
buried her amid wreaths and tears in the graveyard of the small
kirk that lay a mile and a half from Glen.

All the Bart's children were married now except for his eldest
son, Eddy, whose two brothers, Frank and Jack, had married
pleasant, sensible women with backgrounds not so different from
their own. On coming down from Cambridge, Eddy had done
some travelling, qualified for the Bar, led a mild social life, and
been made a partner in the family firm. He had also stood
unsuccessfully as Liberal candidate for the Partick division of
Glasgow, where his father had been successfully returned in 1879.
But Eddy was not political, his interests were entirely centred
round shooting, fishing and forestry. Nor did he have any
ambition to make money, though by now that was hardly
necessary. He was what his father had educated him to be: a
courteous country gentleman. However, he was remarkably
good-looking, and it must have been this which first made him
attractive to Pamela Wyndham.

Eddy was thirty-five when he met Pamela, and she in her
middle twenties. Pamela was the sister of Mary Elcho and George
Wyndham; her family, therefore, were part of the Souls' group,
and so they were already good friends with the Tennant
daughters. It was Pamela's elder sister, Mary, who had been
Laura's special friend and whom she had addressed rhapsodi-
cally in letters as, 'My darling Madonna'. A few years before
meeting Eddy, Pamela had been passionately in love with Harry
Cust. The love had been returned – that is, as much as a
womanizer of Cust's reputation can be capable of deep feeling –

1. *Charles Tennant, the bleachmaker and founder of the Tennant dynasty sits in effigy in Glasgow Necropolis*

2. *A romantic view of St Rollox chemical works, painted in 1844. The 430-foot Tennant chimney – higher than Nelson's column – can be seen centre*

3. Closer to the reality. A contemporary cartoon of the Tennant works that bore the ironic caption: 'A Clear Day At St Rollox'

*4. A little under fifty, and already a wizard of the stock market,
Charles Tennant – grandson of the founder – stands with all the confidence
of a successful entrepreneur. Behind him is his newly built baronial mansion*

5. *Margot and Laura, two of the Bart's daughters, and the ones who
caused the stiff-necked dowagers of Grosvenor Square to turn their heads*

6. Sir Charles Tennant, aged seventy-seven and laden with commercial distinction, poses with two of his treasures

*7. Glen in Peeblesshire. The Tennant seat built by Sir Charles
in 1852 had all the fairytale edges of a rich merchant's fantasy*

8. The Hon. Percy Wyndham at Petworth as a young man. As Pamela's father, he brought one side of the strain of aristocratic blood that was to play such havoc with the merchant genes

9. Pamela Tennant, formerly Wyndham, in the Stone Parlour at Wilsford with her youngest son, Stephen

10. Wilsford Manor, near Amesbury in Wiltshire. This was Pamela's dream house – her Petit Trianon – where she could bring up her children far removed from the hard realities of the world

*11. Eddy Tennant, later 1st Baron Glenconner, with his third son David.
Eddy, dominated by Pamela, took little part in his children's upbringing*

12. Rich Edwardians playing the Simple Life. Pamela frequently caravanned with the children down mossy Wiltshire lanes. Left to right: Clare, Christopher, Bim, and David

*13. Edward Wyndham Tennant (Bim), Pamela and Eddy's eldest son.
The dreamy look and romantic features show how much ground the
Wyndham blood had already gained*

14. Christopher Tennant, who on Bim's death became the heir. As Lord Glenconner, and head of the business, he was to be the rock on whom the family leant in times of trouble

15. *Stephen Tennant at Wilsford with his friend Siegfried Sassoon. Stephen applied make-up from an early age to enhance his beauty, though Lytton Strachey was to remark: 'His lips are too magenta for my taste'*

16. *David Tennant, a celebrated figure among the Bright Young People of the 1920s. His parties were the food of gossip columns, but his own life drifted without direction*

*17. Clare Tennant, my grandmother, taken by Cecil Beaton while married
to her third husband, James Beck. Clare was a leading beauty of her day,
and the camera often followed her*

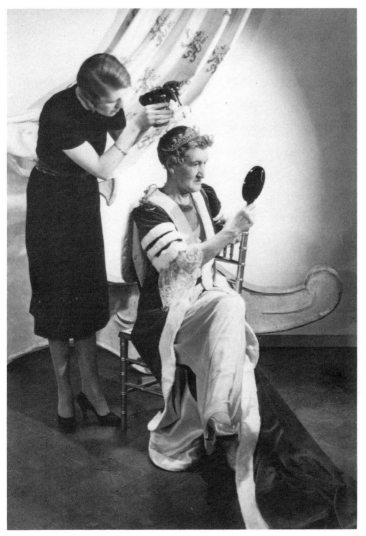

18. By the 1930s Margot was a legendary name and her wit an indulged talking-point. With evident tongue in cheek, she allows Cecil Beaton to photograph her preparing for the Coronation

19. Colin Tennant, now 3rd Baron Glenconner, also in fancy dress, but attending his own coronation on Mustique in 1986 to celebrate his sixtieth birthday

but the affair had been broken off when Cust had to inform her that he must marry another whom he had made pregnant. But it is true that this Adonis of late Victorian England did love Pamela more than any other woman; it was for her that he wrote 'Non Nobis', the only poem of his to last into anthologies and to be reprinted in *The Oxford Book of English Verse*. The final stanza, heroic with self-denial, is a perfect example of that idealized romantic love to which the Souls were prone. But the regret it portrays must have hit Cust the harder since the woman he had married had deceived him with a false pregnancy:

Not unto us, O Lord:
Nay, Lord, but unto her be all things given –
My light and life and earth and sky be blasted –
But let not all that wealth of loss be wasted:
Let Hell afford
The pavement of her Heaven!

Pamela never fully recovered from her love for Cust. Immediately afterwards she was sent to India with her second sister, called Madeline after her mother, and her husband, Charles Adeane, in the hope that distance would make her forget. But less than two years later, when she first met Eddy in Italy, she told him that she could never forget nor forgive Harry. Yet during the weeks that Eddy and Pamela found themselves in Florence together she grew fond of him. He proposed to her out there, and when he had returned to Glen she wrote to him accepting. Pamela realized that since Cust was now married there was little point in prolonging her agony; she may not be able to love Eddy with the same intensity, but at least he would be thoroughly dependable. When Margot heard the news she wrote to her brother, 'You have so much tenderness and so little caprice that you will make the best of husbands.'⁵

But there was an obvious difference between the Tennants and the Wyndhams. The Tennants were merchants who had risen rapidly from nowhere, the Wyndhams were aristocrats and descended from some of the noblest blood in the country. Pamela's father, the Hon. Percy Wyndham, was the younger son of the first Lord Leconfield. The Wyndham family seat was the grand and palatial Petworth in Sussex. Originally a family of squires from Norfolk and then Somerset, the Wyndhams had inherited half the immense Percy estates through descent from the sixth Duke of Somerset, who had built Petworth in the late seventeenth century through marriage to Lady Elizabeth Percy, daughter and heiress of the very rich last Earl of Northumberland. Percy Wyndham's father, George, had been created Lord Leconfield by Queen Victoria not only in recognition of his vast, inherited acreage but also to compensate for his bizarre illegitimacy. George's father, the third Earl of Egremont, had never bothered to marry his wife until she had already borne him six children out of wedlock. (The third earl – Percy's grandfather – became a legendary figure – the patron and friend of Turner, a collector, a Master of Hounds and an agriculturist, an enlightened landlord, he had epitomized the height of civilized aristocracy.) The Wyndhams had blue blood, a patrician intelligence and eccentricity, so the children of Pamela and Eddy were likely to carry some surprisingly different genes from their plain-bred Tennant forebears.

Pamela was a beauty. Describing her on her wedding day in July 1895, Lucy Graham Smith wrote, 'Coming down the aisle after the service she had thrown her veil back and just showed the circlet of brilliants round the small domed head. Her expression was seraphic and she was like a thing inspired . . . I have never seen a bride so lovely.'[6] This delicate beauty was inherited largely from her mother's side. Percy Wyndham's wife, Madeline, was the granddaughter of the Irish hero Lord Edward Fitzgerald, a younger son of the Duke of Leinster, who died in prison for Irish freedom. But the background of Fitzgerald's wife, Pamela – known for her beauty as 'La Belle Pamela' – was shrouded in romance and mystery. It was said, and may be considered almost certain, that she was the daughter of Madame de Genlis and

Philippe Égalité, a cousin of Louis XVI. Madame de Genlis wrote books on education, novels, and was governess to Philippe Égalité's children. She had had a passionate affair with Philippe Égalité, heir to the Orléans dukedom, when he was Duc de Chartres, and the result was Pamela. In an attempt to preserve respectability, Madame de Genlis had presented Pamela as an adopted child, but most people saw through the ruse. For example, it was noticed that with her fine classical features and large brown eyes, Pamela bore a close resemblance to her mother in the former, and to a distinctive Orléans trait in the latter. And beyond this, Philippe Égalité took a more than natural interest in this girl, making a settlement on her. The features of Pamela Fitzgerald descended to her granddaughter, Madeline Wyndham, and on to her great-granddaughter Pamela. And many of the French characteristics were found reappearing in this line of descendants. Pamela Tennant – as she now was – owed much of her beauty to this source, and not a little of her character.

With Pamela the direction of the Tennants was to change dramatically. She had a wilful personality, and she considered her ancestry far superior to that of the Tennants. She saw her background not only as aristocratic, but also as romantic and sensitive; to Pamela, the Tennants were, by contrast, hard and practical. Her childhood home, Clouds, built by the socialistically-minded architect, Philip Webb, reflected all the romantic liberal ideals of her parents. For instance, although indeed a large country house, it was not designed to look 'grand', and Webb had given as much thought to comfort in the servants' quarters as to the Wyndham's own. Inside, Madeline Wyndham had filled the house with the paintings of the Pre-Raphaelites and the chintzes and carpets of William Morris. Glen, on the other hand, lacked poetry to Pamela, and soon after her marriage she was writing to her brother George, 'There is a good deal in the house you would like to change – (it is so *different* to what I have always lived among!) . . . I look around – it is as if Morris were not – nor had been. In my little sitting room I am going to get the Clouds

drawing room chintz – and a pattern of an armchair at home –
and in time get Mamma's sketches on the walls of this room –
and it will look like Clouds.'[7]

Frances Horner may have written in Souls' whimsy to a friend,
'I am glad they have got anyone so delicious as Pamela to take up
Glen,'[8] but beneath the surface a degree of tension must have
been felt. Pamela was not at ease with her sisters-in-law – and in
particular Margot – whom she found to lack rhapsody and
sensibility.

> They do not see the *colour* of others minds quickly [she wrote
> to her sister Mary] – they see the shape of the nose before
> they see the mind of another and the way another behaves
> before they *see* & understand the circumstances that makes
> them behave so ... I cannot understand anyone saying
> Margot is imaginative – when she *is* or seems so – it is
> entirely from sheer *quickness* and alertness & power of
> making everything (even another's wit) her own.[9]

And it irritated Pamela that when she went on a drive across the
rolling Border landscape that Charty should spend the time
knitting; not once did she look at a countryside that was sending
Pamela into ecstasies.

One problem was that at Clouds Pamela had been endlessly
indulged. Madeline and Percy had brought up their children in
an easy-going atmosphere; the normal strictness accorded to
Victorian children was relaxed for them. It was more important
to the parents that their talents be encouraged than that they be
sent to bed early for impertinence to a grown-up. Pamela's
brother George had been brought up to display his knowledge of
politics and literature – 'Hush, George is going to speak!' his
father would announce – Mary and her sister Madeline, to
display their needlework and drawing, and for Pamela the
youngest, to discuss her love of letters, play her mandolin, and
not least to show off her beauty. Life at Clouds was never
intended to touch the ground, with the result that Pamela wished

only to live at the height of Clouds artistic fever. The presence of such a mundane figure as the Bart – committed to commerce and, therefore for Pamela, without the finer aspirations – was a source of constant mockery to her. She found conversation difficult with him, and though she was touched by the softness of his heart, she preferred Glen when he was not there. 'When he is here,' she complained to her brother George, 'dear old thing, though *most kind*; the conversation trails like a winged bird, lower and lower till it gradually settles down among stocks and shares, or the indifferent among the poems of Burns.'[10]

Where Pamela was concerned, Eddy played a back role. His upbringing as a gentleman had taught him that a man does not quarrel with his wife, and anyway, her temper frightened him. On the rare occasions that she went to Glasgow it offended her to see hoardings at the mainline station advertising, 'Charles Tennant & Co., Chemical Manufacturers', and she asked Eddy that they might be removed. One evening at Glen Margot took her to task for treating the Bart in a brusque manner and their hostility to one another was only veiled by the barest social niceties. But Pamela cavassed for Eddy when he again contested the Glasgow seat in 1900, which showed a measure of selflessness since she cared nothing for politics. Soon, though, Eddy and Pamela were house-hunting in Wiltshire. It was not just that she didn't really care for Glen, but that Glen was Sir Charles's home – what better reason could she have to find a home near to her beloved Clouds?

Sir Charles, now in his upper seventies, suddenly decided that he must marry again. He had met a jolly-looking lady in her middle thirties named Marguerite Miles. Like Sir Charles, she was a keen golfer, they got on well and a rapid romance commenced. He had met her in June 1898 and by October he had proposed and been accepted. But the Bart was anxious as to how to break the news of this pending marriage to his children. First of all, he approached his son-in-law, Asquith, who at once related the meeting to his son, Raymond:

The most startling piece of intelligence – since the fall of the French Ministry – is the Bart's announcement that he is about to marry again. The lady is Miss Miles, whom you may have seen on the links at North Berwick, aged about 36 or 37, plain, genial, & a good golf & billiard player. She comes from Lucy's country. He broke the news to me – being nervous of facing his children – on Tuesday evening, in an apologetic and appealing harangue, dwelling on his loneliness, want of companionship, continued virility etc, in a fashion that was at once comic & pathetic. I have prepared them, and today he has gone to Glen where he will have to face the music – for both Charty & Margot are there, as well as Pamela. I have urged them to treat him kindly.[11]

The daughters did not like the idea of a stepmother. After their idyllic Border childhood, they were possessive over Glen and did not want an intruder. They made remarks about Marguerite's distinct lack of looks – 'an enormous shapeless body like a chest of drawers with hardly any curves & those there are in the wrong places,'[12] wrote Charty to Arthur Balfour – and considered the forty-year age gap ridiculous. But they realized that Marguerite had rather a nice character and that she would surely cure the Bart's loneliness. Indeed, she was to do more than this, for in no time she had provided him with a second family. It was an impressive feat for a man of seventy-six to sire between that age and eighty a further four children. Three survived, and two are still living today. The second marriage brought Sir Charles's total child production to sixteen, conceived over a remarkable span of fifty-four years – proof again that the Bart's energy was undiminished.

These silver years of the Bart's were to be doubly blessed by the success of his gold-mining ventures. Whatever other problems might exist, all were eclipsed by the immense dividends paid out by Mysore. Between 1886 and 1913 some £30 million worth of gold was extracted, and between 1896 and 1905 the dividend

return remained consistently over 100 per cent. Every Christmas
the Bart would make generous presents of these shares to his sons
and sons-in-law. Sir Charles had a strong family sense and he
wanted to make his offspring – and their children – secure for
ever. He had become a patriarchal figure, surrounded by children
and grandchildren, and dispensing kindness to all and sundry.
Alfred Lyttelton's son by his second marriage, Oliver Chandos,
remembered him at this time as 'a twinkling, benevolent, white-
whiskered friend of schoolboys', who never shouted at the young
and was more likely to say to one slouching at table, 'Give the boy
some more grapes. He looks tired.'[13]

Yet Sir Charles is criticized by some for not making an even
larger fortune. Why did he not, for instance, expand his
commercial interests even further into Europe – or across Africa?
But surely with mines in Spain and India, and large railroad
holdings in the USA, it was enough? He had been one of the first
to tackle business on an international scale, and his success there
had left behind confidence for a younger generation. Many of the
difficulties he faced in later years were a combination of age and
changing times, which he refused to recognize. As it was, he had
vastly increased the Tennant wealth, built a fine country seat and
amassed a spectacular collection of pictures. On his death he was
to leave a personal fortune of £3 million. What more could any
family want?

But now the Bart's days were ebbing slowly to a close. In
March 1906 he was taken ill while holidaying in Biarritz. He had
formed the habit of going there most years as he enjoyed the mild
spring climate and the golf. Kind Edward VII who was also
staying there – in the same hotel – visited Sir Charles several
times. The Bart was the kind of man of whom the King approved:
immensely rich and almost self-made. He would have known of
him long ago through Margot, by whose audacity he had been
struck when Prince of Wales. The King sent his doctor to attend
him and by May the Bart was able to return to England. But even
the Bart's pugnacious vitality could no longer withstand the

inevitable advance of old age; once back in England he survived
only a few more weeks and died on 4 June. He was in his eighty-
fourth year.

During the life of Sir Charles the Tennants reached their peak.
There had been three generations of determined moneymakers:
was it too much to hope that there might be a fourth? Obituaries
appeared on him in almost every paper as if a great monarch of
commerce had at last slipped away. The long *Times* obituary
spoke of 'his rare combination of shrewdness and courage which
had nothing of the gambler's recklessness in it. He touched no
enterprise unless he was assured that something could be made of
it, and, when once he was assured, nothing daunted him.'[14] *The
Times* also mentioned the distinctive place in society the Tennants
now held since his building of Glen: 'For more than 30 years the
Glen may fairly be described as having been, among all the
country houses of Great Britain, the rallying ground and clearing
house of all that was most alert and alive, whether as regards
promise or achievement, in the personal forces of our time.'

Sir Charles had died in the Surrey house he had built for
himself and Marguerite but his body was taken back to Glen and
buried close to the house, in the little churchyard called Traquair
that had become the burial ground for the Tennants. Flanked by
heathered hills and grazing sheep, it is no more than a simple
whitewashed kirk surrounded by graves. It was here that Sir
Charles, one of the six richest men in Europe, was laid to rest.
Previously his will had been read in which he left the major
portion of his estate to Eddy, but gave £1 million each to his two
younger sons, Frank and Jack. In his excitement, Frank Tennant
had telegraphed his wife on the day of the Bart's funeral, 'I am
very, very happy.' It was not the most appropriate remark, but at
least neither son was to experience the deprivation and jealousies
which are so often the affliction of younger children.

On the death of his father, Eddy immediately inherited a
clutch of directorships, but his role now was more as guardian to
a fortune than the creator of new wealth. This was fortunate, as

the thrust which had driven Sir Charles would not have suited him. 'Eddy lacks drive,'[15] Margot had critically commented on her elder brother as he campaigned in Glasgow for the seat he was to lose a second time. But really there was nowhere for Eddy to go. The money had all been made and Eddy had been educated for the life of a gentleman. If a business crisis occurred Eddy was not the sort to handle it, any more than he might recognize that the country had already begun to decline. Indeed, with such imperial spectacles as the Diamond Jubilee of 1897, the British victory over the Boers in 1902, and the Delhi Durbar of the same year – which Eddy and Pamela had attended – few of Eddy's kind were intended to recognize it. The public-school gentleman had been reared to believe that the British Empire was set to last for a thousand years. For men like Edward Tennant there was absolutely nothing to worry about. And yet, among the reasons for the decline was the gentrification of a merchant class that had once made Britain's industrial empire, and lead the world.

Eddy went to the London office every day as a figurehead. Charles Tennant & Sons had moved some forty years earlier from their first address in Upper Thames Street to Mincing Lane, and some new members had come into the business. The descendants of that Ayrshire Tennant, David, who had been the first to break from poverty to be headmaster at Ayr, were now on the board; and also the grandson of one, William Alexander, who had been coachman to Charles, the bleachmaker. Those Tennant cousins had the young Sir Charles as their superior and as poor relations they had to work hard to prove their worth. This they did, and by the time Eddy arrived they had acquired an interest in the London branch. Likewise the Alexander family, who by the turn of the century had been able to buy two of the Bart's smaller companies. But when Eddy succeeded to the chairmanship of Charles Tennant & Sons it was the Ayrshire cousins who determined the overall policy of the firm. Apart from attending board meetings, signing a few papers, and making a remark here and there, there was really very little for Eddy to do but twiddle his fingers.

Thus he could pursue his fishing, shooting and forestry at will. He also had the time to undertake certain offices of the landed gentleman such as Lord Lieutenant of Peeblesshire and Lord High Commissioner of Scotland – a post he held from 1911 to 1914. While in Wiltshire he and Pamela had built themselves an Arts and Crafts manor house surrounded by an estate of 2,000 acres. The choice of house and setting had been mainly Pamela's, except that through the estate ran the river Avon, where Eddy found some excellent trout fishing. But the placing of Wilsford – as the house is called – was idyllic. Set in the tranquil Avon valley, with the river itself winding at the end of garden, Wilsford was designed to stand outside time. The architect was my grandfather, Detmar Blow, who was popular with a number of Souls' families. He had a reputation for creating houses in harmony with their landscape – and as if they had stood there for several centuries.

Wilsford was built in the Jacobean manner, with gables and mullioned windows, but adopting the traditional local building style of chequered flint and stone. Hints of that romantic socialism, which was part of the Arts and Crafts movement, were not neglected. There are, for instance, no steps leading up to the front door – you enter straight at garden level – it being considered undignified to climb steps as if in homage. For a house built in 1906 there are surprisingly few servants' quarters, but Wilsford was not intended for staffing by the conventional country-house team. There were to be no butler or footmen, but just a few live-in maids, a cook, and otherwise 'help' from the village. None the less, the house was set in several acres of garden with a plentiful supply of gardeners to attend to every horticultural need. This meant that Pamela need only exert herself when she wished to. Sometimes she might make some jam, sprinkle some grain to the chickens, or dead-head a rose or two. Underpinned by Tennant wealth, Pamela could indulge at whim 'the simple life' advocated by William Morris and his contemporaries. But in spite of the Englishness of this rustic Utopia, for

Pamela with her French ancestry, Wilsford was also her Petit Trianon.

It has been rightly said that in the years preceding the First World War, Britain's ruling class lived in ignorance of what was to come. Failing to realize that Britain was no longer supreme, the leisured classes basked in an extravaganza of living based on past glory. Fashions, country-house sports, and house parties were indulged to excess, but the extravaganza was not carried out simply in terms of luxuries. Sometimes, as at Wilsford, it turned to individual fantasy. As her children were born, Pamela saw herself as the Ideal Mother bringing up her infants in an earthly paradise. They were to be sensitive, artistic children with no time for the humdrum and the ordinary. Wilsford, lolling in its gentle valley, was to nurture the sensitive in them; it was a house so much more loving than Glen with its stern architecture and harsh, cold climate. The nursery wing at Wilsford was all thatched, thatch being cosier than tile, and beneath the tip of the wing was an exposed place called 'The Stone Parlour', housing a table, chairs, kitchen dresser and a view down the garden to the Avon. Here Pamela frequently passed her rustic country hours, close to her children, encouraging them to write verses, to draw, and noting down their childish remarks. By the age of six, her eldest son, Bim, had written the following poem:

> I know a face, a lovely face,
> As full of beauty as of grace,
> A face of pleasure, ever bright,
> In utter darkness it gives light.

> A face that is itself like Joy,
> To have seen it I'm a lucky boy,
> But I've a joy that have few other,
> This lovely woman is my MOTHER.[16]

This was not, of course, the way that Tennant offspring had been brought up before. In Glasgow there was no time for such indulgence, and even at Glen neither the Bart nor Emma had believed in pampering. 'I can't bear to see a woman draped in her children,' Margot remarked sharply of Pamela's coddling of her young. But Pamela saw her children as mystical reaffirmations of the Divine Presence – an attitude which was only enhanced by their individual beauty. When later she was to publish her reminiscence of their childhood in her book *The Sayings of the Children* – a book which gained a considerable audience in its day – she wrote opposite the title page under a tender photograph of her eldest three: 'These are my jewels' – 'Every child comes with the message that God is not yet discouraged of Man.'

The children of Eddy and Pamela grew up far removed from the regulated discipline of nannies, walks and suet puddings. Instead, she told them of their wonderful Wyndham ancestry, took them caravanning down Wiltshire lanes, and made fairy stories real for them. The children were born over a ten-year period: first, in 1896, there was my grandmother Clare; then a year later, Edward Wyndham, always called Bim; in 1899 there was Christopher; in 1902, David; and lastly in 1906, Stephen. Eddy hardly approved of the way Pamela indulged them, but he was powerless before her strong will. Frightened as always of her temper, even when she overspent, he preferred to ask the company secretary to speak with her, rather than face her himself. As far as the children were concerned, Pamela was left to behave more or less as she wished.

After the death of Sir Charles the house in Grosvenor Square was sold and a new one acquired by Eddy and Pamela in Queen Anne's Gate. To this more modest eighteenth-century town house a complete wing was added – again by Blow – to create a picture gallery for the Bart's handsome collection. Approaching possessions with a Whig conscience, Eddy opened this gallery to the public – the first of its kind in London. Eddy always displayed a generous disposition towards the less fortunate – even if some might term it the conscience of the rich. For his wife's cousin, for instance – the largely shunned Lord Alfred Douglas – Bosie, footloose in London following the Oscar Wilde

débâcle – Eddy bought a literary magazine named the *Academy*.
Bosie was appointed editor and he gave the magazine a
reputation for provocative content. He attacked Protestantism,
Liberalism, the Lords' Reform, and whenever he possibly could,
Lloyd George. Eddy remained remarkably tolerant of these
attacks against his own party, but finally put his foot down when
Bosie wrote and published a scathing article on Asquith. He told
Bosie that his piece was in 'the worst possible taste' and he had
now decided to sell the *Academy*. But even then Eddy was either
too weak or too kind. Under pressure from a vituperative sub-
editor, who informed Eddy that Bosie was not to be treated in this
way, Eddy gave the magazine to Bosie as a present, while
severing all connection with it himself.

Bosie's actions were made worse in that Eddy was now a
Liberal member, having won the Salisbury seat in the Liberal
landslide of 1905. His behaviour on the *Academy* meant the end of
his friendship with Eddy, and also with his cousin Pamela. But
possibly Eddy was secretly relieved as Bosie's uncertain temper
had led to one or two embarrassing incidents. At a party given at
34 Queen Anne's Gate he had shouted abuse at Robert Ross,
causing a public scene. Douglas had never found Ross easy,
owing to the latter's possessiveness over Wilde, and recently Ross
had complained about the blue-pencilling of one of his articles
offered to the *Academy*. A row had resulted in which Douglas –
now married and claiming to have reformed his habits – attacked
Ross for continuing his low, homosexual practices. The scene at
the Tennants' house in Queen Anne's Gate appears to have been
a recurrence of this row since Marie Belloc-Lowndes, who was a
witness, recalled that 'certain of the words which Lord Alfred had
shouted were quite unknown to me'.[17] It was really not the kind
of set-to that Eddy, on the verge of receiving a peerage, was likely
to enjoy.

The Tennants had been extremely generous to Asquith. With
regular gifts of money first Sir Charles and now Eddy had
enabled Asquith to give up his work at the Bar to concentrate on

his political career. By 1908 Asquith was Prime Minister and Margot installed in Downing Street firmly to leave her mark as a prime minister's wife. Every year Eddy sent Asquith a cheque to help with expenses, and was also kind enough to pay off Margot's repeated bridge debts, much to Pamela's irritation. Even so, the Asquiths frequently found themselves facing financial crisis; whatever the reasons given, Margot's scale of entertaining was never economical. In 1913, Asquith was writing to Eddy, 'I find that with illnesses, operations and constant journeyings etc. this has been a very expensive year. I should therefore be greatly obliged if you could anticipate now what you are kindly in the habit of giving me in the spring.'[18] As usual, Eddy came forward.

In 1911, immediately prior to being appointed Lord High Commissioner, Eddy was offered a peerage. Asquith's thinking must have been in part the Tennants' long service to the Liberal cause, but also he would have seen it as a sound investment for himself. Eddy accepted and, remembering those ancestors who had struggled for so long in poverty, he took the name Glenconner after that farmstead in Ayrshire where 'Auld Glen' had lived, a weathered patriarch of the rural scene. The Tennants were now aristocrats and Eddy an irreproachable figure of the establishment. But the main line of the family had removed themselves yet further from the polluting chimneys of St Rollox. Eddy's brother, Frank, had bought himself a medieval castle in Kent, and nearby was a golf links where he could practise his favourite pastime. With an income of £40,000 a year, there was no need to go near an office. And the youngest brother, Jack, commissioned Edwin Lutyens to build him an immense Whig mansion – carried out in Lutyens's Wrenaissance style – in the same county. Neither did Jack need to see Glasgow again; preferring politics, he became Asquith's private secretary and the Liberal Member for Berwickshire. Beyond the source of their incomes, these Tennants were now respectably distanced from 'trade'. It was left to those poorer Tennant cousins, more recently arrived, to busy themselves between

Mincing Lane and the network of Tennant companies spread across the country.

But apart from the Border fantasy of Glen – so secure in its mock-baronial grandeur from a harsh exterior world – the Wilsford generation of Tennants had weakened their ties from Scotland. A Glasgow cousin might visit Glen now and then, and although there is a street near the works named after my grandmother, Clare, and one after her brother Christopher, these were no more than token gestures. Through Eddy's marriage to Pamela, there was for these children a whole new coterie of relations, whose homes were aristocratic seats rather than merchants' villas. And it was among these houses that my grandmother and her brothers grew up, much as England's aristocracy has always done. For them, West George Street and the smogs of that industrial city, were not even a memory.

9

Wilsford: The Sensitive Ones

The challenge from trade had made little difference to the outlook of England's landed class. Most landowning families remained determinedly unread and stubborn in their views. They never mixed with people from lesser backgrounds and they believed in the rigidity of a class system. These feelings, however, were usually kept well cloaked by the upper-class code of manners. The landed might speak to people from the professional and other classes as if on a level, but they rarely invited them to their homes or had them to stay. In this respect the Wyndhams at Clouds were different. Percy and Madeline Wyndham were liberal in their entertaining and invited whoever appealed to their wide interests. They were one of a small group of country-house owners who wanted to drop the barriers and extend their comfortable homes to others from more varied walks of life. Percy Wyndham favoured the Pre-Raphaelites at a time when they were not sought after, and both William Morris and Sir Edward Burne-Jones were guests at Clouds. In fact Wyndham listened carefully to Morris's socialistic preaching and scored the margin of his *Signs of Change* (1886) with, 'Splendid passage, I hope prophetic – wonderful and impossible as the change in condition, shadowed forth on pages 20 and 21, appears from our present standpoint, it is not more wonderful and impossible than our present standpoint would appear to those who lived thousands of years ago.'[1]

Clouds earned a reputation for warm hospitality to outsiders and its atmosphere of liberality impressed itself upon the children. But with Pamela it had a double edge. When she grew up she chose her friends from among artists, and claimed to give Society second place. She declared that she did not care for 'grand' London life and would refer to London's annual Season as 'those murdered summers'. Yet, as the wife of an Edwardian millionaire and as a recognised Society beauty, Pamela could hardly have sacrificed her position in it completely. Thus throughout the summer she would remove from Wilsford to Queen Anne's Gate to be seen at a ball, a regatta, or the Royal race meeting, while she would spend the fashionable shooting month of August in Scotland at Glen. Whatever her claims, marriage to Eddy Tennant and her own distinguished background made her an inevitable part of that secure 'bred' Society who, in the words of the visiting Duchesse de Gramont, seemed 'to live upon a golden cloud, spending their riches as indolently and naturally as the leaves grow green'. Nor would Pamela have wished to forgo the compliments that society paid her. The Duchesse de Gramont had described her as one of 'a flotilla of white swans, their long necks supporting delicate jewelled heads'[2]; it was not a piece of praise that Pamela would have liked to lose. At Clouds she had been encouraged to show off her beauty to a circle of admirers and she expected constant admiration. Society occasions provided this for her, but it was to Wilsford that she turned to fulfil her yearning spiritual needs.

Pamela had soon filled Wilsford with an assortment of poets, artists and writers. With mellow, silvered-oak panelling and Morris hangings throughout the interior, the atmosphere was conducive to gentle creative talk. The rooms were named after flowers – the Lily Room or the Jessamine Room – so that the house should be suggestive of nothing disturbing. Here Pamela could discuss *belles-lettres* while keeping the true horrors of the world safely at bay. It was at Wilsford that Pamela composed her poems and distributed the finished volumes – all printed on vellum – to her artist friends. 'Given to Detmar Blow in the Celandine Room, Wilsford,' she wrote on the fly-leaf for her architect. When Philip Burne-Jones received his copy of *Windle-straw* he wrote to her in immediate ecstasy, 'I do love 'Windle-straw' – do you mind my telling you so, dear Pamela? Such sweet little verses about such delicious things – all sorts of little things I'd like to have said *myself*! – (and one can't give higher praise that that!). They seem the echoes of such a happy country life – and there are beautiful thoughts too, beautifully expressed.'[3] Wilsford had certainly fulfilled its rhapsodic purpose, but the limitations of Pamela's outlook become quite clear from Burne-Jones's overloaded message.

At Wilsford there was not only the house but the whole surrounding countryside to take the visitor straight into fantasy. Beyond an English garden of yew hedges, tumbling borders and spreading lawns lay the fairy-tale water meadows. Rushes lined the slow-flowing Avon along which Pamela would be punted by her young children on hazy afternoons. Wilsford stated its faith in a rural England that was soon to be idealized by the Georgian poets and nearly as soon desolated by the Depression. Through those water meadows Pamela walked with friends like Sir Henry Newbolt, 'Jack' Squire, the editor of Georgian verse, and the now near-forgotten Georgian poet John Drinkwater. They shared in her universe of country matters and romantic writing. The countryside to Pamela meant lushness, birdsong, and charmingly archaic utterances from the locals. She fell in love, too, with the poetry of that West Country rustic, William Barnes, and published *Village Notes*, a book made up of reported conversations with village people. She liked the rhythm of their oddly pronounced words and their worn clothes, like a dilapidated cowman's hat, enchanted her. It did not occur to her, though, that they spoke and dressed in this way because they were uneducated and poor. Pamela's vision of rural life remained rose-tinted in the extreme.

And yet she was not entirely responsible for her outlook. It had been shaped partly by Clouds where Percy Wyndham could dream of socialism without seriously considering selling his acres. And it was an attitude shared by other liberal landowners who believed that by leading their landed version of the Simple Life they had interpreted Morris's Utopia. What remained dramatically unchanged, however, was the social status. The patronizing cry went up for a house 'with the thatch lovably dripping', and there were Detmar Blow and, in his early days, Edwin Lutyens, to create these homespun havens. Yet to lead this life where there was endless time to linger down country ways, chat to villagers and read novels through the long afternoons, required money. It was one of the sad ironies of Morris's plans for his Utopia that it could never be adopted by the people for whom it was chiefly intended. The poor – whom Morris had intended to elevate – could never afford the ideal house, or find the time to improve their minds. So it was left to the likes of Pamela to interpret this intended socialist dream according to wealth and whim. But with the Tennant money, and Eddy so helpfully in the background, Pamela could take the dream and the whim further than most. Wilsford was a further irritant to Pamela's sister-in-law Margot, who noted sarcastically that Pamela and Eddy had built themselves a house stone by stone, with their own hands. It merely confirmed Margot's opinion that Pamela was not 'a citizen of the world' and that the death of a half-tamed canary would mean more to her than the loss of a whole regiment.

Though outward appearances were always kept, Eddy soon began to tire Pamela. Beyond an interest in nature, and Eddy's was more prosaic than hers, they had no common enthusiasms. He was not particularly interested in either literature or the visual arts, and of his own Tennant collection he was once heard to remark of a painting, 'Jolly nice pair of bunnies there, aren't they?' He may have had a fine sense of public duty, but this was not enough for Pamela. Through Eddy she had met the Liberal politicians, Sir Edward Grey, who was soon to be Foreign Secretary. Grey was at first a good friend of Eddy's, but Pamela found him more than sympathetic. He had a passion for birds, could talk about books, and was generally Eddy's intellectual superior. A relationship started between them, but whether it became physical or remained purely spiritual, has never been definitely known. No love letters survive, though strong suggestions have been made that it was more than platonic.

In Edwardian England moral standards were cynical, not romantic. Society girls must certainly not have sexual love affairs before marriage, but after marriage was another matter. It was assumed that a woman married for security rather than love, and that therefore she would need a deeper attachment sooner or later. But to keep the bloodlines and inheritance in order, it was expected that the first two children be by her husband. After that, and even the most staid dowagers agreed, it really didn't matter. And so, in not a few families, there was confusion as to who was truly whose father – though the children grew up in innocence of this conundrum, and a husband always took on a child as his own. With Pamela, hints of this confusion spread to the Tennants.

Clare and Bim – the first two born – were clearly by Eddy. Both have a look of their father and both distinctly resemble each other. But in some of Pamela's later children there was less of a resemblance in their physical appearance. Two of Pamela's reputed boyfriends, not long after her marriage to Eddy, were Detmar Blow and Ivor Guest, later Lord Wimborne. Guest, the heir to a steel fortune, became Viceroy of Ireland during the First World War. He came unstuck there through being obliged to follow the policy of the Chief Secretary and the English cabinet which had led to the Easter Rising. After his resignation, an able mind soured and he did very little with his promise. He lived as a cultivated rich man, who never had to exert himself even for the slightest trifle. 'Footman – toothpick' or 'Footman – my hat', were commands frequently in the air at Wimborne House in London and at his Northamptonshire seat, Ashby St Ledgers. When he visited the Ritz Hotel, which lay next door to Wimborne House, the chauffeur would back the car twenty yards up the road and deposit him there. Ivor Guest had a considerable reputation as a womanizer; he knew how to flatter and how to charm, and with her vanity, Pamela would easily have fallen under his spell. Both as Ivor Guest and as Lord Wimborne, he was a frequent visitor to the Tennants' London homes.

Guest might have been a suitably suave attendant in the drawing room, yet Detmar Blow was a far more likely choice of lover for Pamela. He had been a friend of Pamela's family since he had repaired the tower on their church at East Knoyle in the early 1890s. He was one of the artists to whom Clouds opened its doors, and as Pamela's chosen architect he was often in her company from the late 1890s onwards. He had a strong Byronic face and he dressed in a slightly wayward manner which would have appealed to her idea of 'the artist'. As a younger friend and disciple of William Morris, he had imbibed his idealistic socialism, and this also she would have liked. He believed, too, in a rustic out-of-doors life that was part of the back-to-the-land ethos of the Arts and Crafts movement; he liked to travel in a gypsy caravan sketching buildings as he went. Detmar's Bohemian leanings provided flights of excitement that Pamela's more constricted Society world denied her. Detmar fulfilled her concept of the romantic artist, but the physical affair did not last. Finally he was to find Pamela too emotionally demanding, and he had to snuff out his candle when he heard her coming down the passage.

Pamela's relationship with Sir Edward Grey – which would have taken place shortly after Blow – was talked about at the time. Writing to his wartime sweetheart, Venetia Stanley, Asquith remarked, 'Edward Grey came to see me to talk over the military situation. He is in better spirits than he was, and Margot elicited from him at tea-time that our Pamela was arriving, to take her usual part in his weekly rest cure.'[4] Before and after the death of his wife Dorothy, in a carriage accident in 1906, Grey had lived in Queen Anne's Gate, just a stone's throw from the Tennant house at number 34. He was a quiet and rather reserved man, filled with all those codes of honour and principle that made the perfect gentleman. It was Grey's high sense of trust that had led him to believe that Germany could be pacified into non-aggression, which in turn led H. G. Wells to remark that the British Empire had been lost on the playing fields of Eton. Grey always felt himself partly responsible for the outbreak of the First World War. Should he not have let Germany know many years earlier how Britain would react if treaties were violated? Might not that have halted Germany's growing confidence as aggressor? Had his policy of intervention with other countries in fact worsened the developing crisis? The chivalrous gentleman in Grey was prepared to blame himself – although whatever he had done the outcome would probably have been the same. Europe wanted a war. And yet he had known when he made that declaration on the 4 August 1914, that the stability of the old world was to go for ever. It was to Eddy that Grey had turned, as they stood at the window of his room in the Foreign Office, to make his prophetic comment, 'The lamps are going out all over Europe; we shall not see them lit again in our lifetime.'

In spite of Grey's reputation for integrity, it is possible that he fathered one of Pamela's children. Behind this model of good behaviour some passions must have stirred. Much as he adored Dorothy, she had an aversion to sexual intercourse, and the marriage was never consummated. If Grey was in any way human – and he was – it would have been only natural for him to look elsewhere. In 1902 Pamela's third son, David, was born; and he grew up to bear some resemblance to Edward Grey. How much Eddy knew of Pamela's affairs can never be known, but he remained as close in friendship to Grey as ever. He even left Grey a sum of money in his will. It is probable that Eddy recognized Pamela's character and chose not to interfere; he also had the advantage in that he was not a jealous man. Marie Belloc-Lowndes – a regular guest at the various Tennant houses – heard Eddy state at the dinner table in London that he did not know what jealousy was like. For Pamela, whose nature was the opposite, this brought on a sudden fit of tears and she had to leave the room. Once, when a lady friend of Eddy's had sent him a present of a wicker chair, Pamela had ordered the servants to burn it.

Marie Belloc-Lowndes – who was partly French – and Osbert Sitwell noticed the foreign strain in Pamela's behaviour. Most of her contemporaries did not cling to their children, and the fieriness of her feelings – checked only at times by an aristocratic manner and reserve – was hardly a British characteristic. They were struck by this Continental side of Pamela, which both saw as confirmation of her ancestry. Osbert Sitwell, who was to know her well through a later friendship with Bim, wrote in his autobiography of these contradictory aspects of her character. 'She was', he said, '– though she in no way realized it – far from being a rather remote, reasonable woman, under which guise she saw herself, presented herself, and was accepted, but, to the contrary, remained violently and enchantingly prejudiced in a thousand directions.'[5] He noted in particular, as an example of this impulsive spirit, a remarkable ability to champion those in whom others had long ago lost faith: 'In her sitting-room . . . stood always a collection of photographs of the most astonishing rakes and rips, in whom she still believed, and whose conduct she would unflaggingly, and with the greatest display of ingenuity defend, or, where defence was plainly outside the capacity of any human being, ignore. All her black sheep, as it were, became swans.'[6]

With her wilful temperament, Pamela could hate as actively as she could love. Towards her first and greatest attachment, Harry Cust, she maintained a fierce loyalty. Considered one of the most promising members of young England, Cust's life had drifted to disappointment. After a brief moment of hope when editor of the *Pall Mall Gazette* – a distinguished literary and political weekly owned by Jacob Astor – Cust had sunk into an unhappy marriage, drink and apathy. He rose late, dawdled to his club, wrote a few letters, and dawdled home again. Sometimes he would send Pamela little poetic missives, reminiscent of their attachment:

Now – & Then!
Here is the Spring,
Late on the Wing,

& Where are *you*,
Child of the Blue,
And *when*.[7]

In his decline Pamela stood by him and they always referred to 'Non Nobis' as 'our' poem. But towards Margot Asquith Pamela kept up only the barest civilities. In the first place there was jealousy on both sides, and Pamela could exacerbate the hostilities by the use of her withering tongue. Whenever family circumstances brought them together – as inevitably they did – stormclouds were never far distant. Writing of a visit from Pamela in 1903, Raymond Asquith makes clear the tension: 'Pamela Tennant arrives this evening: it will be interesting to see how she and Margot get on: the allegory she wrote in which Margot figures as a princess in a glass house, herself as a beetle beloved by God, and my father as a Muscovy duck, has made things a little strained.'[8]

Pamela's strongest emotions were spent on her children. She offered them a demanding love and expected in return their undivided attention. The price of this love was that their worlds must revolve around her. At a tender age she turned the children into her captive admirers. As an acclaimed beauty, immortalized by John Singer Sargent in *The Wyndham Sisters*, his renowned study of aristocratic finesse, it was no more nor less than she expected. Her children were her guarantors of admiration. Yet where she felt secure from attention, Pamela could show a generous heart; but the children were not all equal in her affections. She demanded most from her eldest son, Bim, and least from her daughter, Clare. She complained that Clare was temperamental, given to tantrums, and that her heart was cold.

Pamela would often say that Clare's eyes were 'as cold as Scotch pebbles'; but Pamela had a grievance. Clare was growing up to be as beautiful as her mother, and for Pamela this was a disturbing threat. Whenever she could, therefore, she would put her daughter down.

A clear account of Pamela's disparate feelings can be found in her *Sayings of the Children*. This book, received so sentimentally in its day, was an indulgence of Pamela's preferences. Each child is numbered by order of birth – One, Two, Three, Four, and Five. Clare, who is One, usually says hard, unkind things. When Clare's doll is broken, her mother asks her how. 'Well, it happened this morning; it happened when I was very quietly breaking her, in bed.'[9] Three, who is Christopher, makes practical remarks, 'Brown one ons, brown one ons,'[10] he says, wearing his first pair of brown breeches. From Four and Five – David and Stephen – come poetic imaginings and protestations of love for their mother. 'What would you do if one day Daddy were to tell you that I had died?' Pamela asks Four. 'I would kill myself beside you,'[11] he replies, sending his mother into ecstasies. But the finest and most noble sayings are reserved for Bim, who is Two. 'When I say my prayers you know, sometimes joking thoughts come instead of them. And then I make myself see one thing only. And that is God, with his arms wide open.'[12]

In the following extract Pamela makes plain her adoration of Bim and her dislike of Clare:

Once Two and One were having an argument, their Mother listening as she sat near by at her work.

'There's only one thing, the story says so, that you can get without money. And at last the Prince found it. It was love.'

'Only one thing?' Two asked, 'I should have said three.' And then very softly his Mother heard him murmur, 'Love, a rose, and Paradise.'

She said nothing, thinking here indeed was an answer

beyond anything story could devise; but the sister happened to be in a prosaic mood.

'Not a rose,' she replied, in a square-toed manner, 'because you've got to pay your gardener and roses come out of some sort of shop. And then there are the spades and things.'

The Mother listened anxiously, thinking the discussion closed. 'He'll find nothing to say to that,' she said to herself sadly, and she looked towards them as they sat playing on the floor together.

But she might have trusted that golden spirit, when had he ever failed her?

He was placing little wooden bricks one upon the other.

'Not the wild roses,' he said contendedly, 'the wild roses come to us for nothing.'[3]

Thus, though the Tennants now had money enough for hours and weeks of leisure, there was tension in their lives: in spite of surface appearances, Wilsford was not the happy homestead that Glen had been to Margot and her sisters. Pamela's wish to make her childrens' lives the substance of a fairy tale was distorted by her own uncontrolled emotional impulses. To indulge the children might all be part of the liberation that had led on from Pre-Raphaelite interiors and the Simple Life, but Pamela had confused indulgence with possession. It was as if they lived under orders to love her, and one default brought out her terrible anger. For the temper that she so disliked in Clare was no more than a mirror of her own.

Peace was only kept by the contagious high spirits of Bim. He knew how to play his mother and as her favourite his constant protestations of love satisfied her. When he went to prep school he wrote back saying that he had Wilsford violets pressed into his prayer book. One day a boy made a jeering reference to his mother and Bim was given permission to fight the boy in front of the whole school and beat him hollow. His letters home were filled with admiration for her: 'Some one said here to-day that they had seen something in a magazine about your being the loveliest lady in England. I felt jubilant indeed! ... Then somebody – I suppose in fun – asked me if you went in for the 'Throne' beauty prizes. That made me laugh. To think of the silly women who do go in for them, when if you appeared they would say 'here cometh one the latchet of whose shoe we are unworthy to unloose.'[14] In another he wrote: 'You can't think how I love Wilsford. Just think of the Dinghy Cut, Round House, village boys, b. Brown, and best of all the most lovely face in the world, which of course belongs to you.'[15]

Every year – usually for part of the summer and at Christmas – the family went to Glen. In 1905 the house had been badly burnt by fire when Pamela, Eddy and the children were all there. On this occasion Pamela's whimsy vanished and she became very calm, remembering the terrible fire that had destroyed Clouds only three years after it was built. Then they had been caught unawares in the early morning, but the Glen fire happened in the afternoon. After five minutes of what she described as 'quite *sickening* fear & a sense of overwhelming remembrance,' Pamela threw herself into the fray. Backwards and forwards across the courtyard she went 'with my dress filled with books, my long underskirts (for we were in tea-gowns) swishing heavy with wet and mud, in a melancholy way round my ankles'.[16]

It took just over two years to rebuild Glen and the man chosen for the task was Robert Lorimer, the Edinburgh-based Scots architect who understood the baronial style. Apart from a central block, the exterior of the house was undamaged, but Lorimer made several alterations both inside and out. Instead of the former bleak sheets of plate-glass, so fashionable in Victorian windows, he put glazing bars, giving the house a less gaunt appearance. Inside, he enlarged the main staircase, which previously had been rather cramped, and remodelled the rooms to have a spacious Edwardian look. But whatever changes were made to Glen nothing could replace Wilsford in Pamela's heart.

Writing to her brother George shortly after moving back there, she confided, 'We are enjoying ourselves here – the children *are* so happy that it compensates for the (always to me) excruciating wrench of leaving Wilsford.'[17]

But beyond the fact of Wilsford's perfect setting, the West Country was filled with Pamela's own family. Clouds was only a short journey away and Pamela took the children over frequently to see their Wyndham grandmother. 'Gan-gan', as the grandchildren called Madeline Wyndham, would surely be a more stimulating force on the children's imagination than those tough, unfeeling Tennants. And indeed with her shawls, home-made enamel brooches, air of vagueness, and eye for creating warm and loving rooms, Madeline instilled a sensitivity into the souls of these children: none of them ever forgot either Clouds or her. Also at Clouds was Pamela's brother, George, who filled the children with dreams of romance and chivalry, lived on a perpetual poetic 'high', gave advice to the children on their drawings, their poems, and encouraged them to revel in the distant past. 'I should have been very happy to have lived in those days riding through forests in quest of adventure,'[18] he wrote to one of them.

George and Pamela shared literary aspirations and their correspondence is full of literary recommendations and asides. 'I am reading a good deal,' Pamela writes from Glen, 'The Making of England, by Green, and Masson's Essays on Chatterton & Swift – also writing and correcting proofs *hard*.'[19] George writes, 'I write verse again, and I read nothing except Virgil, Catullus, Shakespeare, Walter Scott and Boccaccio. . . . So I live, getting younger and younger, loathing the thought of going back into the pig-stye of Politics.'[20] In 1905, two years earlier, he had suddenly resigned as Chief Secretary of Ireland owing to an oversight he had made when under pressure. Wyndham was not born for the cut and thrust of life any more than his sister Pamela had been. However, he had seen through the Irish Land Act, which for the first time enabled tenants to buy the freehold of their farms. Within five years over 200,000 tenants had taken up the

Government aid offered, and possessed their holdings. It was fitting for the romantic Wyndham that he should have fulfilled the dreams of his Irish ancestor, Lord Edward Fitzgerald, and played such an instrumental part in freeing the Irish from British domination. His liberal conscience made George the ideal landlord at Clouds when he inherited on the death of his father in 1911 – for if he was not born for rough and tumble, he had been made for that combination of *littérateur*, scholar, sportsman and landlord. Speaking of his writing, T. S. Eliot saw him as, 'this peculiar English type, the aristocrat, the Imperialist, the Romantic, riding to hounds across his prose, looking with wonder upon the world as upon a fairyland'.[21]

The Wyndhams took over the moulding of the young Tennants, and the vigour of Mincing Lane might seem a thousand miles away and St Rollox a thousand years ago. They, too, were being brought up to view the world as fairyland. To see it as a land of hunting and poetry, secured by ancient aristocratic patronage. 'I rejoice in Bim's poem,' writes George to Pamela, 'it is delightful. But never instigate him. If he writes that now, leave him alone. Encourage him to ride and sail a boat or shoot birds. His brain will dart out only too soon. Muffle it in hardy fatigue.'[22] Bim, who ultimately became head of the family, was not a man of business, as a more rigorous Glasgow childhood might have fostered in him, but an artist and an aristocrat, safe in the cradle of the Empire. Pamela liked to remind herself how similar to Uncle George Bim was turning out.

Stanway, the home of Pamela's eldest sister Mary was not far from Wilsford. The Elchos, who had been principal players during the heyday of the Souls, now lived rather separate lives, with Mary based at Stanway. She was in many ways Pamela's opposite. She had a dignified beauty, but no vanity; she was interested in the arts, but without Pamela's preciousness; and she was not possessive with her children. Osbert Sitwell, who knew Mary Elcho – or Wemyss as she became – claimed that her unaffected nature came from her being surrounded by the

astringent wit of the Charterises, her husband's family. Yet
Pamela had her Tennant sisters-in-law, who hardly lacked for the
appropriate word. It was more that Pamela had been the
indulged one of the three sisters, while Mary and her sister
Madeline had been brought up not to question her superiority.
Thus Mary was always fond, welcoming, and loyal to Pamela.
When Margot, for instance, wrote to her complaining of Pamela's
self-centredness, Mary defended her. 'I know you'll forget any
little hardnesses of speech about your Pamela,' wrote Margot in a
half apology, 'I could not bear you to think me stupid enough not
to see her extra out-of-the-way cleverness.'[23]

The net of Tennant cousins had now widened considerably,
and first cousins to the Wilsford children were half those blue-
blooded families who had made up the core of the Souls. There
were Charterises, Listers, Wyndhams, and Adeanes. Lytteltons
were step-cousins, and on a less blue-blooded though intellectual
level, there were Asquiths. The cousins were a close band, seeing
each other frequently, staying in each other's houses, and being
pages or bridesmaids at one another's weddings. Some of the girl
cousins shared a private education, for at the time it was not done
among the upper classes to send their daughters to school. Few
Society girls were seriously educated beyond a smattering of
learning from a home governess, but here was a slight exception.
Alfred Lyttelton's second wife, Edith, who was involved in a
number of public works, arranged proper schooling for several
relations and their friends at her house in Westminster. Among
the cousins who attended were Clare and her cousin Kathleen
Tennant – a daughter of Eddy's brother Frank – and their cousin
Elizabeth Asquith. Essays were set, the classics read, and the
plays of Shakespeare recited – a considerable advance from the
days when girls were taught little beyond reading, writing and
social etiquette. One of the brightest girls was Elizabeth Asquith,
which was hardly a surprise. Since the Prime Minister had scored
his double first, all Asquith children were expected to excel. But
Elizabeth also had a forthright tongue, and she was one of the few

to talk of her Aunt Pamela without effusiveness. Unable to take Pamela's affectations any more, Elizabeth addressed some tart sentences on the matter to Mary Charteris, another niece:

> Aunt Pamela has surpassed herself by sending both Aunt Lucy and mother photographs of Bim – very much touched up, à la hyper-nut. His exuberance has the effect of starch on me – I gradually stiffen until I find myself thinking platitudes in perfect silence. I really got fond of Clare but she jars on me more than anyone at times. She keeps all her limitations in silhouette. Aunt Pamela has sent me a little cardboard song called 'The Holy Hay' words by Pamela Glenconner, music by Henry William Brown. I admire people who can give their essence so cheaply.[24]

Elizabeth might have been harsh in her judgement of Bim, who had a difficult course to steer with his mother, but she stated Pamela's excesses accurately. Yet what hope was there for Pamela to understand life as it must be lived for most people, with the tissue of make-believe she had constructed around her? There is no doubt that she read widely but she did not relate her reading to very much outside her ivory tower of 'art and letters'. Her books of prose and poetry – which appeared with a certain regularity – are the thoughts of a sensitive lady limited by her own material ease. To write of village ways, folklore, and the sentimental in family life suggests a Lady Bountiful approach to literature, yet the books sold. Pamela's dreamy vision of rustic habits and knickerbockered children had its demand. But among the more imaginative of her child studies was one called *The Children and the Pictures*. Here Pamela made the subjects of the Tennant collection come alive and talk to Clare, Bim and Christopher. 'I can see him in his dressing-gown and slippers, the light shining on the mahogany door; his clean white hair, and shrewd face,' says Romney's Mrs Inchbald to Clare. 'How he loved us. We shall never have *that* again,'[25] she concludes, remembering the Bart.

Sometimes the pictures tell their own story, and sometimes – as in the two Morland paintings – the children of the subjects come out and play with the three young Tennants. Once again Pamela's irritation at Clare is felt; Bim plays soldiers with Morland's soldier children, and gives Raeburn's Leslie Boy a black eye. The three Tennants are quickly seduced by their mother's fantasy, and begin to lead their waking lives among the pictures. Lulled into the past by the stories they tell, Christopher wishes he had asked Mrs Inchbald what they did to smugglers when caught. Bim finds the present very dull by comparison. 'Nothing nice happens nowadays,' he says. 'No smuggling, no highwaymen, no pirates; *nothing*. People go about in top hats.'[26]

Pamela's fantasy kingdom – her Never-Never Land of that eternal childhood planned for her children – was brought to an abrupt halt by the outbreak of war. School had not prevented her from filling the children's heads with dreams of Wilsford and herself, and she kept them at home from school at the slightest excuse. Bim had gone off to Winchester and Christopher to Dartmouth's naval college, but David spent only one term at Sherborne and Stephen no more than a few days at school. The reason for removing David was that he caught diphtheria, and Stephen went home because he cried. Throughout the war she was able to keep these two by her side, having them privately tutored in the house. Yet after 1914 Pamela's mind was constantly on Bim. Fired by those ideals which had inspired so many of Bim's background, he had left Winchester one year early to enlist. At seventeen, he became the youngest Wykehamist to join up, and in another year's time he was the youngest member of the Brigade of Guards to be sent to France.

If Bim had grown up to believe in knights in shining armour, so too had his sister Clare. It was to Clare that George Wyndham had written of 'riding through forests in quest of adventure' and she had fallen in love with the idea of a mounted hero. But she had also inherited her uncle's passion for foxhunting and the youth of the hunting field in those days was largely made up of dashing young cavalry officers ready for action. So when war broke out, what could seem more romantic than to marry one? Clare was eighteen in 1914, with a beauty that far surpassed her mother's. Pamela had not bothered about her very much, and Clare was unhappy and anxious to escape from home. To marry an officer became her ambition, and she wrote to her cousin Mary Charteris, who was working as a nurse, 'It must be fun being among so many of the military. After all, they are the only people . . .'[27] Clare's first love was an officer in the Coldstream Guards named Victor Gordon-Ives, but he was killed only six weeks after war had been declared. Clare was distraught. 'I can't bear it at all,' she wrote to Mary, '& can hardly stop crying. I loved him very much, and I fear he was in pain – he died of his wounds on Sep. 16th – He was so dear & kind & I have such vivid pictures of him in my mind, it cuts very hard.'[28]

But Victor Gordon-Ives had a reputation among the ladies, so Clare was probably well rid of him. Next, though, she had found herself a fully fledged cavalry officer – a young lieutenant in the Life Guards. Adrian Bethell perfectly fitted Clare's requirement of a cavalry officer who hunted; also, as the heir to a decent-sized estate in East Yorkshire, he had certain material means, and beyond that, he was a gentleman. If there was going to be a match, Pamela and Eddy considered this an excellent one. Clare's cousin, Charles Lister, wrote to their aunt Lucy Graham Smith, 'Clare's young man sounds very attractive, and I should think a great riding man, which is what she wants.'[29] Adrian was exactly the type she wanted, and in a state of high excitement she wrote again to Mary:

I am so *very, very, very* happy – I can hardly write sense! & I keep on thinking it someone else and not me! I've been engaged a fortnight today at 11.45, because I looked at my watch – & have been quite *gaga* ever since. He is such an angel – & loves horses & has hundreds, & has given me the *most* lovely ring that ever was seen. I wish everyone was as happy as me – my only sadness is the thought of his going

back to that *Hell* – but he will be a Capt. by then I think –
which is a tiny bit safer.[30]

Clare and Adrian were married in August 1915, and like a fairy
tale six white horses drew the carriage that took them from the
church in Westminster to the Tennant house in Queen Anne's
Gate. Afterwards there was a honeymoon at Stanway and then
Adrian was obliged to return to France. Moments of happiness
were by necessity shortlived; already the war had taken its toll of
Clare's cousins. 'Oh why was I born for this time?' wrote Cynthia
Asquith, another cousin and sister of Mary Charteris, 'Before one
is thirty to know more dead than living people? Stanway, Clouds,
Gosford – all the settings of one's life – given up to ghosts.'[31] And
within another year Cynthia and Mary had lost two brothers,
while two young Wyndham cousins – Percy and George – were
already dead. And by early 1915 even that optimism which had
sent Bim to enlist at such a tender age, was beginning to wane.
He had written to his cousin Mary on the loss of two out of three
of his closest friends: 'I suppose I shall find some more, but none
for some time. But one can't expect to keep friends long in these
days, can one?'[32]

Christopher had gone as a young cadet to fight in the
Dardanelles campaign, but David did not leave school until 1916.
In order to deflect some of the nanny's consuming interest in
Stephen, Pamela adopted a child. She generally disliked nannies
because there was always the possibility that the child would
grow fonder of the nanny than of her, but, now, with a strange
baby to fill the nursery, there could be no danger of her losing
Stephen. Every day she fussed and cosseted Stephen; when the
time came for school, Bim felt it wise to write in advance to his
old prep-school master, 'You won't find Stephen an easy chap in
some ways. He's non-combatant by nature, and a conscientious
objector to things essentially manly, such as jumping on other
little boys' faces, and having his own jumped on.'[33]

While the Tennant companies became the main Government

agents for explosive materials, Bim sent brave letters back from France. He was determined that his mother should know that he had nothing to fear, and in spite of shell blasts and close artillery fire, he reassured her always that he was 'in the highest possible spirits'. He sent, too, high-blown protestations of his love for her and poems about Wilsford. Osbert Sitwell came to know Bim at this time; they were in the same Company for a while and shared a dug-out. Sitwell found Bim 'compact of energy as a cracker', and said that 'to be in his company was like having an electric battery in the room, invigorating without being in the least tiring'.[34] He also gave endless praise to Bim's character, and it does seem that Bim had rare qualities. 'A spirit higher than any I have ever known,' wrote Sitwell in his autobiography, and at eighteen Bim was still a romantic – an idealist – about people and life. But there was one poem, which he did not send his mother, that shows an inevitable scepticism being brought home by the horror of war. It is called 'The Mad Soldier',[35] and it opens as follows:

I dropp'd here three weeks ago, yes – I know,
And it's bitter cold at night, since the fight –
I could tell you if I chose – no one knows
Excep' me and four or five, what ain't alive.
I can see them all asleep, three men deep,
And they're nowhere near a fire – but our wire
Has 'em fast as fast can be. Can't you see
When the flare goes up? Ssh! boys; what's that noise?
Do you know what these rats eat? Body-meat!

This soldier who has dreamt himself alive when he is dead, was a bitter statement from a young man who was known in the regiment for his enthusiasm as 'the Boy-Wonder'. He wrote it in June 1916 and later it was published in Edith Sitwell's modern-verse anthology, *Wheels* (1919). That summer Blackwood's published Bim's first volume of poetry. Pamela helped him to select them and gave him endless praise. Bim wrote: 'Tell me –

do you really think my poems are worth publishing? It is because you think them good, and not because you are my Mother that you like them, isn't it?'[36] It is understandable that Bim should have been unsure: all his brief life his mother had secured him in her world but let him find no such security in any other. When home on leave, he went to dances but there would always be a note pushed under his door: 'Goodnight darling Love . . . Endless love to you and God's blessing – & may I never fail you – even in little things. Mummie.' She called his girlfriends 'the hell-kittens', thereby hopefully diminishing their chances. But Pamela need not have worried, for Bim did love her, and also knew how to give her the compliments she needed.

In May 1916 Pamela, at the age of forty-five, gave birth to a second daughter. But the child, named Hester, died only a few hours after she was born. The death of this baby sent Pamela into a deep depression, reminding her that she was past the age for childbearing. She had the child buried in the garden at Queen Anne's Gate, and circulated her waxen photograph to all her family. From the trenches, Bim did his best to cheer her up:

> You must not say you have lost nerve and confidence, because you have not – and I trust you absolutely in everything. What a perfect time we will have together when I get home, please write and tell me you are happier, you who are so young and so lovely, I can't bear to think of your feeling otherwise . . . You have all the resiliency of youth, and always will have.'[37]

But Bim never did come home. He was killed in the battle of the Somme on 22 September that year. A sniper shot him and he fell instantly. All through that summer he had sent home happy, brave letters, but once the Somme offensive had got under way he knew that his hopes must be slight. Nineteen thousand were killed on its first day – 1 July – and also Bim's nineteenth birthday, and the carnage did not stop. 'Death and decomposition strew the ground,' Bim wrote to his mother on 18 September.

A few days before Margot's stepson, Raymond Asquith, had
gone, along with so many of Bim's friends and cousins. 'It is a
terrible list,'[38] he told his mother in the same letter. Then, on the
eve of his own last battle, Bim wrote out some farewells. He wrote
to his old prep-school master: 'I so often think of West Downs
days, and how happy they were. Then on my birthday in 1911
you talked to me so splendidly on what I was going to do with my
life. We never thought it would be this way!'[39] He ended with
Brutus' farewell to Cassius, which he used again in a long letter of
goodbye written to Pamela. In this letter, he thought of his
fighting Wyndham ancestors, his pride at being a Grenadier, and
quoted a line from that poem which Harry Cust had written to
her: 'High heart, high speech, high deeds, 'mid honouring eyes.'
And in a last paragraph, he let her know that he had never loved
anyone but her:

> I always carry four photies of you when we go into action,
> one is in my pocket-book, two in that little leather book, and
> one round my neck, and I have kept my little medal of the
> Blessed Virgin. Your love for me and my love for you, have
> made my whole life one of the happiest there has ever been;
> Brutus's farewell to Cassius sounds in my heart: 'If not
> farewell; and if we meet again, we shall smile.' Now all my
> blessings go with you, and with all we love. God bless you,
> and give you peace.
>   Eternal Love,
>   from BIM[40]

Pamela was devastated. She published his last letter in *The
Times*, and also one of his tenderest poems, 'Home Thoughts in
Lavantie'. Bim's boy heroism touched hearts, and spoke for all
those young men who had first answered Kitchener's call. 'I
thank you for giving us all that last glorious message,' wrote Sir
Henry Newbolt of the letter, 'to read it made the tears start, not
for sorrow but for pride, and the pure sense of beauty.'[41] Bim had
indeed fulfilled that upbringing of chivalry, and many saw him

'in that company of the knights where the King of Glory passes on His way',[42] but what true consolation could this bring to Pamela? She collected his writings and wrote a life – such as it had been – and published privately all the letters written on his death, but still there was the void. She placed a memorial to him in Salisbury Cathedral, in the church at Wilsford, and in the kirk at Traquair. Each tablet had some saying that might bring him back to her; in the cathedral she took as epitaph the remark to her, of a private soldier, 'When danger was greatest his smile was loveliest.' But however much she rehearsed his life, the living form of the adored son was gone. To find him again Pamela turned to spiritualism.

Other Tennant cousins had been killed in the war – Mark and Henry, the sons respectively of Frank and Jack – but Bim stood at the head of the family, and his death left its shadow. Through Pamela's influence he was unlike his background; instead of that reserve taught at home and in school he had warmth and spontaneity. Even Margot remarked how she preferred Bim to Raymond, who was born, she complained, 'with hardly any emotion'.[43] Asquith and Margot had shed, she wrote, 'scalding tears'[44] over the letter. It was a credit to Pamela's upbringing that she had always encouraged a naturalness of feeling in her children. So far, Bim had responded to this best of all, but what might have happened had he lived? As ultimate head of the family, would he one day have been expected to occupy that office in Mincing Lane? 'Sometimes I think that if I live I shall be a poet one day,' he had told his mother from the Front. But whatever his dreams – or those of others for him – they no longer held any place. It was only that the spirit of what-might-have-been now filled the room at Glen and Wilsford. Life went on, but now as if something irreplaceable was missing.

Christopher returned from his Mediterranean war unscathed. In 1915 he was still under age for action and he had missed danger in the Dardanelles and at Gallipoli. He was now the eldest son, but there were times ahead when he was to feel that he should have been the one to go and not Bim. The code of primogeniture and Pamela's deep love for Bim took its toll. And although Pamela admired Christopher as a splendid son, and although he was now the eldest, it was not on his shoulders that she began to lean. Needing again an emotional dependence, it was to her third son, David, that she turned. She reminded herself that her brother George had said, 'They're all delightful, but David is the star of your company, Pamela.'[45] She took David to read Shelley over George's grave at Clouds, while she in turn recited over the graves of her parents. One result of her domination of David was to inhibit him in the naturalness she so desired.

But where was Eddy in all of this? 'My father was such a dull man, I can't even remember what he looked like,' said Stephen to this great-nephew. His remark suggests the extent to which Eddy stayed behind the scenes and was encouraged to remain there by Pamela. That patriarchal influence that had once ruled the Tennant family had gone. Eddy's gentlemanly ways had quite stripped him of ambition. When a New York paper announced the Glenconners' arrival there with, 'British Tycoon Arrives', the young Stephen, who was with his mother, looked up and asked, 'Are you a tycoon, Daddy?' Eddy went sheepish and mumbled, 'I suppose I am.' But this is hardly how the Bart would have taken it. And beyond the occasional quiet remonstration at Pamela's cosseting of his children, he said little. He had taken on the reserve of his type – the country gentleman – and wanted no more than peace to pursue his forestry and fishing. Quite suddenly, two years after the end of the First World War, he died while undergoing an operation. He was only sixty-one years old and his youngest son but a boy of fourteen. With Eddy dead, the matriarchal influence was left to reign supreme.

After his death Pamela felt guilty about Eddy. Perhaps she could have been nicer to him and tried to appreciate more those qualities of decency that he had possessed. Margot complained bitterly that Pamela had neglected Eddy shamefully in his last days, but Margot had an extra grudge as she suspected Pamela of being behind Eddy's recent refusals to pay any more of her bridge debts. Now, to make up for anything that had lacked, Pamela sought Eddy too through her medium: the spirit world became her obsession. But around her were four children, three of them already adults. They had looks, wealth, intelligence and charm. They seemed made for the fabled 1920s that were about to open before them, and indeed three of them became part of the history of their times. With so much in their favour, it did not seem possible that any of them could fail.

10

Lost Lives

By 1917 Clare had left Adrian, but he knew nothing of this until he returned on leave from the Front. Expecting to find her in the house they had taken off Hyde Park, he found only the servants. Soon, however, a friend of Clare's arrived to explain that she had run off with another man. It was a considerable shock to Bethell who was a thoroughly respectable young squire. A little later a taxi drew up and Clare got out. Bethell advanced to meet her, still believing it could not be true. 'If you so much as touch me, I shall scream so the police will hear,'' was Clare's greeting. Clearly the marriage had come badly unstuck and within a few months a divorce was pending. But Clare was only twenty and there was a baby hardly more than a year old.

Clare's divorce was the first that had happened in the Tennant family, and her abrupt departure from a husband she had known only two years became a scandal. It might be possible to have discreet affairs after marriage, but to leave a husband and request a divorce was severely frowned on. And beyond that, it was simply not done for a married woman to run off abandoning her baby. Clare's fresh suitor was the Hon. Lionel Tennyson, grandson of the poet, but unlike his grandfather rather more of a roué than a man of substance. Heavy debts had already obliged his father to transfer him from the Coldstream Guards to the Rifle Brigade, whose base at Winchester he considered a safe distance from London. But this made small difference to Lionel who had only to acquire a season ticket up to town. Night clubs and gambling were, for Lionel, irresistible pleasures; and it was in London that he had begun his courtship of Clare. But it was not long before Society was talking of this clandestine romance, and in fairly knowledgeable terms. The gossip reached the young Prince of Wales, then serving on the Italian Front. He wrote of it to his friend and confidante of the day, Lady Coke: 'What stories there are about Mrs Adrian Bethell; she and Lionel Tennyson seem to be or to have been on *exceptionally* intimate terms, though I've never even seen her so it doesn't interest me in the least!'[2]

By the end of 1917 Clare's divorce had gone through; Bethell was granted custody of the baby daughter and Clare was the guilty party through her adultery with Lionel Tennyson. It was rare for the wife to be sued, but Adrien Bethell was deeply grieved by this wreck of his life at such an early stage. Also, Clare did not mind being named as the respondent; in a sense it showed that she was in demand, and this flattered her vanity. Yet, though later friends like Lord David Cecil felt Clare rose above any stigma attached to this early divorce, she remained sensitive to Society's judgement of her at the time. 'It was like walking down Regent Street with the fleur-de-lis branded on one's shoulder,' she confided to a relation, comparing herself to a scarlet woman in eighteenth-century France. And, indeed, the talk of her indiscretion continued to reverberate, once again drawing the interest of the Prince of Wales. He wrote to his confidante:

> What do you think of the Bethell divorce? I've never even seen her, tho' I feel sorry for her as Lionel Tennyson is an absolute rotter & doesn't really love her, so I hear, anyhow not enough to want to marry her tho' he'll simply have to!!!!! One can hardly believe he'll be such a beast not to, tho' on the other hand it might be better for her if he didn't under those circumstances; what a mess for a woman of 20 to have got into!!!![3]

Clare married Lionel just two days after her decree absolute from Bethell, on 27 March 1918. On the surface Lionel promised a more exciting life than Adrian Bethell could offer. Bethell might have had a large estate in East Yorkshire, but it was a long way from the fashionable nightlife of London where Clare wanted to be seen and admired. With a certain dreariness of tone she would repeat the Bethell postal address – Rise Park, Hull – as if it indicated a prison sentence in the back of beyond. With Lionel she could be constantly under the spotlight of attention, and she was also attracted by his fame as a sportsman. She had quite forgotten her need for a foxhunting man; Tennyson's fame was as a cricketer, and it was his one activity that spoke in his favour. During the 1913 to 1914 season he had played for England in five test matches, and in 1921 he was to captain England against Australia. It was at this time that he performed a feat which remained in the minds of cricketers for generations. Playing with one broken hand, he batted sixty-seven runs single-handed. Clare believed she had found herself a hero.

Pamela and Eddy were distressed by the way Clare had simply severed herself from her daughter. Where could such coldness have sprung from? Whatever Pamela might say against the Tennants it had not come from them; if anything, the Tennants, with their thick merchant blood, were family-minded to a degree. The Bart had taken infinite trouble over the well-being of his offspring; likewise Eddy has provided handsomely for all of his. Clare had received a motor car – an expensive gift at that date – on her marriage to Adrian, and £100,000 in settlement. This streak of wilfulness, which in Clare's case was capable of inflicting terrible hurt, had certainly come from her own mother. As Pamela always had to have her way, so too did Clare, but with her the wilfulness appeared in monstrous proportion. Pamela might be vain and hot-headed, but she was not unkind to children, and even towards Clare, whose temperament she disliked, her letters show concern. Eddy and Pamela felt deeply for their first grandchild, whose childhood was spent between the solidity of the Yorkshire squirearchy and the sensitivities of Wilsford.

On the death of his father, Christopher succeeded to the family business. Like Eddy, he suddenly found himself the heir to chairmanship, directorships and, of course, a large fortune. But unlike his father Christopher wished to be an active businessman. He went every day to Tennant's in Mincing Lane and worked closely with those poorer Tennants who now owned a substantial share of the business. In fact by dint of hard work, these far-back Ayrshire cousins were no longer poor, and as far as the business was concerned they stood on an almost equal footing with their more famous kinsmen. Because he had inherited through the accident of his brother's death, Christopher believed all the more strongly in the duty of family responsibility. And a part of that duty was to ensure that the business continued to prosper.

The 1920s were years of dramatic change for the chemical empire first assembled by Charles Tennant in 1800. Much of the machinery at the St Rollox works was now outmoded, and in 1923 the great Tennant chimney had to be dynamited. With its demolition Glasgow lost one of its most significant landmarks and reminders – poisonous though the fumes had been – of her burst through to industrial glory. In 1926 St Rollox, for long a company within United Alkali – that group of manufacturers who had sworn allegiance with the Bart as first president – now became part of a large new chemical enterprise called Imperial Chemical Industries. The making of ICI was the result of a long-awaited merger of Brunner, Mond, Nobel's, United Alkali and British Dyestuffs, carried out to protect the whole of the British chemical industry against their increasingly powerful rival – Germany. Tennant's were well compensated, but it meant the end of their association with chemicals. Charles Tennant & Co. of Mincing Lane, and other dependent companies, might diversify their interests and hold their reputation as a sound – and rich – private business, but with St Rollox gone the making of the family fortune was now history.

But this was of no concern to Pamela who, in the meantime, had been bringing up her youngest son Stephen to believe he would have been happier as a girl. Safe in her Wiltshire retreat, Pamela had indulged a further fantasy that in order to compensate for Clare's failure as a daughter, all she had to do was to turn her youngest boy into a female for a while. Until about the age of six she had dressed Stephen in flowing Regency-type gowns, although at prep school age she had set him free to be a boy. But of course it was too late. Stephen had rather taken to this idea of loose clothes, and Pamela should not have been surprised when at seventeen he came into the drawing room with a large beauty spot marked on his face. Soon he was going a step further and applying a great deal of make-up – foundation creams, powder, mascara, rouged lips – anything, in fact, that would enhance his handsome face. Like his mother and his sister, who were such perfect examples, Stephen too wanted accolades to his beauty.

In 1922 a sobering influence had come into the lives of the young Tennants. Pamela had married her old-time friend and admirer, Sir Edward Grey, now Lord Grey of Fallodon. They were married quietly in the church that stands adjacent to Wilsford Manor, drawn together not simply by the strong ties of affection but by their shared love of nature. There were aviaries at Wilsford and at Fallodon, Grey's Northumberland home, and together Grey and Pamela would sit talking to the birds, who ate freely from their hands and perched for hours on their shoulders. The sight of the communing pair, however, was too much for Margot; one morning at Wilsford she could not resist opening her window to shout, 'And I know a damned robin too, when I see one!' But Pamela gave Grey the peace he needed after the horror of war, for though she could help him write his memoirs in his near-blindness, politics were otherwise banished. It was only Pamela's little granddaughter, Diana – my mother – who had that memory of dancing round the nursery at Glen on Armistice Day and would sometimes tug at his sleeve to ask, 'Will there be another war? Will there be another war?' The subject always made him shake, and brought the same answer: 'There will never ever be another war,' he would repeat.

By the 1920s Margot had achieved a legendary status. Her consistently outspoken behaviour had made her a household name, and this was enhanced by the publication of her autobiography in 1920. Here she spoke frankly about people in high places and her own amorous attachments before marriage. Autobiography was still a reticent craft, and Margot's book became a best-seller. But many misread her high spirits, and saw the Tennants as dangerously fast. One reviewer, who took her fiercely to task, simply said that now that she had painted her own portrait, 'scandal may take a long vacation'. The reviewer, whose name was Harold Begbie, wrote under the strange pseudonym of 'A Gentleman with a Duster', and saw it as his duty to clean up the mirrors of those in the public eye. He had already published *The Mirrors of Downing Street* in which he exposed what he believed to be the appalling weaknesses in our rulers, and in that volume he had devoted a chapter to the moral collapse of H. H. Asquith. Shortly after the appearance of Margot's autobiography Begbie published another harsh criticism of well-known figures in *The Glass of Fashion*, and this time gave a chapter to the indiscretion and vulgarity of Margot Asquith. He claimed that Margot was nothing short of a sensationalist, and declared that, 'If the world went on its way, carrying the taper of modesty through the darkness of this human night, she would pin Catherine wheels to her front, fasten a Roman candle at her brow, and advance brandishing a rocket in either hand.'[4]

Of course Margot liked attention, but Mr Bebgie's assessment of her was absurdly prudish. He vented disgust that a woman of fifty-six should detail an incident of a Prussian officer 'picking her up' in the Dresden opera house when a young, unmarried woman. He described the memoirs as 'this long pilgrimage through Vanity Fair', crowned by the final egocentric wish for 'a crowded memorial service'. In fact Margot's memoirs were a much-needed relief from those Society books where ladies of title spoke of visits to large country estates or parties in large town houses and little else. Begbie might claim that 'Mrs Asquith's sensational career has not been good for the spiritual life of English society', yet who but the plainest Puritan would have wanted her different? Throughout the 1920s and 1930s Margot's witticisms were quoted and capped by all from bright under-graduates to bewildered dowagers. So much so, that apocryphal wit was allowed to slip in. She is supposed, for instance, never to have answered Jean Harlow, on calling her 'Margo*t*' (hard 't') with, 'The 't' is silent, as in Harlow.' While it is true that after an unsuccessful trip to the USA, where she had gone to read her memoirs, she did pronounce, 'If I'd been Columbus, I would never have mentioned it.'

After Asquith's retirement from politics Margot, as Countess of Oxford, came into her own again, much as she had, though in a different way, as a precocious girl. Behaviour that had once startled smart London, had now hardened with age into definite eccentricity. She carried about with her, for example, an obsession for the greatness of 'Henry' and would sometimes say unexpectedly to neighbours quietly dozing in a railway carriage, 'I can clearly see you would like to hear about my husband.' She became convinced that most illnesses were spread by the teeth, and could turn abruptly on her unsuspecting hostess with, 'Have them out!' She also took to going to every wedding she possibly could – usually only to inspect the bride – and a friend, Sir Michael Duff, recalls her stopping him on the stairs at a reception to say, 'Darling, don't go up – the bride – simply hideous.' And then, after Henry's death in 1928, Margot would stride up and down the drawing-rooms of the country houses of younger friends, reliving the glorious days of the Liberal Party when her husband was leader, and she 10 Downing Street's most famous hostess. But never was there a kind word for the man who had unseated Henry in the midst of battle: Lloyd George, to Margot, was always 'a low cad' or 'the rottenest man I ever knew'.

Only Margot and Lucy now survived of the Bart's daughters, though of his sons there were still Frank and Jack. Charty Ribblesdale had died of the dreaded family ailment, tuberculosis,

some years before the First World War. But at least she was
spared the sadness of seeing her second son, Charles, killed in
that bloodbath. The Ribblesdales' eldest son, Tommy – an officer
in the tenth Hussars – had died in Somaliland in 1904 and now,
with both his sons dead, Ribblesdale suffered from bouts of acute
melancholia. And Lucy Graham Smith, though still in her
Wiltshire hunting-box, had long been crippled with a creeping
bone disease. It was only Margot who remained as a vivid
reminder of the Tennants' rapid rise to social recognition. But
Pamela did not like to be reminded of Tennants, and in particular
of Margot. If she had a criticism of her children, it was to tell one
or other that they were getting like Margot. It irritated Pamela if
Margot came too close to her children. But this was to happen as
Clare's second marriage began to break down.

Lionel Tennyson might have glamour as a cricketer, but after a
few years the reckless gambling and drinking became too much
for Clare. For several seasons they had taken a hunting-box near
fashionable Melton, where they hunted with the Quorn, Cottes-
more and Belvoir, but hunting was not really Lionel's game. He
preferred the evening to the daytime when there was liberal
drinking and cards, and at the latter he proceeded to lose a fair
amount of his wife's money. They had had two children but by
1926 Clare had found a lover, an American named James Beck,
who had few working commitments and was in England to meet
Society. In January 1927, Diana Cooper went to dine with Clare
and left the following record:

> I dined last night with Clare Tennyson in Gloucester Place.
> I arrived first. She was looking as pretty as be damned. I
> never saw her lovelier. She at once entreated me not to
> mention the fact that 'her old friend Jimmy Beck' as she
> called him was coming to dinner. As there were five other
> guests the precaution seemed hardly worth while. Maud
> Russell looking very middle-aged, Buffles looking like an ox
> and Sheila looking like a cow – Beck and another American

called Cox completed the party. Beck is quite a pleasant
nice-looking fellow but seems to possess no unusual quality.
Clare was very much *la femme delaissée* apologising for the
wine (which was quite good) saying she had had to buy it
herself and knew nothing of such things. She is much
worried poor little creature – Lionel has the detectives on
her all the time, and Edward Grey of Fallodon is
continually giving her lectures down the telephone.[5]

Pamela showed a genuine concern at the collapse of her
daughter's second marriage. Both she and Grey urged her not to
marry Beck; having failed in two marriages, was it really wise to
embark on a third? But Margot was encouraging Clare to marry
again, and this annoyed Pamela. 'I am rather distressed at the
line Margot is taking now in Clare's affairs,' Pamela wrote to her
sister Mary Wemyss, 'she has a certain amount of influence over
Clare, who feels – rightly in general – that she [Margot] has so
much more knowledge of the world than I have.'[6] The
implication was, of course, that she, Pamela, was too sensitive to
know about the world, while Margot, with the toughness of her
background, would know it all too well. Pamela was right to
recognize the almost wilful muddle that Clare was creating
around her. Clare admitted that she could not see any view that
was not immediately before her: 'an inch-view', her mother
remarked, and concluded that poor Clare was 'spiritually
shortsighted'.

Yet in that world of country-house visiting, smart night-clubs,
and Society places of rendezvous – such as the Ritz foyer or the
Embassy club – Clare was an undisputed success. Her beauty
and what Society friends called her 'wit' – which was often the
cutting remark – were in demand. Liking comfort and admiration, Clare was equally fully committed to the country-house
scene. Having abandoned with her first marriage the opportunity
of living in a country house, she made up for it by spending most
of the year circulating round them. These were days when

one often stayed for three weeks at a time – there being such a
plentiful supply of servants – and Clare took full advantage of the
lengthy stay. As she increasingly became a personality and
leading beauty of the period, she was expected to be self-
indulgent and vain. To feed her skin, Clare bathed every day in
milk and Robert Heber-Percy remembers her staying with the
eccentric Lord Berners at Faringdon, stretched out all morning
on a sofa, the feet raised on the far arm to let the blood circulate
and so preserve her youth. Conrad Russell, the friend and Balliol
contemporary of Raymond Asquith, wrote an account of meeting
Clare in one of those country houses – Heveningham in Suffolk –
and caught some of the flavour of her vanity and, also, her
appeal. The letter is to his sister, Flora, and dated August 1928,
when Clare was thirty-two:

> The guests are a man called Green who makes boilers in
> Yorkshire & Mrs Beck – only I call her Mrs Tennyson as it
> seems wrong to be too well informed about her husbands.
> She is very very lovely & wears green velvet pantaloons in
> the evening. In the morning she is dressed only in a small
> tight fitting Union Jack which certainly does not hide
> overmuch of her charms; & in the afternoon she is dressed
> in a sweater & white shorts as if for the Oxford &
> Cambridge Boat Race. I am stunned by her beauty & can't
> take my eyes off her.[7]

In 1928 Clare married James Beck, as predicted. The marriage
was purely physical on Clare's part as Beck had very little
socially to recommend him. He did not really fit into her world of
country-house sports and after dinner bridge. The only point in
his favour was an ability to play the piano – albeit with the
theatricality of Liberace – but this was not enough. 'And what
about Beck!' Clare's friends like the late Lord Rosebery would
say, across the dining-table at Mentmore. Society might have
been snobbish in not taking him to its heart, but Beck was snob
enough himself to submit to this humiliation. On occasion even

Clare would mock him – which was cruel – and encourage him to look silly by making him jump sheep hurdles – which of course he could not do – in the parks of her ducal friends. An indication as to how Beck bored people is well put in a letter from Diana Cooper to her husband Duff. Diana, Clare and Beck were all guests of Mrs Laura Corrigan, a rich American, who entertained lavishly in her Venetian *palazzo*. The letter describes a row between Clare and 'Jimmy'; these were not infrequent:

> Clare cried on the balcony. Jimmy Beck took a bad fall at the Gondola landing – unfortunately – not *in* the water. The whole of our Palace and the servants were kept awake by yells, sobs, screams from the Beck room. At one moment it was thought we ought to interfere. All the noise and hysteria was on Clare's side and the cause was straight jealousy – isn't it unbelievable. That paunched horror.[8]

On marrying James Beck, Clare had further children, this time twins – a boy and a girl. In all, she now had five children, and to most of them she was totally indifferent. Society, enjoying her company, chose not to judge her too harshly for this abandonment of her own flesh and blood. Diana, who was my mother, had not seen her since she was one-and-a-half; her two sons by Lionel saw her more frequently, though they spent a large part of their childhood with Tennyson cousins. She brought up the Beck twins – as they were called – but in a distinctly unmaternal way. They were lovingly posed beside her for the endless stream of Society photographs, but beyond that it was made clear that she had no time for them. And indeed she didn't. When her marriage to Beck ended in 1939, the twins called to say goodbye before returning to America: that they were two homeless children of ten was of no matter. 'It was such a bore,' Clare said to a friend, 'I was in the bath when they called, so I just waved from a window.'

Wilsford had been intended as a haven of security from which Pamela's and Eddy's children could step strong into the world: now its perfect nurturing was turning horribly sour. Pamela was distraught at Clare's behaviour and wrote to her first son-in-law, Adrian Bethell, saying that she had given her children too much love and here was the result. But Pamela only saw herself as the adoring mother and never once analysed that other motives might be involved. She did not recognize that her hardness towards Clare might possibly have left deep marks and warped her character. She did not see for a moment that any jealousy or possessiveness on her part could exist where her own children were concerned. Yet, by contradiction, when her treasured David told her that he wished to marry Lady Ursula Grosvenor, the daughter of Bend'Or, Duke of Westminster, she told him that if he did this, he was 'placing a pistol' at her head.

So much of Pamela's life had become a dream, making less and less contact with reality. Now, she held continual séances – either at Wilsford or in London – so that she might speak with Bim, and sometimes Eddy. In the mornings at Wilsford she would sit at the edge of her granddaughter Diana's bed and tell her of last night's conversation with Bim. But her experiences with the Other Side were given serious coverage when she published a book on them entitled *The Earthen Vessel*. One of her companions in spiritualism was her Wiltshire neighbour, Sir Oliver Lodge, the well-known physicist who was partly responsible for the invention of the radio. He too had lost a son in the war, and was to publish tracts on speaking with the dead; he also lost some credibility in his profession for indulging what was regarded as a game for fantasists.

Or else Pamela visited Clouds, where her nephew Dick Wyndham now lived. The house had not lost its atmosphere, and every time she saw it her childhood came back. There was her mother coming laden with shawls to give to the concert audience; there was 'Papa' crossing and re-crossing the hall in his 'flapping slipper-heels'; and there was the young Pamela playing her guitar. But most of all there came back to her the memory of that summer of 1893 when Harry Cust had broken his news to her. She had told her sister-in-law, Sibell Grosvenor, that at every

New Year she read through the letters of that sad affair, and the tears always streamed down her cheeks. When she went to Clouds she would stand on the same hearthstone in the hall where she had heard Cust explain the muddle he had made. She remembered, too, the words he had told her that were in his mind. 'Whatever I was doing, and whatever I did, sad, mad, and bad, I always said to myself, "I have got Pamela, like a star in a cupboard to come back to." '9

Pamela's emotional demands fell heavily, though in different ways – on both David and Stephen. Her son David was her kind of man, and she once said to him, 'What a child we could have.' He had dark looks and there was an aristocratic hauteur in his face – he was also very masculine. She expected a great deal of David; for her he was someone who could clearly make a success of any career he chose. But to bring up a child not to fail can impose an unfair burden. David wavered between careers, not sure that he could be the success that his mother expected. First of all he trained as an engineer in Cambridge – at which he showed great skill; then he became one of the first BBC radio announcers, and was praised for his clear speaking voice. But this did not last either. In 1925 he performed a volte-face on a conventional career and opened a night-club.

At the same time as David was planning his club, he was living with a young actress, Hermione Baddeley. They had already had a child, and it was not until about a year later that they decided to marry. Pamela's former relief that at least his girlfriends were not on the stage was now in vain; in fact most of her dreams for David to fulfil some ideal destiny of her own whimsical imaginings were best forgotten. David wanted to live among Bohemians and saw himself, with his money and his club, as a patron of starving artists. The rich members – meaning chiefly the aristocracy and 'the county' – were to pay the normal rate while David's poor artist friends were to have food and drink for a peppercorn sum. The club was called the Gargoyle and situated in the heart of London's West End, just off Dean Street in Soho.

From an upstairs bar you descended to the floor below where there was a restaurant and also a dance floor. This room was comfortable, rather plush, with dining-tables and banquettes. The odd Matisse painting moved around the club's rooms, which began a myth that the dining-room had been modelled after a painting by him. But since so many rakish stories were to blossom from the Gargoyle, myth suited the club well. In the evenings there would occasionally be a cabaret, or David's wife would do something impromptu, or David himself might sing to his guitar. David's wife was an asset in bringing in members, since she was one of the rising names in revue theatre. For many years Hermione Baddeley was synonymous with the Gargoyle, and David and Hermione leaders of that fast-living coterie 'the Bright Young People'. For many of them the Gargoyle became a second home.

With the fortune established, and a quantity of Wyndham blood, David and Stephen were happy to shed that need for respectability which had dominated the lives of the Tennant men of the previous generation. Eddy's two brothers, Frank and Jack, might continue to live as respectable country gentlemen, but Pamela's children felt no commitment to such conventional yardsticks. They felt themselves now to be aristocrats and they were determined to enjoy the properties of this new dimension. They took it as a kind of bonus to the individual status that Pamela had already made them believe they held. When David's cousin Dick Wyndham told him one day that he really hadn't done very much with his life so far, David replied, 'Well, I've crossed the Sahara, opened the Gargoyle – and I'm an Honourable.' Clare ticked off a close friend when she wrote to her forgetting her title on the envelope. And in a lighter vein, David, rousing a farmer late at night to request the use of his petrol pump, announced, 'We're titled folk from town.'

It was Pamela's wish that Stephen should show precocious talent in every direction. When, as a child, his mother had asked him what the flowers were saying, Stephen told her that they said, 'Stephen, Stephen, Stephen.' Pamela concluded that he would be a poet. Just as she had treasured all Bim's early verses, so she carefully folded away every piece of Stephen's writing or drawing. A poem written when he was seven she was convinced showed the inspiration of William Blake, while his drawings were stuck into an album with inscriptions like, 'Stephen's most beautiful Easter card to me. Wilsford 1914'. She had brought Stephen up not only to the expectation of great beauty, but also of genius. In later years this always haunted Stephen and he would write on the flyleaf of books, 'Arthur Waley said to Sachie (Sitwell), "I think Stephen has genius." Sachie said to me, "Arthur is usually right." ' Stephen held his first London exhibition at the Dorien Leigh Galleries at the age of sixteen, and was soon a pupil at the Slade.

His work at this time showed an easy facility for caricature with an occasional influence of Aubrey Beardsley. The drawings were witty and displayed Stephen's extravagant interest in fashion – he was adept at capturing haughty dowagers or racy 1920s flappers. At the Slade he made an immediate friendship with a fellow student who at once understood his exotic humour, romantic flights, and the sheer excitement of being young. Rex Whistler had arrived at the Slade in 1923, the same year as Stephen, and he wrote to an old Haileybury school chum saying that they had got 'rather a "case" '. 'Case' was the Haileybury term for a schoolboy crush, but Whistler did not mean that his infatuation was necessarily sexual, though it was certainly emotional. Stephen had a delicate and exquisite beauty, which his contemporaries compared to Shelley, but Rex's attraction for Stephen was primarily his sense of 'fun' and high-tuned poetic sensibilities. In their lunch hours they would talk of their favourite poets, and in particular of Edgar Allan Poe. They quoted Poe in their letters, thinking often of lines from 'Ulalume', 'To One in Paradise', and most of all of 'Annabel Lee'. So much so, that 'a Kingdom by the sea' became their watchword, and whenever Rex wrote to Stephen he inscribed it on the back of the envelope in decorative script.

Under Stephen's influence a new host of people came to
Wilsford. In childhood the visitors had been relations, or
Pamela's Pre-Raphaelite-hued 'artistic' friends. Now, the faster
pace of the 1920s asserted itself, with frequent visits from the
three Sitwells, Whistler and Cecil Beaton. For Rex Whistler,
Wilsford was a background quite different from his own. 'I'm
going down this weekend to stay at Lord Grey of Fallodon's
house in Wiltshire!!!',[10] he wrote to a friend. But this did not
mean that Whistler was ashamed of his more humble origins – it
was just that in the Tennant household he could live the escape
into fantasy that was to dominate so much of his drawing. Soon
Rex was accompanying Stephen on a recuperative holiday to
Switzerland – for Stephen had fallen a temporary victim of
tuberculosis – accompanied by Stephen's doctor, his nanny, and
his brother Christopher's valet. Before the journey Stephen and
Rex spent weeks discussing and writing to each other about their
alpine wardrobe. Frequently Rex felt that Stephen was appropriating
all the best colours, and eventually he complained that
there was nothing for him to wear but black. Stephen relented,
but even so, their possibly matching scarves gave Rex cause for
worry: 'Our jades are sure to be different,' he wrote, 'though your
description is rather like mine. Not a pure green quite, but a
brightish milky colour. You need not, however, fear in me a rival,
charming and beautiful though I know my appearance to
be . . .'[11]

Like Pamela and Clare, Stephen expected to be first and for all
eyes to be turned on him. His need for admiration was
paramount, and began to overtake the zeal with which he should
have been applying himself to his painting. On one of the first
occasions on which Cecil Beaton had seen him Stephen was
riding the papier-mâché horses at an Olympia circus, dressed in a
black leather coat, with large chinchilla collar, and blowing
kisses to left and right. Beaton recorded that it created 'an
unforgettable sight', and he was soon swept away with an
enthusiasm to be Stephen. The night before he had met Stephen

at a society party and decided at once that Stephen's world was for him. 'The photograph orders of Miss Franks and that Jew can go to Hell,'[12] he wrote in his diary, seeing before him the pathway to a new group of glittering young aristocratic stars. But Beaton's snobbery did not allow him to see that there might be terrible shortcomings in Stephen's enviable background. On his first visit to Wilsford in 1926, Beaton thought only of his escape from his middle-class parentage and of his chance in this grander world. What mattered was that Lady Grey and her children had welcomed this outsider into their rarefied milieu.

With Whistler it had been different. He was not entirely taken in by Pamela's outward displays of warmth and graciousness. Looking back he could not think of Wilsford as a happy house, for all its intended romance. 'There was,' as Rex's brother Laurence has put it, 'always the sense of steel in the caress.'[13]

While Clare was embarking on her third marriage, and David opening his arms to Bohemia, Stephen began the most important relationship of his life. Through the Sitwells Stephen had met Siegfried Sassoon. Since being hailed as a hero in literary circles for his anti-war verse, Sassoon had shifted from his almost exclusively hunting friendships to the more sophisticated worlds of Renishaw, Garsington and Bloomsbury. The war had broken his innocence and those simple good people of the hunting field were never to be the same to him. Their philistinism now irked him, and his recognition of his homosexuality set up another barrier within him. After the war Sassoon had had an affair with a painter named Gabriel Atkin, and in the early 1920s another with a German, Prince Philip of Hesse, whom Sassoon had told Stephen was like 'a cuddly teddy bear'. But Stephen, thin and ethereal, was the direct opposite and Sassoon fell violently in love with him.

They set off almost at once on what Stephen has described as 'a honeymoon' to Sicily. It was March 1928, and together they roamed the island looking at the ancient remains and the spring flowers. Of the two, Stephen was the more decorative, wearing

couture pyjamas in 'soft mushroom pink' and bringing with him
a pet parrot. Sassoon's appearance was always ruggedly masculine, as befitted his role in their relationship. At times Stephen
found 'S.S.' – as his friends often called him – rather boastful, in
particular since his *Memoirs of a Fox-hunting Man* (1927) had just
been accepted for publication by Faber and Faber, where T. S.
Eliot sat. 'Don't you realize I'm a Faber author,'[14] he would say
to Stephen, who was not in the least impressed by the publishing
grades. But Sassoon was obsessively in love with him – 'I would
gladly die for him,' he wrote – and Sicily was the highpoint in a
romance that was ultimately doomed. To immortalize their time
there, Sassoon afterwards composed his poem 'In Sicily'[15]:

> Because we two can never again come back
> On time's one forward track, –
> Never again first-happily explore
> This valley of rocks and vines and orange-trees,
> Half Biblical and half Hesperides,
> With dark blue seas calling from a shell-strewn shore:
> > By the strange power of Spring's resistless green
> > Let us be true to what we have shared and seen,
> > And as our amulet this idyll save.
> > And since the unreturning day must die,
> > Let it forever be lit by an evening sky
> > And the wild myrtle grow upon its grave.

Sassoon took Stephen to meet his famous friends. There were
visits to Thomas Hardy at Max Gate and to T. E. Lawrence at
Clouds Hill. Stephen was struck by how short Hardy was, and
how he had to stand on a chair to carve the goose. When they
visited Lawrence he told Stephen how he read the plays of
Shakespeare constantly and otherwise just enjoyed cutting the
logs and stacking them by the fire. Pamela showed no interest in
Stephen's jaunts. She was engrossed in spiritualism, and on the
day he visited Hardy barely looked up from her latest spiritualist
tract. In the autumn of 1928 Stephen went abroad again, this

time to France, and Sassoon joined him. He did not return to England until the third week in November, when a telegram summoned him. Pamela had died of a sudden stroke at Wilsford.

Pamela's death had happened while she was alone at Wilsford. None of her children could reach her before she died, and Edward Grey made the night journey from Northumberland on a specially ordered train in the hope that he might find her alive. But Christopher met him in the early hours of the morning at King's Cross station to break the news. 'Lord Grey heard the tragic news calmly, but then the pent-up emotion of the seven hours' tension in the express became too much for him, and he broke down,' newspapers reported throughout the country the next day. And within days Pamela had received a mass of obituary notices which praised her for her beauty and her devotion to her children. The notices glowed with praise and many ran on for several columns. 'Model Wife and Mother' – 'Never Grew Old', goes one; 'Charming Personality', reads another; and, of course 'Her Feathered Friends' – 'A Lover of Birds'. Indeed, one paper described a touching scene of Pamela in her Wilsford aviary:

> If birds can feel loss, the scores of birds in the big aviary at the Manor will miss Lady Grey sorely. She was passionately fond of birds, and every day while she was at Wilsford she would sit in the aviary and the birds would perch on her head, shoulders, and arms. Whenever she walked outside she had one or more birds perched on her shoulder.[16]

Stories were related of how, when shopping in Newcastle from Fallodon, Pamela would walk through the streets with a favourite parrot, Koko, perched on her arm. Another told of when, as wife to the Lord High Commissioner to the Church of Scotland (as Eddy became), she had suddenly stopped the procession in the middle of Edinburgh, alighted from her carriage and gone into a bird shop hung with cages. She had bought every caged bird on the spot and asked for them to be delivered to her at Holyrood. Later, she took the cages into the King's Park there and set every bird free. *The Times* obituary mentioned her 'rare gifts of spirit of mind', and went on to say that 'she will be long and sincerely mourned in many a household, humble as well as great . . .'. Pamela, it was clearly noted, though a patrician to her fingertips, had had the common touch. But perhaps it was John Buchan's wife, then Lady Tweedsmuir, who captured Pamela more accurately when she wrote of her in her memoirs as 'an Olympian character, because of her aloofness from mundane things. She floated to and fro between Wilsford and the Glen, appreciating their different beauties, and so well buttressed by wealth tht she never had to catch a bus or think about the price of fish.'[17]

Clare gave a sob when told of her mother's death and announced, 'It's the end of my childhood.'[18] David, who was left Wilsford by his mother and the large personal fortune Eddy had bequeathed her, sold the house and estate to Stephen, saying he had no wish to live with his mother's ghost. Christopher, settled at Glen and busy in the City, took it all with an air of detachment, while the orphan baby that Pamela had adopted on Stephen's birth and named Barnaby had run away to sea in his early teens, and was not there to sorrow. The most affected were Pamela's eldest grandchild, Diana, who had received from her the love denied by Clare, and also, desperately, Stephen. Cecil Beaton, who had succumbed to Pamela's definite charm and also her status as a *grande dame*, wrote in his diary of his own reactions and fears for Stephen. A friend had brought him the news, and the shock was the greater since Pamela had been in good health and was only fifty-seven:

> . . . My life stopped still . . . I couldn't believe that it was true – she must be mixing up the name. She assured me & still I couldn't believe it. Why Lady Grey had been so particularly well of late. I know that she had suffered from her heart but she had since her visit to her pet cure hospital

felt so well, looked so well – that she could die was something that one had never reckoned with. There would be no one to look after the ill-birds, there would be no one to look after the parrots – no one to look after Stephen. Poor Stephen, & how false & frivolous my letters written to him last week would seem at this moment – Poor Poor Stephen. I could not believe it until I had made sure – until I had read it in the newspapers. I couldn't believe that my hostess of the happiest weeks I have ever spent in my life, was dead. The weeks in that glorious vividly sunny garden in the south of France – where there was a theatrical display of primulas, bougainvillaeas, pansies, roses, tulips – lovely swamps of pastel coloured flowers – I couldn't believe it – Lady Grey sitting on the loggia putting sprigs of peach blossom into the birds' cages, & talking about Emily Dickinson.[19]

Beaton had written again in his diary after seeing photographs of the funderal at Wilsford 'with Lord Grey & David, hatless, stunned & emaciated, holding funeral flowers in the rain . . . I am most upset & fussed now that there is no one to look after Stephen – to look after his health & to keep him from doing silly things.' And not long afterwards Stephen did decline, but there was an appointed guardian. Before, it had always been his mother who had taken the villas in the South of France for his tuberculosis, or the apartment in Paris when he no longer enjoyed school; now Siegfried Sassoon would look after him. But whether Stephen wanted Sassoon so close to him was another matter.

With another attack of tuberculosis, brought on by the death of Pamela, Stephen left for Bavaria at the end of 1928. He went as a paying guest to a select guest-house near Garmisch, owned by a respectable German couple who had been impoverished by the country's economic collapse. Stephen invited several friends to join him there and by April – which was his birthday month – there were Rex Whistler, William Walton, Edith Olivier – a country neighbour, and Sassoon. Everyone adored the warm atmosphere of the guest-house – which was largely created by the abundant personality of Johanna Hirth – and Edith Olivier remarked in her diary, 'I feel that anyone who is guided to this place . . . *must* be a *chosen person* . . . Stephen has been led here for great purpose – that the loveliness in him may grow and the other side vanish.'[20] By 'the other side' Edith Olivier meant not his illness, but the vanity and self-centredness which she saw endangering his life and creating havoc of his work. But the specialist who came from Heidelberg to treat his ailing lung wondered 'how anyone so heavenly – so "underlich" – so spiritual can face this rude world'. While Sassoon, who stood closest to this vision 'of a Fra Angelico' – as the Heidelberg doctor described Stephen – skipped from room to room in an excitement of infatuation. How different this Siegfried was – everyone thought – from the morose poet so often encountered in London.

Back in England Sassoon could not leave Stephen alone. At the beginning Stephen had certainly reciprocated his love; with his strong masculine features Sassoon was very much the physical type for which Stephen longed. Once, when alone in London and missing Stephen, Sassoon had been tempted to try to seduce Rex Whistler. He felt that certain indications had been given which meant Whistler would respond, but he noted in his diary, '. . . if I were to try the experiment I should find myself betraying Stephen, who has given me his whole heart'.[21] But now, as Sassoon's love grew more and more possessive, Stephen did not know that he wanted to let go his whole heart. By the end of 1929 Sassoon was living at Wilsford, nursing the intermittently sick Stephen. The recurrent bouts of tuberculosis suited Sassoon as he could keep a constant vigil at the bedside. But he also made Stephen a prisoner, permitting visitors to see him for only half an hour at a time, and many of these were old friends like Rex Whistler. Eventually Stephen could stand it no longer and Sassoon was dismissed from the house.

In Sassoon's diaries Stephen emerges as a monster of egotism and wilfulness, but it is strange that Sassoon didn't realize the kind of background he was stepping into. Given Pamela, Stephen's wealth and looks, did he honestly believe that Stephen was of the sort with whom to settle down into marital bliss? Sassoon was the victim of an obsession and it is hardly fair to run down the character of the love object simply because things have not gone your way. But the obsession had gone deep with Sassoon, for even after he had been dismissed from Wilsford he took a house nearby, where he waited for a year or more, in case Stephen should want him back. Stephen was cruel now, for sometimes he would call him back only to reject him again. By the middle 1930s Sassoon had drifted out of Stephen's life, yet the mark he had made was to last for ever.

After Sassoon Stephen never again experienced the illusions and torments of the love affair. 'There is an hour that we could be happy all our lives, could we but find it,' he repeats frequently in his journals. From now on he started to travel among seaports, where he had a series of fleeting passions with sailors. Or else there would be friends from the nearby military camps round Salisbury, but nothing lasting. But it was his travels to France that meant most to him. First it would be Paris and visits to Jean Cocteau (who dubbed him 'Le Carnival de Venise'), and then on to Marseille, where he was gathering notes for a novel. A certain louche atmosphere in the old quarter of Marseille had caught Stephen's fancy; here he was going to write a humming tale of the maritime boulevard; the title was to be 'Lascar', which pleased him as the anagram of 'rascal'. But this novel, conceived in the late 1930s, was never to be completed. He wrote blurbs for it – 'a husky yarn about seamen and cargoes' – and painted its jacket in a series of vivid boulevard scenes, but the book itself lay abandoned. The stamina that Stephen's Glasgow ancestors had had to construct St Rollox was not in him. His indulged childhood had made him believe that he was already a star, and that beauty was sufficient for immortality.

Meanwhile, David's attempt to break away from his background was not as easily accomplished. He wanted to mix with artists but he found it difficult to lose the *grand seigneur* manner that came with his upbringing. The Gargoyle was precisely what London needed in those decades given over to pleasure, but David found that he had to drink if his barriers of shyness were to be broken down. Inevitably the club attracted not a few heavy drinkers – drink being almost the password for freedom in years that were busy shedding stiff pre-First World War conventions – but unlike Augustus John or Dylan Thomas, David had no pressing activities to occupy him in his spells of lucidity. However drunk he became he always retained a dignity. It was only that as the years went on his life increasingly lacked direction, and yet, as the host of the Gargoyle, and the giver of several celebrated parties, the late 1920s and the 1930s would not have been the same without him.

It was very much due to David's personality that the Gargoyle attracted its wide membership, and from the day it opened became *the* place to go. Evelyn Waugh took Anthony Powell there, who found the kind of night-club setting that was later to serve him in his novel of English life, *A Dance to the Music of Time* (12 vols, 1951–75). Many of the characters in the book took their composites from Gargoyle regulars, as did several in the fiction of Evelyn Waugh and Henry Green. The Gargoyle was where you found 'life', and David himself was part of it.

David could be by turns histrionic, witty, and appallingly rude. 'So you're the two nancy boys I'm told I'm longing to meet,' he once said to a distinguished music critic and his friend. But rudeness was a part of the Bright Young breakaways' language, like throwing daring and irregular parties to show that they wished to have nothing to do with their parents' formal behaviour. David and Hermione gave one of the first – a Pyjama and Bottle party. A few months later that same year Eddie Gathorne Hardy, Brian Howard, Elizabeth Ponsonby and Bebe Plunket-Greene (all leaders, with David, of the Bright Young

People) gave a Bathing Suit Bottle party at the St George's Swimming Baths in Buckingham Palace Road. Such events continued regularly for a number of years, and invariably as the evening wore on and the drinking grew heavier, scuffles or rows were not unusual. One surviver of the period remembered just such a scene occurring at one of David's: 'It ended in a free fight, I found myself in the middle of a jealous fracas, scuffle and scrimmage, which although it had nothing to do with me, resulted in my dress being torn off and tufts of my hair held up as trophies.'[22]

With a private income of £15,000 a year, David did not have to worry about anything except fun. He bought a house in Wiltshire – not far away from Clouds – and kept a fleet of cars and a Gypsy Moth aeroplane. He drove very fast down country lanes in racing cars of the latest model, or took his plane on trips to Paris. He filled his Wiltshire house with London friends and rarely saw 'the county' whom he referred to as 'the mugwumps'. And since many of his friends were writers, David saw no reason why he shouldn't exercise himself in this direction too. Sometimes he would read aloud from his travel diaries, but he never developed a natural style and marred his text with patronizing interjections such as 'the peasants were awfully kind to us'. Close as David tried to come to other worlds, he remained trapped: Bohemian as his life might be, it was impossible for him to forget his background. He wanted to be Bohemian, and he wanted to be thought an aristocrat, and the newness of the Tennant wealth made him insecure. Deep down within himself, these were all further reasons for drinking. Happiness for David could only exist when the fun was sufficiently charged. Without night-clubs, parties and other 'kicks', despair could all too easily reassert itself. Brian Howard, the most publicized decadent of the 1920s, wrote an imaginative tale of flying to Paris with David in his plane. In spite of Howard's highly coloured telling, the excerpt provides a fitting example of how David drew his life-blood from the short-lived pleasure:

'Oh, David! Did you see how frightened the angels were!'
'Yes,' he screams back, 'we are nine thousand feet high. I
thought Heaven was higher, didn't you?' 'David,' I scream
'look – look!' For we are entering the largest amphitheatre
in the cosmos. The amphitheatre of Heaven. On either side
clouds as large as continents form two enormous curving
walls. Beneath us are clouds. The sun, whizzing along
above us, has lit a white fire within each cloud. They seem
incandescent. All is empty. The people of Heaven have run
away. The clouds divide beneath us. I see that each cloud
stands upon a pillar of rainbow. A broken, brilliant rainbow
connects each cloud with the suburbs of London. 'Brian!'
David screams to me, 'I am the new Satan. Milton must
now write *Paradise Lost* again. I conquer Paradise.'[23]

David, Clare and Stephen inhabited quite different worlds,
and rarely met. David disliked Clare's country-house friends,
Stephen and David had little in common, while Clare was
ashamed of Stephen's femininity. The Tennant family, once so
united, had split apart. It was only Christopher, the eldest, who
held them together, seeing each through their separate troubles.
Christopher made Glen a refuge for Clare's abandoned children;
when David's drinking became too heavy Chistopher would
organize the cure; and when Stephen's spending cut severely into
his capital, it was Christopher who took control. By escaping to
naval college at twelve, Christopher had been fortunate to free
himself from Pamela's emotional bondage and maintain a
balanced viewpoint. As a child, I used to wonder at his air of
aloofness as he strolled, hands in pockets, around the rooms at
Glen. I knew he was not a cold person, but I was puzzled by the
way he kept his emotions constantly disengaged. Later I realized
that watching the disintegrating lives of his brothers and sister
must have given him a terrible fear of letting go.

Because nothing did improve for David, Clare and Stephen.
The actual world where people have to live and make a

semblance of togetherness, remained as remote to them as a foreign planet. My mother, Diana, was seventeen before she saw Clare again. More than fifteen years had passed since their last meeting. Diana had come to London from Yorkshire and decided that she would look up her mother – which is not an unnatural desire in offspring. But apart from some tears of shock on seeing for the first time this ignored daughter who so resembled her, the greeting was chilly. She made no attempt to know her, and during the few weeks that Diana stayed with her in Charles Street, she gave her no affection. Clare's heart was dead and her mind without conscience. And towards her twins by Beck she showed no further interest: once they had left for the USA she neither wrote to nor contacted them again. Yet, as the 1930s moved to the 1940s and to the 1950s, for what was Clare preparing herself? She had behind her three failed marriages and children she did not love. At fifty she still looked thirty – everyone said, a freak of youthfulness – but at sixty there could be nothing sadder, surely, than a fading Society beauty advancing into late middle age alone.

Throughout the 1940s and 1950s, Stephen still dreamed of the great novel he would soon publish. He kept up a wide contact with other writers, as if being with them would somehow spur him into activity. Elizabeth Bowen, Willa Cather, Rosamond Lehmann and Virginia Woolf were his stimulants to creativity. Whatever comment they made about his writing would be noted carefully in his journal. 'Her realization of how beautiful & exceptional this novel is stabilizes my own belief in it,' he wrote, on discussing 'Lascar' with Elizabeth Bowen. In the middle-1930s Virginia Woolf had lent him her house in Sussex for a week, but even the ascetic bookishness of Monk's House did not seem to have the desired effect. Nor, it would seem, did Virginia Woolf expect to find there an outpouring of Stephen's imaginative prose. 'We're just off to see what Stephen Tennant has done to Monk's House,' she writes to Lady Tweedsmuir, 'Bath salts – scents everywhere I expect, if not Stephen himself.'[24] The

following year she wrote to her sister, Vanessa, 'Voices sometimes reach me from the outer world: . . . Stephen Tennant wants
me to drive in his Victoria with him, talking intimately.'[25] All the
time he needed reassurance from established writers that he too
could do it. Stephen's background, so filled with privilege on the
surface, had only made him deeply insecure.

Yet, of the two younger brothers and Clare, it must be Stephen
who was to disappoint least. If Pamela wished for sensitive,
artistic children, then Stephen had not let her down. Over the
years he has filled volumes of journals with his yearnings, literary
curiousness and maxims for the day. The journals, executed in a
flowery script of different-coloured inks with an illustration
frequently placed on the page, are works of art in their own right.
They reveal Stephen in his many contradictory aspects. 'I shall
always be a stranger on this wonderful earth – never acclima-
tized, never *apprivoisé* – nor reconciled . . . I exist, I sing. I leave
some whisper of the world – to catch an echo – a vibration, in
spray & iridescence.' And from the Hotel Russell in London in
1938, 'Oh, if only I could ask time to stand still, it is so heavenly
to be young . . . I have finished a drawing for the book "Lascar",
and now I am going to bed – the music from the Hotel lounge is
very seductive at this distance. I am sniffing a delicious Wilsford
rose, oh what a perfume! – a pale pink one. This evening I looked
very beautiful.' From a journal dated 1941: 'A man asked me how
old I was. "Are you 21?" he said . . . A delicious rather pensive
fatigue envelopes me today . . . Willy Maugham says, "Write
from 9 to 1 whatever happens – work regularly – never wait for
inspiration."' Finally, there is a quote: 'the restless swallow fits
my restless mind,' and set not far below it, 'Dark eyes, I would go
to the end of the world for dark eyes . . .'

By 1950, 100 years had passed since John Tennant, his mind
on commerce, had said, 'I don't care much for Italian gardens.'
The great fortune that had been made through enterprise, and
guarded by diligence, was now about to be dispersed. The share
that had gone to David and Stephen had not as yet been

increased by industry, but spent by whim and fancy. Clare's settlement had been largely exhausted through the frivolities of Lionel Tennyson and the indolence of Jimmy Beck. Thirty-four Queen Anne's Gate had been sold and, following Eddy's death, ten of the best pictures in the Tennant collection had gone, sold for death duties in New York. But the group of Tennant companies was still there, and they were still lucrative. Yet it was only a matter of time before even this asset was realized. What survived was Pamela's vain and spoilt temperament, cancelling out with ease the more dependable characteristics of the Tennants. It was this aspect of which all her descendants now had reason to be wary.

11

The Blood Remains

Since the sale of St Rollox, the Mincing Lane firm had been branching out in a number of profitable areas. Because of their name, Charles Tennant & Sons remained one of the main agents of chemical products. In 1928 the firm had become sole agents for a Jerusalem-based company manufacturing potash and bromine. This company – Potato Potash – produced the largest quantity sold within the British Empire; the two substances were vital for many other chemical manufactures and pharmaceutical products. There was also Tennant's role as agents for steel, pig iron, and rubber: Charles Tennant & Sons had been among the first members of the London Metal Exchange in 1877, and the company now had further income through representing on it a variety of leading copper producers. In Trinidad there was a large citrus and mahogany estate to manage, and in 1940 the company reached back to its roots and acquired a sand mine at Loch Aline. During the Second World War, Britain leant heavily on it for the manufacture of glass. The family business had moved well into the twentieth century, and would still keep the Tennant family high above the breadline for generations to come.

But Eddy's preference for forestry over business had meant that the majority shareholding had passed to the Ayrshire cousins. It was William Tennant, then head of the Ayrshire side, who had run the office and taken the company into several of its successful areas. These Tennants had a capacity for hard work and sound business thinking that the Glen Tennants, on becoming landed nobility, had rather abandoned. However, Christopher, conscious of his new responsibility as family guardian, had been determined to reverse this. Committing himself fully to a City life, he had gone every day to Mincing Lane and immersed himself in the affairs of the firm. William Tennant, aware that his side owed their sudden riches to their enterprising kinsman, made the honourable gesture. On seeing that Christopher was prepared to settle down as a businessman, William sold back the majority shareholding to his cousin.

Comfortable though Christopher's material circumstances now were, his life had not been without its personal dramas. His first marriage, made in 1925 on the encouragement of his mother, had come adrift. It was another instance of Pamela's need to dominate her children, in imagining that because she was fond of the girl's father, her son would be happy for ever with the daughter. But out of this marriage had come Colin and James, those older cousins whom I met on early visits to Glen. A second marriage, made ten years later, produced three more children – Emma, Toby, and Catherine – who were also growing up when I went to the house as a child. Christopher never spoke about these personal matters – he did not believe in such discussions. It was an area for which he had firmly shut himself off. Once, when my parents' marriage was breaking down, he told me that I must not go talking about the reasons to my school friends. For fear of losing hold himself, Christopher trained himself to keep a distance from trouble and believed that others should do the same.

His detachment was also Christopher's answer to dealing with a family situation that had come tragically unstuck. When I asked him about my grandmother's behaviour he would reply that in youth she had been very wilful: my grandfather Bethell was a country squire which had not been right for her. To myself I wondered if anyone would have been right for her – Bethell, Tennyson and Beck all dispatched. Perhaps it was only the moment's attention she had been after and had vanished in pursuit of other compliments. Looking at incidents in her life would seem to confirm this. 'He kissed me on the lips as he dropped me off,' Clare would say to friends after some relative stranger had given her a lift home. But soon after the Second World War a distinguished general had kissed her on the Palladian bridge at Wilton. Clare said to herself that this surely was true love. She was, at the time, just under fifty, and still acclaimed as a great beauty: her skin had remained as firm and young as that of a girl in her twenties. General Sir 'Monkey' Morgan was a pink-faced military man who had been largely responsible for the successful planning of D-Day. But what on earth did Clare see in him? everyone asked. Friends concluded that she must be in love with the medals. None the less, Clare persisted in believing that very soon a fourth marriage would take place. Here, she claimed, is the man for whom she had searched a lifetime. But the General already had a wife, he was thoroughly conditioned by convention, and all he really wanted from Clare was a touch of romance on the side. Vanity, however, soon got the better of Clare. She wrote to the wife telling her that her husband only cared for Clare. The General, who had been earnestly keeping the delicate matter from his wife, was horrified and fled straight home. And that was Clare's last attempt to secure a stable relationship.

By the Second World War David, too, was divorced. He had left Hermione Baddeley for Virginia Parsons, a pretty grand-daughter of Sir Beerbohm Tree. The change had happened partly through Hermione having had an affair while David had been gone on a long trip to China, and partly through the restlessness that David's money and the night-club scene he lived by provoked. Before war broke out, he had already joined up with an artillery regiment, though he was soon to find that he was unsuited to being an officer. His hatred of giving orders to the men, dislike of discipline, and the guilt of a superior background all brought on a nervous breakdown. After a time in hospital the

Army's medical board decided that David was of the wrong temperament for active service. They needed officers who would not be haunted by such anxieties. David returned to his former career as a BBC announcer, and for a while he was happy to be back reading the news. But before a year was up his easy switch to boredom, accompanied by depressions and a conviction of doom, set him drinking again. He was obliged to leave the BBC, but then found the job that possibly made him most content during the war. He went to work as a chef on a boat that travelled British waters delivering provisions to different ports. When required to, David could show degrees of professionalism and skill, and he did so with his cooking. At last he had a *métier* that gave him a kind of classlessness – he enjoyed the camaraderie with the men, and on leave he took them to the Gargoyle. But by early 1945 it was over; David was once again in his club, and intermittently drinking.

The war had been a wonderful period for the Gargoyle. It was filled with raffish officers on leave, determined to break a little loose after the rigours of army discipline. It was one of these young officers who made the remark over lunch there to the novelist Anthony Powell, that became 'awfully chic to be killed'[1] in *The Soldier's Art*. Alongside the officers were Society girls, Soho Bohemians, and many slightly ageing faces from the 1920s – the insulting shriek, for instance, of Brian Howard was never far distant. As elsewhere in London, night-club entertainment was never in such demand as when the bombs were falling.

By the late 1940s, however, the Gargoyle began to show a steady falling away of membership. The years of grim post-Second World War austerity had set in and few could afford to go out. A handful of regulars might be there, but those Friday and Saturday crowds no longer filled the restaurant bookings as before. Such threatening signs always sent David into a panic. Like many of the rich, he always worried about money – as if he had none – while at the same time spending it. These anxieties, of course, were unnecessary; apart from his father's trust, he had the large sum inherited from his mother, and also a 25 per cent interest in the Tennant business. But the fear of impending poverty never left him. There were times when he would suddenly sell a small object just for the sake of realizing a few hundred pounds. One day he sold a Georgian coffee pot and showed the cash to Virginia with delight. The Gargoyle, fallen on hard times, sent him back to his only release from anxiety – drink. But the drinking bouts could be broken by excitable high spirits, when everything as quickly went back to radiance and tranquillity. There were blissful evenings and days; evenings when the Gargoyle bandleader would strike up the ball theme from *La Traviata* whenever David and Virginia entered. But living with an alcoholic is not easy, and in 1952 Virginia fell in love. Her lover was the Marquess of Bath, and David was shattered. Henry Bath was also good-looking, and beyond that he had assets of birth which David felt he could not match. The undercurrent of inadequacy, stemming from Pamela's emotional idealization of him, returned. David drank, and drank hard.

A painful double divorce took place. Henry Bath left his first wife Daphne, and Virginia left David. Soon after the collapse of his marriage David sold the Gargoyle; the club that for thirty years had been the pulse of London's Bohemia closed. On its sale David left England for Spain, where he built a house up in the mountains, not far from a quiet fishing village called Torremolinos. David had always like Spain, and he was one of the first to discover that now densely populated area. In the 1950s tourism there was unknown, and with peace at last in his mountain home one might think that he could come to terms with his many neuroses, but the solitude haunted him, bringing on drinking now accompanied by heavy sedation. To quell his loneliness, although she was now remarried, Virginia went out each year to see him, and also his daughter Pauline, but after a few years Virginia had to stop as David considered them married again. Then, in the early 1960s, David married for the third time. His new wife was young enough to be his daughter, and could not understand the complications of his background but at least, for David, she was company. The restlessness, however, had not deserted him. Prompted by his nephew, Colin, having recently bought the island of Mustique in the West Indies, David thought, why not move there? Schemes and inventions had always been a part of his life and he settled for St Lucia where he had the idea of starting a round-the-islands air service. In the 1960s this did not exist for the smaller islands; if he could make it work he could also recapture his love of flying. But the scheme ended in disaster and David lost a considerable amount of money. He went back to Spain, disillusioned and without purpose, and died of a heart attack one morning in 1968.

I never knew my great-uncle David. He was never at Glen when I went there as a child, and because of his estrangement from my grandmother, he rarely saw her offspring. But I knew that he drank, because I recall stories – perhaps exaggerated in my child's imagination – of bottles flying through the air. Years later I was told that David would refer to his ailments as 'suppressed rage'. There was, indeed, an element of rage in all Pamela's children. Clare's tempers were legendary and some said that a reason she never grew old came from her instant ability to express rage. And Stephen, too, with his unpredictable humours and need to startle was also in a condition of anger. But in childhood I did not know what had gone wrong with their lives, although I was aware that there was this uncontrollable strain in the blood. Its source was in Pamela's demand to be noticed and my grandmother, I was told, had passed it on to me. Sometimes, when I had flown into childish tantrums, I would sit in the drive pouring the gravel over my head. At this point my relations would shake their heads despairingly: 'It's Clare', they would murmur, in worried tones, to the assembled company.

My mother wanted desperately to see her mother, and throughout my childhood and early adolescence we lived in the hope that this might happen. They had not met or corresponded since my mother had stayed with her in Charles Street in the middle 1930s and it was now the 1950s. When I looked at a photograph taken of them by Cecil Beaton for a *Vogue* series on mothers and daughters I felt a chill. How outsiders would be deceived by that united pair. 'Uncle Christopher will talk to her,' my mother would say to us. Holidays after holidays we would wait for this visit from our grandmother. Then one day my mother said, 'It's useless. There's nothing to be done.' And so we went on glimpsing her from the tops of buses going down Sloane Street, and there was no longer any question that we might meet her. Clare could not accept her issue. My mother never recovered from the rejection, and though it did not diminish her character, the wound was always there.

Following her affair with the General, Clare reverted from Beck to Tennyson, changing her name by deed poll. She now claimed that Lionel Tennyson was the one man she had loved and she clung to her sons by this marriage as if they were the tokens of a great affection. And as those glamorous decades faded where she had reached the pinnacle of her fame, she needed these two guardians of the shrine. I remember my mother described this act of guardianship to us when she had gone to her cousin Emma Tennant's coming-out dance in the 1950s. 'Harold and Mark stood stiffly on either side of my mother, who sat in a sulk for the whole evening,' she commented. The irritation at not being the very centre of attention was sufficient to send Clare into a fit of temperamental anger, just as Pamela, at Fallodon, or Glen, or Wilsford, would leave the dining table to face the wall if she was not the talking point. Perhaps it was fortunate that at sixty Clare was discovered to have an advanced heart condition. Society gave a brittle laugh when told that her doctor should have diagnosed the condition earlier: how could he have found her heart, they gibed, since she did not have one. But the angina worsened, she found regular breathing and climbing stairs difficult, and it was appropriate that when taken gravely ill she should have been at Glen. Unable to make a home for herself, or for others, in life, it was always to this Tennant home that she had returned for protection. At Glen Clare could be a girl again, and whatever guilt might lurk within her could vanish. It was there that she died, with Christopher's arms around her, on a summer's night in 1960.

Clare was buried in the churchyard at Traquair where her grandfather, Sir Charles, and her tragic aunt Laura lay. But in spite of the change brought by the Wilsford upbringing, the Tennant blood had not been entirely lost, and outside the main line there were still signs of the old temperament. The three daughters of Sir Charles by his second marriage had turned out sound, dependable characters, cast exactly in the former Tennant mould. Peggy, Katherine and Nancy may not have had the beauty of their Wilsford connections, but they had a strong sense of public service. You dress like parsons' daughters, their half-sister Margot used to tease them, and they were the happier for it. No vanities clouded their brows, no jealousies for attention, and they looked on the Wilsford developments with alarm. Two were made Dames of the British Empire for their work in public areas – and were as industrious as those early people who had founded St Rollox. These three daughters of the Bart – and two survive today – had the Tennant blood untainted. Unlike the Wilsford Tennants, they knew where they were going.

Because of the resolutions he had made, Christopher had known his direction. By the 1960s, as chairman of Charles Tennant & Sons, he had come to head an extremely desirable network of companies, and had no intention to sell. In fact C. Tennant & Sons were considering further expansion and adding another substantial company – the British Metal Corporation BMC – to their list. But just as Tennants were negotiating to buy the BMC, the large mining-based group, Consolidated Gold-fields, put in a bid for Tennants. The mining group had, in the first instance, intended to buy the BMC but Consolidated's bankers, Schroeder Wagg, were already acting for Tennant's and they could not negotiate for both. Consolidated, therefore, seeking a seat on the London Metal Exchange – which Tennant's already had – changed tracks and bid for them. The year was 1963 and the offer to Tennant's was £2½ million. Christopher's partner Ernest Tennant – the son of Ayrshire William – had died the year before and Christopher was left to make the decision alone. Had Ernest Tennant lived it is almost certain that he would not have favoured a sale; it was here that for once Christopher faltered. He was sixty-four and he wanted to retire, he did not feel that his eldest son cared for the business, and the offer was a good one. In that year Charles Tennant & Sons was sold to Consolidated Goldfields and the Tennant family's long-established source of revenue through commerce came to an end. For a few years Christopher continued as chairman under the new organization. But by the mid-1960s Ernest's son, Julian, had become the new chairman of Tennant's, now the property of the vast mining concern.

What had happened to Colin, Christopher's son and heir? Once again the chairmanship had gone back to the Ayrshire cousins. The reason was that although Colin worked in his father's firm, he was hardly ever there. His interests were not in the City, but in a demanding social life. He preferred large country houses, smart people, and being noticed. I realized now that the Ford Thunderbird, which I had seen parked outside the door at Glen as a child, was an integral part of this life. Also, there was no need for Colin to sit day after day in the dim obscurity of a City office. He was young, indulged with money, and he found it more satisfying to be written up as one of London's most eligible bachelors and the escort of Princess Margaret. But it was because of his reputation as a socialite and his acknowledged lack of interest that Consolidated Goldfields would have been reluctant to accept his candidature. Colin always felt bitter about this, and unfairly blamed his father, though he had received over £1 million from the sale as compensation and the freedom to lead the life he chose. The ownership of Mustique – and all the gossip-column attention that has gone with it – was to prove more in keeping with his character than checking company reports in Mincing Lane.

The need to be noticed had become a feature among Pamela's

descendants. My mother, who according to Christopher had many of his mother's qualities, was an example. After a children's party where other mothers were present, we would always be asked, 'Who was the most beautiful woman in the room?' And the same would go for a wedding. The answer, of course, we knew: 'You, Mummy.' We were fortunate in that bearing such a strong resemblance to Clare, she did not age, and she had also had her own success as one of the prettiest débutantes of her day. But the need to be reassured and to be an idol to her children, were characteristics that had nothing to do with the plain-speaking Bethells. And I was often interested to notice the ease with which her Tennant side seemed to have checked those solid, landed genes. Her behaviour was impulsive, and her reaction to a situation was usually more emotional than considered. In the 1950s she had once executed a solo dance on the floor of the Café de Paris night club, which was then still a rather conventional Society night spot. Going to a party once at St James's Palace and not knowing the right door, she had taken one of the silent sentries and tickled him hard in the ribs; that way, she said, the man would have to speak.

There were not just signs of Pamela but also of Aunt Margot. It was Margot who, as an adult woman, had leapt on to the shuffleboard in the great hall at Stanway to give her version of a Spanish flamenco. As children we grew used to my mother's outbreaks, to her need for admiration – embarrassed though we sometimes were – for they often came as a welcome relief from too much upper-class stuffiness. 'You should have been on the boards, Diana,' a Bethell relative said to her one day after she had left the company bewildered by her eccentric behaviour.

A further change in Tennant temperament was an instinct to dramatize under pressure. Pamela's brother, George, had soon fallen back on drink when his troubles in Ireland became too intense. Nerves that had once stood fierce attacks on St Rollox' pollution could now be wrecked by the slightest domestic upheaval. Shortly after the selling of Tennants, Colin had a nervous collapse, prompted in part by the unreasoned belief that his father had abandoned him. Early signs occurred while driving up to Scotland. Colin felt himself 'dissolving into gold dust' as he too appropriately put it, and a car was sent to collect him from the motorway. He was to spend some time under treatment and only regained his confidence once he had started to develop his island of Mustique. Colin had bought the island for £40,000 and his plan was to turn it into a resort for the rich. He had given a piece of land to Princess Margaret as a wedding present, which immediately made the island attractive to prospective purchasers. He began to settle there for most of the year and attempted to calm his inherited insecurities by lavish spending. Colin, too, was afflicted by the need for admiration and any flight of extravagance was worth it, so long as it was noticed. 'The Tennants,' he said to me one day at Glen, 'have been destroyed by their vanity.'[2]

With my mother I watched both these traits at work to a sadly premature death. Rejection by Clare, a broken marriage, and near financial destitution brought this genetic frailty more readily to the surface. Diana's cry for attention was found in artificial stimulants. Once at Glen she had started on a potent nerve calmant medicine, which she would take in excessively heavy doses. 'Diana's gone to her room and come down quite another person,' Christopher's wife Elizabeth remarked with tactful English understatement. Later my mother progressed to barbiturate sedatives, which she would mix freely with alcohol and amphetamines. It was not a matter of daily intake but whenever she felt oppressed or insecure. Soon, however, the sedatives became an addiction and began to attack her health. She lived on an almost perpetual high and her blood pressure responded at an equal pace. All the searing lines that she would quote to us from Tennessee Williams or *Gone With the Wind* did nothing to answer her need for a colossal affection and audience. She announced that she would die young of a stroke like her grandmother Pamela – indeed, she had no wish to face physical decay – and a month after her fifty-first birthday she sustained a massive haemorrhage. 'Your mother did have a lot of suffering which she had done nothing to deserve,'[3] Uncle Christopher wrote sympathetically from Corfu.

Christopher had made Glen and the estate over to Colin at the same time as he retired from the business. But with Christopher gone from Glen the family centre had gone too. Under Christopher Glen had been a home for all his relations, but with Colin's more volatile temperament this was no longer to be. Colin preferred to entertain ephemeral celebrities, Glen was used less often, and the Tennants' link with Scotland was now slight. Christopher had built himself a house on Corfu, and if the cousins saw each other, it was there rather than in Scotland. They had all grown up since those days of playing He along the passages at Glen. Emma, whom I remember as an emergent débutante, had turned her back on society to become a novelist, at which she was achieving success. She had returned to the Tennants' former radicalism but by now, brought up in a setting of impregnable financial security, it fitted less well. James, the next brother to Colin, had filled himself with an unbalanced envy of Colin's senior position and hardly anyone saw him at all. Toby, who had been that keen sportsman teaching us to catch trout in the burns, had settled down as a sheep farmer in Roxburghshire – a refreshing throwback, perhaps, to Auld Glen at Ochiltree. Corfu, as Glen had once been, became the Tennant centre and then, in 1983, Christopher died. Colin became the third Baron Glenconner, but the wealth and the estates had considerably diminished since Eddy had been the first.

By 1980 that impressive collection of paintings formed by Sir Charles barely existed at all. The selling had begun in the 1920s to pay death duties, and had been taken up again in the late 1950s and 1960s to raise cash. There was still the odd picture at Glen, but nothing on the scale that I remember even as a child. In some places a picture had been replaced by a less valuable one – for instance a Landseer now hangs in the hall where

Constable's 'Waterloo Bridge' once was – but the Romneys, Hoppners and Gainsboroughs had all vanished. The estate, which had grown to 10,000 acres since Sir Charles first acquired it, was now permanently let to a local farmer, and the house itself available for renting at £1,000 per day. Colin had used Glen through the 1960s and for much of the 1970s, but his increasing attachment to the West Indies made him easily bored by the place. He has said that he could leave Glen tomorrow and not miss it. Glen, the house that had served to turn the Tennants from merchants into gentlemen, and to establish them with a landed image, was no longer of interest.

By the yardstick that measures success by solidity, the Tennants had fallen. Glen let, the business sold, and Wilsford running to weed does not proclaim a family that has held on to its possessions. The odd member – like Colin – may still be backed by large sums of capital, but the overall impression suggests decline. Yet in the decline there remains a flourish and an insistence not to conform. Until his recent death this was best seen in the survival of Stephen. At Wilsford Stephen had created a setting that would stand outside of time. Gone were the dark furnishings of his mother's day, the William Morris hangings, and the Arts and Crafts Jacobean panelling. In their place Stephen had introduced garish wallpapers, rococo tables, glittering chandeliers, walls of mirrored glass, with polar bear and leopardskin rugs to tumble throughout the house. The formal English garden had gone too, and instead palm trees and cypresses swayed against Wilsford's chequered flint and stone walls. In an area he called 'the Amazon garden' shrubs and exotic plants crowded together, separated only by pathways of sand, leading to small pools where fountains trickled. 'Who mothered me? Who fathered me? – no earthly parentage surely blessed me thus?' Stephen wrote in his journal.

In the 1940s and 1950s Stephen had several exhibitions of paintings, and he became a cult among the highly sophisticated. His unintentional funny remarks would race in circles round his friends. During the Second World War he had made journeyings to the foyer of the London Ritz, where he could frequently be found near the golden fountain. One day his friend Sir Michael Duff came in, escorted by two GIs – the USA having recently joined the Allies. Sir Michael was hesitant that Stephen might notice him in his present rather masculine company – and notice him Stephen did. 'Darling boys, come *all* this way to save us,' Stephen moaned in wistful tones . . . 'Cru-el war,' he added, and vanished again. Nancy Mitford roared and declared it her favourite 'Stephen' story.

Possessors of Stephen's pen-and-ink watercolours of sailors in louche bars or Ganymedes draped in vine leaves, could claim to be connoisseurs in the byways of English art. 'Ah, a Stephen Tennant,' the discerning visitor would say, spotting in a corner a vivid profusion of coloured inks. But had Stephen painted more and turned himself into a professional it is possible that his reputation would have entered the mainstream. The Society hostess Christabel Aberconway once said to Osbert Sitwell how much she thought Stephen owed to Rex Whistler. 'The other way round, you mean,'[4] the observant Sitwell replied. Except that the delight of Stephen's work is that they are the creations of a fantasist who has never cared about the commercial market. And Stephen's desire for fame, too, was only of interest when it was make-believe. He liked the glamorous film-star postcards he had done of himself, each signed 'Yours cordially'; or to daub on the back of a painting, 'The world famous but very modest Stephen Tennant,' but actual fame would have meant exposure and work he might not have wished to do. That could be both vulgar and tiring: so Stephen let his talents drift.

Time passed and Stephen grew older. The legendary beauty who had been fêted in bar, drawing room and boulevard grew plump, and though no less cocottish, touches of the dowager appeared. The powder remained as firmly on his face, but Stephen went a little less often to the Ritz, the Hotel Russell, or abroad. He had always been very proud to be taken for a woman, this being for Stephen the final accolade that may be given to an outstanding appearance: years before when ordering his breakfast by telephone at the Ritz, he had noted in his journal 'He said, "Yes, Madam," ' In his early fifties, as if he had been on the stage long enough, he took to his bed. Lulled by the peace of Wilsford – where nothing disturbs but the distant song of birds – he could compose himself away from a world that had always been too harsh for him to take. He felt safe now with his life spread out across his bed; he could pick at incidents as he pleased. For the next thirty years Stephen lay back and remembered.

Propped up by pillows, with amber beads resting in his hands, he cut back through time. He remembered the scent that 'S.S.' gave him in Sicily, and the barman in Marseille who sang to him, and Aunt Margot dancing at the Savoy with E. M. Forster's policeman boyfriend. 'The Chief of Police is my greatest friend,' Margot had said to P. C. Buckingham as they tangoed across the floor. He remembered days at St Moritz and the afternoon when a busload of tourists had stopped to clap and cheer him because he was so beautiful. Virginia Woolf called him her 'bird of paradise' and Osbert Sitwell said he was 'the last professional beauty'. Jean Cocteau told him never to read newspapers: 'You and I are too sensitive,' he had said. But why had Jean brought that strange man to tea – Genet was his name – who had stolen his lovely sapphire cufflinks? Baudelaire was quite right about the French: 'Crépuscule du soir – ami du criminel'. Surrounded by the friends and thoughts of a lifetime – his bed strewn with scents, jewels, stuffed animals and letters – Stephen lay back and remembered.

Over eighteen years I often sat in my uncle's darkened bedroom discussing memories and other random matters that came to mind. I let the conversation run as he liked, for it made Stephen more fluent. 'I'm so glad we're not like all those other Tennants, just interested in making money,' he said to me one day, a dim memory that somewhere long ago chimneys had belched filth into the air. And on that day he wanted to talk about the family. 'Clare's awful, vile temper – I can hear her now when she was shut in her room at twelve. You should have heard the terrible screams that came out – like a caged tigress . . . But she had a very intelligent silence.' Stephen paused to finger a jewel, examine a piece of jade, and try a new scent. 'Give me your hand, Simon dear. Do let me spray some of this on, it's *so* good. I love the name. It's called Just Call Me Maxi.' He paused again, rearranging a pile of loose letters and poems. 'My brother David was a strange person . . . I never really understood him. I don't know why my mother was so fond of him.' A further pause and then suddenly he recited a line of his favourite French poet, Anna de Noailles: 'Nomade, solitaire, et toujours étonné.' Stephen closed his eyes and thought of the Orient. 'Do you know "The Fiddler of Dooney"?' he said, interrupting his own reverie. His voice turned singsong and romantic as he intoned the Irish ballad: '. . . And dance like a wave of the sea.' He recited the poem again. We sat in silence for two or three minutes. 'I think there's no doubt that I do have great beauty. Have you ever noticed, Simon, the shape of my nose? I have my mother's nose. If I lie like this you can see the nostrils . . . lovely, aren't they?' Stephen stared ahead at the chink of sunlight filtering through creeper and mullioned window into the room. 'My brother Christopher sends me lovely shells from Corfu. But I'm afraid Christopher has the world's values. I could *never* have the world's values.' Stephen rested back and let his eyelids fall.

There is no estate surrounding Wilsford now. The 2,000 acres were sold in the 1930s at a bottom price. There are no gardeners in the garden and rough grass and dock spread everywhere. You cannot go down to fish the Avon as great-grandfather Eddy and Grey did in those years before 1914: marsh weed and nettle grip you at the waist. The white gates that once opened to Pamela's victoria are closed and the paintwork grimed by a green fungus. But the house itself has been enhanced by the decay. With the gables cobwebbed in creeper and the roof's stone tiles padded by moss, no effort is required to drift down through the centuries.

Now that Stephen has gone, and when the house is sold, who will remember the dream? The garden will be tidied, the fishing made practical, and the house rubbed down. The dream, so purposeful in its execution, had foundered on the bedrock of its whimsicality. And yet, there will always be the graves in the churchyard: Pamela, David, my mother, Stephen – and like the listeners of the de la Mare poem, only they shall know.

The Tennants had become insubstantial. The dynasty that Charles Tennant of St Rollox had begun and trusted to stand firm in his native Glasgow had failed him. The mausoleum that lies beneath his statue there was never to be filled – and today the empty vaults bear witness to the desertion. Nor is there any landmark left of old St Rollox – no building where we can say, 'Here sat Tennant at his ledgers.' But a rumour persists that when you pass the site by train, the air can suddenly cloud with the vapours of a century's-old chemical refuse. One nine five West George Street is replaced by an office block, and the area so altered by modern building that it is hard to recapture the rattle of merchants' carriages. Bit by bit the Tennants were being removed from history. There is no plaque to mark the residence of that bold financier, the Bart, in Grosvenor Square; and at 34 Queen Anne's Gate the ballroom erected to hold forever the Tennant collection has recently been gutted. And if one day Glen should go, what then would remain? There would be the recording of incidents and people in memoirs and biography, but all would be not quite dead. There would be the blood and, recurring through the generations, a temperament that many descendants might find hard to bear.

Notes and Sources

2 Poverty in Ayrshire

page 14   *1*   'wrath upon this people' H. Grey Graham, *The Social Life of Scotland in the Eighteenth Century*, p. 149.

14   *2*   'to any other nation' T. C. Smout, *A History of The Scottish People 1560–1830*, p. 106.

14   *3*   'Sleat for his pleasure' *Ibid.*, p. 105.

15   *4*   'of their hands and arms' Grey Graham, *op. cit.*, p. 148.

17   *5*   'of Ayrshire farmer' A. Murdoch, *Ochiltree, its History and Reminiscences*, p. 242.

18   *6*   'of Natural Philosophy' Notes on David Tennant by his decendant Charles Tennant.

19   *7*   'nominated by the Council' *Ibid.*

20   *8*   'mutual affection' Smout, *op. cit.*, p. 282.

20   *9*   'and sometimes down' Henry Hamilton, *An Economic History of Scotland in the Eighteenth Century*, p. xiv.

22   *10*   'variety of expressions' David Daiches, *Robert Burns and his World*, p. 11.

22   *11*   'in virtuous habits' *Ibid.*, p. 13.

24   *12*   'as the landlords' Smout, *op. cit.*, p. 314.

24   *13*   'to your Country' J. de Lancey Ferguson, *The Letters of Robert Burns*, vol. 2, p. 37.

24   *14*   'shall determine me' *Ibid.*, vol. 1, pp. 182–3.

25   *15*   'the bargain practicable' *Ibid.*, p. 197.

page 25 *16* 'never engaged in it!' Daiches, *op. cit.*, p. 98.

26 *17* The letter–poem is 'Letter to James Tennant, Glenconner.
1786'. James Tennant was the eldest surviving son of Auld
Glen. He remained a miller at Ochiltree, never leaving his
earthy roots. See *Poems and Songs of Robert Burns*, Collins,
1981.

3 Making Bleach

31 *1* 'to be expected' W. Higgins, *An Essay on the Theory and
Practice of Bleaching*, p. 78.

33 *2* 'than Dr Black' Smout, *op. cit.*, p. 508.

33 *3* 'révolution chimique' J. R. Partington, *A History of
Chemistry*, vol. 3.

34 *4* 'managing it themselves' W. Higgins, *op. cit.*, p. 42.

35 *5* 'any important invention' G. Blair, *Glasgow Necropolis*,
p. 164.

36 *6* 'small towns in Europe' C. A. Oakley, *Second City*, p. 10.

37 *7* 'acid it consumes' J. Liebig, *Familiar Letters on Chemistry*,
p. 31.

37 *8* Sir Walter Scott, *The Antiquary*, 1816, chapter 15.

38 *9* 'we ourselves sell' Tennant Letter Book for 1801, ICI
Archives.

4 The Largest Chemical Empire

40 *1* 'the actual results' Nancy Crathorne, *Tennant's Stalk*, p. 73.

42 *2* 'of those tenements' Edmund Burke, *Reflections on the
Revolution in France*, see Introduction, p. 31.

43 *3* 'if you *dare*' P. Mackenzie, *Reminiscences of Glasgow and the
West of Scotland*, vol. 1, p. 306.

44 *4* 'the rest is gone' Donald Southgate, *The Passing of the Whigs*,
p. 21.

page 44   *5* 'wont to despise' *Ibid.*, p. 22.

45   *6* 'flashing with fire' Mackenzie, *op. cit.*, vol. 2, p. 248.

47   *7* 'throughout the year' Liebig, *op. cit.*, p. 28.

48   *8* 'the Killingworth Colliery' Crathorne, *op. cit.*, pp. 90–1.

49   *9* 'of the community' *Glasgow Herald*, 26 September 1831.

50   *10* 'when it is naught' J. M. Reid, *A History of the Merchant House in Glasgow*, privately published by the Merchant House, p. 25.

50   *11* 'which you want' Adam Smith, *The Wealth of Nations*, p. 116.

51   *12* 'with their situations' Tennant Papers 1763–1840, unpublished manuscript, p. 64.

5 A Fortune and a Concubine

55   *1* 'in Great Britain' Andrew Gibb, *Glasgow – The Making of a City*, pp. 107–8.

56   *2* 'passing over it' St Rollox Emission Depositions, c. 1822. Mitchell Library, Glasgow.

56   *3* 'buildings going up' *Ibid.*

57   *4* 'for a few weeks' *Ibid.*

57   *5* 'I've got it . . . I've got it' Crathorne, *op.cit.*, p. 107.

58   *6* 'of the place – THE Chimney' George Dodd in *The Land We Live In*, vol. 2, p. 320.

59   *7* 'the whole world' J. D. Burn, *Commercial Enterprise and Social Progress*, p. 114.

59   *8* 'the price this year' Crathorne, *op. cit.*, p. 101.

60   *9* 'no more Italian gardens' *Ibid.*, p. 102.

62   *10* 'picture is complete' H. J. Tennant, *Sir Charles Tennant, His Forebears and Descendants*, p. 32.

63   *11* 'so much employed' Crathorne, *op. cit.*, p. 102.

64   *12* 'dispute his claim' David Murray, 'Notes on the Tennant Family', unpublished manuscript, p. 101.

65   *13* 'is being sold' E. L. Woodward, *The Age of Reform*, p. 124.

page 66   *14* 'inch of the ground' Burn, *op. cit.*, p. 119.

67   *15* 'father had built' *One Hundred Glasgow Men*, vol. 2, p. 310.

6 A Great Entrepreneur

69   *1* 'The devil you have' Crathorne, *op. cit.*, p. 124

70   *2* 'Sublime in thought', *Ibid.*, p. 120.

71   *3* 'not abiding sorrows' Margot Asquith, *Autobiography*, vol. 1, p. 6.

76   *4* '"*ciel ouvert*" at Tharsis' Crathorne, *op. cit.*, p. 134.

77   *5* 'sharply defined mouth' S. G. Checkland, *The Mines of Tharsis*, p. 100.

77   *6* *Octavia* is the novel that bears a portrait of Margot's father.

77   *7* 'shareholders' meeting' Charles Tennant to his second wife Marguerite, 26 July 1900, Crathorne Papers.

78   *8* 'companions or recreations' H. J. Tennant, *op. cit.*, pp. 33–4.

80   *9* 'knew were coming' Alexander Crum to Charles Gairdner, 26 April 1883. Bank of Scotland Archives.

81   *10* 'trafficked in the shares' North British *Daily Mail*, 26 April 1883.

81   *11* 'find fault with' Frederick Pitman to Charles Gairdner, 26 April 1883, Bank of Scotland Archives.

83   *12* 'were squeezed out' W. J. Reader, *Imperial Chemical Industries – A History*, vol. 1, p. 101.

84   *13* 'and you cannot' *Ibid.*, p. 110.

84   *14* 'a good deal' H. J. Tennant to Lord Rosebery, 21 June 1884, Rosebery Papers.

84   *15* 'do you remember?' Lord Ribblesdale to Lord Rosebery, 2 December 1882, Rosebery Papers.

85   *16* 'almost touching' *Ibid.*, 13 January 1882.

86   *17* 'else was new' Barbara Wilson, *Dear Youth*, p. 155.

86   *18* 'projected pleasure scheme' *Ibid.*, p. 157.

7 Entering Society

88   *1* 'the Tennant family' Lady Frances Balfour, *Ne Obliviscaris*, p. 392.

89   *2* 'child of the heather' Margot Asquith, *op. cit.*, p. 26.

91   *3* 'of the dance' A. G. C. Liddell, *Notes from the Life of an Ordinary Mortal*, p. 227.

93   *4* 'the large full moon' Maurice Baring, *The Puppet Show of Memory*, William Heinemann, 1922, pp. 167–8.

94   *5* 'I live too fast', David Newsome, *On the Edge of Paradise*, John Murray, 1980, p. 48.

94   *6* 'have you no conversation?' John Tennant, unpublished memoir, Chandos Archives.

94   *7* 'many books for me' Jane Abdy and Charlotte Gere, *The Souls*, Sidgwick and Jackson, p. 11, 1984.

95   *8* 'Tennant family' A. G. C. Liddell, *op. cit.*, p. 226.

96   *9* 'like the stars' E. Lyttelton, *Alfred Lyttelton*, p. 125.

97 *10* 'countless unborn souls' Laura Tennant to Mary Elcho, 1884, Stanway Papers.

97 *11* 'towards the sky' Laura Tennant to Alfred Lyttelton, c. 1885, Chandos Archives.

98 *12* 'to the stars' *Ibid.*, undated, Chandos Archives.

98 *13* 'houses and shooting' Alfred Lyttelton to Laura Tennant, 1885, Chandos Archives.

98 *14* 'future cherubic state' Laura Tennant to Frances Horner, May 1883, Mells Papers.

98 *15* 'neat and well' Mary Gladstone Drew, 'Laura', unpublished manuscript, p. 73, Chandos Archives.

99 *16* 'noblest in us' and 'in the papers' *Ibid.*, p. 65.

99 *17* 'salute her soul' Margot Asquith, *op. cit.*, p. 46.

99 *18* 'has ever been' *The Times*, obituary Sir Charles Tennant, 6 June 1906.

100 *19* 'a very long life' Mary Gladstone Drew, *op. cit.*, p. 82, Chandos Archives.

100 *20* 'understood so much' A. C. Benson to Alfred Lyttelton, April 1886, Chandos Archives.

page 100 *21* 'darkened hoplessly' Sir Edward Burne-Jones to Alfred
Lyttelton, April 1886, Chandos Archives.

100 *22* 'her memory is sweet' Henry James to Alfred Lyttelton,
April 1886, Chandos Archives.

100 *23* 'temperament and impulse' Margot Asquith, *op. cit.*, p. 26.

101 *24* 'more retiring nature' Journal kept by Charlotte
Ribblesdale and Frances Horner on a visit to
Oberammergau, August 1890. Charty's response to
Frances Horner's entry here was: 'On the contrary opinion
was divided. It is melancholy to be so cloyed by devotion as
not to be capable of recognising it.' Unpublished
manuscript, Mells Papers.

101 *25* 'society and admiration' E. F. Benson, *Dodo*, p. 79.

102 *26* 'uneducated person' Daphne Bennett, *Margot*, p. 97.

102 *27* 'up with old Duffs' Margot Tennant to George Curzon, 11
November, 1889, Curzon Papers.

102 *28* 'excellent thing for us' Frances Warwick, *Life's Ebb and
Flow*, Hutchinson, 1929, p. 72.

103 *29* 'before breakfast' Lady Cynthia Asquith, *Haply I May
Remember*, p. 51.

104 *30* 'her like again' Frances Horner, *Time Remembered*, p. 162.

104 *31* 'rhythm under me' Margot Tennant to Frances Horner, 23
January 1889, Mells Papers.

104 *32* he's rich, isn't he?' Margot Tennant to Lord Rosebery,
February 1885, Rosebery Papers.

106 *33* 'under no illusions' Michael and Eleanor Brock (eds.), *H.
H. Asquith: Letters to Venetia Stanley*, p. 8.

106 *34* 'shall be my law' Bennett, *op. cit.*, p. 111.

107 *35* 'failings of the aristocracy' A Gentleman with a Duster, *The
Glass of Fashion*, p. 56.

8 New Aristocrats

109 *1* 'unworthy of Scotchmen' Peter L. Payne, *Colvilles and the
Scottish Steel Industry*, p. 62.

page 111 *2* 'full of radicals', John Jolliffe, *Raymond Asquith*, p. 33.

111 *3* 'pretty aquiline nose' Wilson, *op. cit.*, p. 156.

111 *4* 'in her heart' Lucy Graham Smith, unpublished journal, 1 January – 30 December 1895, p. 109.

113 *5* 'best of husbands' Margot Asquith to Edward Tennant, 15 April 1895, Glen Papers.

114 *6* 'bride so lovely' Graham Smith, *op. cit.*, p. 144.

116 *7* 'look like Clouds' Pamela Tennant to George Wyndham, 21 August 1895, Grosvenor Papers.

116 *8* 'take up Glen' Frances Horner to D. D. Lyttelton, 1898, Mells Papers.

116 *9* 'everything . . . her own' Pamela Tennant to Mary Elcho, 23 October 1897, Stanway Papers.

117 *10* 'poems of Burns' Pamela Tennant to George Wyndham, 24 August 1898, Grosvenor Papers.

118 *11* 'treat him kindly' H. H. Asquith to Raymond Asquith, 27 October 1898, Mells Papers.

119 *12* 'the wrong places' Charty Ribblesdale to A. J. Balfour, 28 October 1898, Balfour Papers.

119 *13* 'he looks tired' Lord Chandos to Nancy Crathorne, 30 March 1966, Crathorne Papers.

120 *14* 'nothing daunted him' *The Times*, obituary Sir Charles Tennant, 6 June 1906.

121 *15* 'Eddy lacks drive' Bennett, *op. cit.*, p. 162.

123 *16* 'is my MOTHER' Pamela Glenconner, *The Sayings of the Children*, p. 132.

125 *17* 'unknown to me' Marie Belloc-Lowndes, *A Passing World*, p. 179.

126 *18* 'in the spring' H. H. Asquith to Lord Glenconner, 13 December 1913, Glen Papers.

9 Wilsford: The Sensitive Ones

128 *1* 'of years ago' Max Egremont, *The Cousins*, p. 21.

page 129   *2* 'delicate jewelled heads' Barbara Tuchman, *The Proud Tower*, p. 16.

130   *3* 'beautifully expressed' Philip Burne-Jones to Pamela Tennant, 22 May 1905, Wilsford Manor Papers.

133   *4* 'weekly rest cure' Michael and Eleanor Brock (eds.), *op. cit.*, p. 249.

135   *5* 'thousand directions' Osbert Sitwell, *Laughter in the Next Room*, p. 100.

135   *6* 'became swans' *Ibid.*, p. 100.

136   *7* 'And *when*' Wilsford Manor Papers.

136   *8* 'a little strained' Jolliffe, *op. cit.*, p. 108.

137   *9* 'breaking her, in bed' Pamela Glenconner, *op. cit.*, p. 3.

137   *10* 'brown one ons' *Ibid.*, p. 54.

137   *11* 'myself beside you' *Ibid.*, p. 52.

137   *12* 'arms wide open' *Ibid.*, p. 63.

138   *13* 'us for nothing' *Ibid.*, pp. 63–64.

139   *14* 'unworthy to unloose' Pamela Glenconner, *Edward Wyndham Tennant*, p. 58.

139   *15* 'belongs to you' *Ibid.*, p. 60.

139   *16* 'round my ankles' Pamela Tennant to Mary Elcho, 7 February 1905, Stanway Papers.

140   *17* 'of leaving Wilsford' Pamela Tennant to George Wyndham, 23 August 1907, Grosvenor Papers.

140   *18* 'quest of adventure' George Wyndham to his niece Clare Tennant, 15 July 1905. Quoted in *Edward Wyndham Tennant*, p. 28.

140   *19* 'proofs *hard*' Pamela Tennant to George Wyndham, 23 August 1907, Grosvenor Papers.

140   *20* 'into the pig-stye of Politics' George Wyndham to Pamela Tennant, 18 January 1907. Quoted in J. W. Mackail and Guy Wyndham (eds.), *Life and Letters of George Wyndham*, vol. 2, p. 561.

141   *21* 'upon a fairyland' Egremont, *op. cit.*, p. 178.

141   *22* 'in hardy fatigue' George Wyndham to Pamela Tennant, 18 January 1907, Mackail and Wyndham, *op. cit.*, p. 562.

page 142   *23*   'out-of-the-way cleverness' Margot Asquith to Mary Elcho, c. 1900, Stanway Papers.

143   *24*   'essence so cheaply' Elizabeth Asquith to Mary Charteris, 27 December 1914.

143   *25*   'have *that* again' Pamela Tennant, *The Children and the Pictures*, p. 9.

144   *26*   'in top hats' *Ibid.*, p. 198.

145   *27*   'only people' Clare Tennant to her cousin Mary Charteris, 5 November, 1914.

145   *28*   'cuts very hard' *Ibid.*, September – October, 1914

145   *29*   'what she wants' *Charles Lister: Letters and Recollections with a memoir by his father Lord Ribblesdale*, T. Fisher Unwin, 1917, p. 22.

146   *30*   'tiny bit safer' *Ibid.*, 3 July 1915.

146   *31*   'given up to ghosts' Lady Cynthia Asquith: *Diaries 1915–1918*, p. 97.

146   *32*   'in these days, can one?' Edward ('Bim') Wyndham Tennant to his cousin Mary Charteris, 18 March 1915.

146   *33*   'his own jumped on' *Edward Wyndham Tennant*, p. 80.

147   *34*   'in the least tiring' Sitwell, *op. cit.*, p. 97.

147   *35*   'The Mad Soldier' was published in 1919 in the first number of *Wheels*.

148   *36*   'like them, isn't it' *Edward Wyndham Tennant*, p. 204.

148   *37*   'always will have' *Ibid.*, p. 197.

149   *38*   'a terrible list' *Ibid.*, p. 233.

149   *39*   'be this way' *Ibid.*, p. 81.

149   *40*   'Eternal love, from BIM' *Ibid.*, p. 235.

149   *41*   'sense of beauty', *Free*, a volume compiled by Pamela Glenconner, containing letters written on the death of Bim Tennant and privately printed 1917, p. 157.

150   *42*   'on His way' *Ibid.*, p. 48.

150   *43*   'hardly any emotion' *Ibid.*, p. 54.

150   *44*   'scalding tears' *Ibid.*

151   *45*   'your company, Pamela' Pamela Grey to Mary Wemyss, 13 March 1928, Stanway Papers.

10 Lost Lives

page 153 *1* 'the police will hear' Told to the author by a close friend of Clare's and witness of the occasion.

154 *2* 'in the least!' HRH The Prince of Wales to Lady Coke, 4 September 1917.

154 *3* 'to have got into!!!!' *Ibid.*, 30 December 1917.

158 *4* 'in either hand' A Gentleman with a Duster, *op. cit.*, p. 38.

161 *5* 'down the telephone' Artemis Cooper (ed.), *A Durable Fire*, p. 244.

161 *6* 'than I have' Pamela Grey (formerly Glenconner) to Mary Wemyss (formerly Elcho), 9 June 1928, Stanway Papers.

162 *7* 'my eyes off her' Conrad Russell to Flora Russell, 19 August 1928.

163 *8* 'That paunched horror' Cooper, *op. cit.*, p. 269.

165 *9* 'come back to' Pamela Grey to Mary Wemyss, 13 March 1928, Stanway Papers.

168 *10* 'house in Wiltshire!!!' Laurence Whistler, *The Laughter and the Urn*, p. 64.

168 *11* 'my appearance to be. . .' Rex Whistler to Stephen Tennant, 19 October 1924.

169 *12* 'go to Hell' Hugo Vickers, *Cecil Beaton*, p. 86.

169 *13* 'in the caress' Whistler, *op. cit.*, p. 65.

170 *14* 'a Faber author' Told to the author by Stephen Tennant.

170 *15* 'In Sicily' was first published in Faber's Ariel Poems series, no. 27, 1930. It was illustrated by Stephen Tennant.

171 *16* 'on her shoulder' *Glasgow Bulletin*, 20 November 1928.

172 *17* 'price of fish' Susan Lady Tweedsmuir, *The Edwardian Lady*, Duckworth, 1966, pp. 87–8.

172 *18* 'the end of my childhood' James M. Beck, *The Years That Were*, Pageant, 1965, p. 135.

age 173   *19* 'talking about Emily Dickinson', Cecil Beaton,
                unpublished diary, 20 November 1928.

173   20 'other side vanish' Whistler, *op. cit.*, p. 136.

174   21 'given me his whole heart' Whistler, *op. cit.*, p. 131.

177   22 'up as trophies' Marie-Jacqueline Lancaster (ed.), *Brian
            Howard: Portrait of a Failure*, p. 266.

178   23 'I conquer Paradise' *ibid*, pp. 280–1.

179   24 'if not Stephen himself' N. Nicolson and J. Trautmann
            (eds.) *Letters of Virginia Woolf*, vol. 5, Chatto and
            Windus, 1982, p. 413.

180   25 'talking intimately' *Ibid.*, vol. 6, p. 57.

11 The Blood Remains

185   *1* 'chic to be killed' Anthony Powell, *The Soldier's Art*, p. 78.

192   2 'by their vanity' Colin Tennant to the author at Glen,
            1979.

193   3 'nothing to deserve' Christopher, 2nd Baron Glenconner
            to the author and his brother, 16 August 1967.

195   4 'round you mean' Whistler, *op. cit.*, p. 81.

Bibliography

Asquith, Lady Cynthia. *Diaries 1915–1918*, Hutchinson, 1968
   Haply I May Remember, Barrie, 1950
Asquith, Margot. *Autobiography*, 2 vols., Thornton Butterworth,
   1920–22
   Octavia, Cassell, 1928

Balfour, Lady Frances. *Ne Obliviscaris*, Hodder & Stoughton, 1930
Begbie, Harold (pseud. A Gentleman with a Duster). *The Glass of
   Fashion*, Putnam, 1921, (American edition)
Belloc-Lowndes, Marie. *A Passing World*, Macmillan, 1948
Bennett, Daphne. *Margot*, Gollancz, 1984
Benson, E. F. *Dodo*, Methuen, 1894
Blair, George. *Glasgow Necropolis*, Glasgow, 1857
Boyd, W. *Education in Ayrshire through Seven Centuries*, University of
   London, 1961
Brock, Michael and Eleanor (eds.). *H. H. Asquith: Letters to Venetia
   Stanley*, Oxford University Press, 1982
Brown, P. Hume. *History of Scotland*, vol. 13., Cambridge
   University Press, 1911
Burke, Edmund. *Reflections on the Revolution in France*, first published
   1790, Penguin Books, 1983
Burn, J. D. *Commercial Enterprise and Social Progress*, London, 1958

Campbell, W. A. *The Chemical Industry*, Longman, 1971
Checkland, S. G. *The Mines of Tharsis*, Allen & Unwin, 1967

The Upas Tree: Glasgow 1875–1975, University of Glasgow, 1981

Clement, A. G. and Robertson, R. H. S. *Scotland's Scientific Heritage*, Oliver and Boyd, Edinburgh, 1961

Clow, A. and N. L. *The Chemical Revolution*, Batchworth Press, 1952

Cooper, Artemis (ed.) *A Durable Fire: The letters of Duff and Diana Cooper 1913–1950*, Hamish Hamilton, 1983

Crathorne, Nancy. *Tennant's Stalk*, Macmillan, 1973

Croft Dickinson, W. (ed.). *The History of the Reformation in Scotland by John Knox*, Thomas Nelson, 1949

Croft-Cooke, R. *Bosie: The Story of Lord Alfred Douglas*, W. H. Allen, 1963

Daiches, David. *The Paradox of Scottish Culture*, Oxford University Press, 1964.
Robert Burns and his World, Thames & Hudson, 1971

Dodd, George. *The Land We Live In*, vol. 2, London, 1847

Dugdale, James. 'Sir Charles Tennant: The Story of a Victorian Collector', *Connoisseur*, September 1971

Egremont, Max. *The Cousins*, Collins, 1977

Ensor, R. C. K. *England 1870–1914*, Oxford University Press, 1936

Enterprise, An account of the activities and aims of the Tennant companies, Adprint, 1945

Gibb, Andrew. *Glasgow – The Making of a City*, Croom Helm, 1983

Glenconner, Pamela. *The Sayings of the Children*, Blackwell, 1918
Edward Wyndham Tennant, John Lane, 1919

Graham, H. Grey, *The Social Life of Scotland in the 18th century*, A. & C. Black, 1950

Haber, L. F. *The Chemical Industry during the Nineteenth Century*, Oxford University Press, 1958

Hamilton, H. *The Industrial Revolution in Scotland*, Oxford University Press, 1932
An Economic History of Scotland in the Eighteenth Century, Oxford University Press, 1963

Hardie and Pratt. *A History of the Modern British Chemical Industry*, Pergamon, 1963

Higgins, S. H. *A History of Bleaching*, Longman, 1924

Higgins, W. *An Essay on the Theory and Practice of Bleaching*, Dublin Society, 1799

Hobsbawm, E. J. *Industry and Empire*, Penguin Books, 1983

Horner, Frances. *Time Remembered*, William Heinemann, 1933

Hume, David. *Writings on Economics*, Thomas Nelson, 1955

Jolliffe, John, *Raymond Asquith, Life and Letters*, Collins, 1980

Kent, A. (ed.). *An 18th-Century Lectureship in Chemistry*, Jackson, 1950

Lancaster, Marie-Jacqueline (ed.). *Brian Howard: Portrait of a Failure*, Anthony Blond, 1968

de Lancey Ferguson, J. (ed.). *The Letters of Robert Burns*, Clarendon Press, 1931

Liddell, A. G. C. *Notes from the Life of an Ordinary Mortal*, John Murray, 1911

Liebeg, Justus. *Familiar Letters on Chemistry*, London, 1845

Lister, Beatrix (ed.). *Emma Lady Ribblesdale, Letters and Diaries*, privately printed, 1930

Lyttelton, Edith. *Alfred Lyttelton*, Longman, 1917

Macintosh, George. *Biographical Memoirs of the late Charles Macintosh F.R.S. of Campsie and Dunchatton*, privately printed, 1847

Mackail, J. W. and Wyndham, Guy. *Life and Letters of George Wyndham*, 2 vols., Hutchinson, 1925

Mackenzie, Peter. *Reminiscences of Glasgow and the West of Scotland*, 2 vols., John Tweed, Glasgow, 1865–8

Meikle, H. W. *Scotland and the French Revolution*, Frank Cass, 1912

Murdoch, Alexander, *Ochiltree, its History and Reminiscences*, London, 1911

Murray, N. *The Scottish Handloom Weavers*, J. Donald, Edinburgh, 1978

Oakley, C. A. *The Second City*, Blackie, 1975
One Hundred Glasgow Men, vol. 2, Maclehose, Glasgow, 1886

Paine, Thomas. *Rights of Man*, first published 1791, Penguin
   Books 1983
Partington, J. R. *A History of Chemistry*, vol. 3, Macmillan,
   1962
Payne, Peter L. *Colvilles and the Scottish Steel Industry*, Clarendon,
   1979

Reader, W. J. *Imperial Chemical Industries – A History*, vol. 1. *The
   Forerunners 1870–1926*, Oxford University Press, 1970
Reid, J. M. *Scotland's Progress*, Eyre & Spottiswoode, 1971
Ribblesdale, Lord. *Impressions and Memories*, Cassell, 1927
Rose, Kenneth. *Superior Person*, Weidenfeld & Nicolson, 1969

Scott, Sir Walter. *The Antiquary*, 1816
Sitwell, Osbert. *Laughter in the Next Room*, Macmillan, 1949
Slaven, Anthony, *The Development of the West of Scotland: 1750–1960*,
   Routledge & Kegan Paul, 1975
Smith, Adam. *The Wealth of Nations*, first published 1776, Penguin
   Books, 1982
Smout, T. C. *A History of the Scottish People 1560–1830*, Collins,
   1969
Southgate, Donald. *The Passing of the Whigs*, Macmillan, 1962
Stewart, George. *Curiosities of Glasgow Citizenship*, Glasgow, 1881
Strang, John, *Glasgow and its Clubs*, Glasgow, 1884

Tennant, E. W. D. *One Hundred and Forty Years of the Tennant
   Companies 1797–1937*, privately printed, 1937
   True Account, Max Parrish, 1957
Tennant, H. J. *Sir Charles Tennant. His Forebears and Descendants*,
   privately printed, 1932
Tennant, Pamela. *Village Notes*, William Heinemann, 1900
   The Children and the Pictures, William Heinemann, 1908
Tennyson, Lionel, Lord. *From Verse to Worse*, Cassell, 1933
Trevelyan, G. M. *Grey of Fallodon*, Longman, 1937

Bibliography

Tuchman Barbara. *The Proud Tower*, Hamish Hamilton, 1966

Vickers, Hugo. *Cecil Beaton*, Weidenfeld & Nicolson, 1985

Weber, Max. *The Protestant Ethic and the Spirit of Capitalism*, Allen and Unwin, 1967

Wilson, Barbara. *Dear Youth*, Macmillan, 1937

Whistler, Laurence. *The Laughter and the Urn*, Weidenfeld & Nicolson, 1985

Woodward, E. L. *The Age of Reform*, Oxford University Press, 1962

Wyndham, Violet. *Madame de Genlis*, André Deutsch, 1958

Index